Sharon Ashwood is a novelist, desk jockey and enthusiast for the weird and spooky. She has an English literature degree but works as a finance geek. Interests include growing her to-be-read pile and playing with the toy graveyard on her desk. Sharon is the winner of the 2011 RITA® Award for Best Paranormal Romance. She lives in the Pacific Northwest and is owned by the Demon Lord of Kitty Badness.

ENCHANTER REDEEMED

SHARON ASHWOOD

MILLS & BOON

First Published in Great Britain 2018
by Mills & Boon, an imprint of HarperCollins*Publishers*
1 London Bridge Street, London, SE1 9GF

Enchanter Redeemed © 2018 Naomi Lester

ISBN: 978-0-263-26673-3

49-0218

MIX
Paper from
responsible sources
FSC® C007454

This book is produced from independently certified FSC™ paper to ensure responsible forest management.

For more information visit: www.harpercollins.co.uk/green

Printed and bound in Spain
by CPI, Barcelona

This is for all you readers who like a bit of
magic and romance in your stories,
preferably at the same time.

Prologue

Merlin had destroyed the world as he knew it. The question was what to do next.

As with many disasters, the beginning had been innocent enough. He'd lived in the kingdom of Camelot as the enchanter to King Arthur. Those were eventful years—someone was *always* trying to murder the king, antagonize a dragon or start a war. Often it was his rival in magic, Morgan LaFaye, who wanted Arthur's crown for herself. In nearly every case, the first person Arthur called was Merlin, whether for magic, for advice or even just to complain. In that brief, wonderful time, the solitary enchanter had been part of a community. He'd had friends and drinking partners. He'd even kept pets.

Not that things were perfect. In those days demons roamed the mortal realms, causing untold suffering to everyone in their path. The witches, fae and human lords formed an alliance under Camelot's banner to cast the demons out. Thousands of soldiers massed to do battle, but it was Merlin's magic they counted on for victory. Merlin delivered and they won, but at a terrible cost. As a side effect of his final spell, the fae suffered irreparable damage and fled to nurse their wounds. In a parting shot, the fae swore to return and wreak vengeance on King Arthur and all of humankind.

No one knew when this attack would come. So, once again, Camelot turned to Merlin for answers. With a heavy heart, he summoned all the knights of Camelot to the

Church of the Holy Well and put them into an enchanted sleep. For centuries they lay upon their tombs as stone statues, set to awaken when it was time to fight once more.

Centuries rolled by, and Merlin wandered many enchanted lands in search of a cure for the fae. Meanwhile, the Medievaland theme park bought the Church of the Holy Well and the stone knights and shipped them all to Carlyle, Washington, as a tourist attraction. In the process, many of Arthur's knights were sold as museum pieces and curiosities.

When Merlin returned to the mortal realms, no one knew where the knights of the famous Round Table had gone. Camelot was in ruins. The fae—who had chosen Morgan LaFaye as their new and wicked queen—picked this moment to return, seeking vengeance. And, just in case his day wasn't bad enough, the demons were back—including his ex.

Chapter 1

Sorcerer, enchanter, wizard, witch, warlock—they were all job descriptions that were synonymous with "idiot." A person could be born of witch stock and blessed or cursed with natural talents, but it was lunacy to make magic a profession.

This raised the question of precisely why Merlin Ambrosius had been a professional enchanter for over two thousand years and had earned the laughable title of Merlin the Wise. By most standards, he was the most powerful magic user in the land, but that wasn't always an advantage. While Regular Joe Enchanter might have a bad day and blow up his cauldron, Merlin had ripped the souls out of the entire fae race. Merlin the Wise? Not so much.

And now here he was, about to peer through a portal torn through time and space to spy on the scariest creepy-crawlies to ever sprout horns.

His workshop was on the top level of an old warehouse, while the bottom floor was occupied by an automotive repair shop. It was a good arrangement, since Merlin preferred to work at night when the employees had gone home and wouldn't be tempted to ask about funny smells, indoor hailstorms or a flock of flying toads. Today, though, the shop was shut and he had the place to himself. This was a definite bonus, even if it meant getting up before noon. Superstar wizard or not, stalking demons on a sunny afternoon was slightly less terrifying than on a dark and stormy night.

The ritual circle was drawn in chalk in the middle of the floor and the scant furniture pushed aside. The curtains were pulled, softening the light. Empty space yawned up to the rafters, the shadows untouched by the dozen sweet-scented candles flickering in the draft. A hush blanketed the room. Merlin sat cross-legged in the middle of the circle, his comfortable jeans and faded T-shirt at odds with the solemnity of the magic. The truth was, ritual robes didn't matter. Only strength of will and focus would help with this kind of work—which was, in effect, eavesdropping.

Merlin needed information. Specifically, he needed to know what Camelot's enemies had been doing in recent months, because rumors were flying on the magical grapevine, blog sites and social media accounts—not to mention Camelot's spy network. On one hand, there were the fae. They had been far too quiet since the autumn—no attacks, no gratuitous death threats, no random monsters unleashed to trample a city—and the silence was making everyone nervous.

On the other hand, the demon courts were stirring. Arthur, with Merlin's help, had thrown the hellspawn back into the Abyss during Camelot's glory days. But no banishment lasted forever and sooner or later the demons would try to return. Was that what was going on?

He cupped his scrying stone in the palms of his hands, willing answers to flow his way. The stone was cool, smooth and heavy and he concentrated until it was the only object filling his senses. Popular culture loved the image of a wizard with a crystal ball, but to tune into Radio Demon, dark red agate was best. The good stuff was rare, and Merlin had searched for centuries for a flawless globe the size of a small pumpkin. When he'd finally found what he wanted, it had cost enough gold to purchase a small country, but it had been one of his go-to tools ever since.

He spoke a word, and the solid rock dissolved into a cloud of dark gray streaked like a bloody sunset. He still held a hard sphere, but it was like a bubble now. Inside was a window into a complex web of realities that included Faery, the Forest Sauvage, the Crystal Mountains and many more separate but connected realms. He nudged the vision until he was staring into the demon territory called the Abyss.

The mist parted and Merlin had a view of two figures. It wasn't the best angle—he was somewhere above and to the left—but that was an advantage. Spy holes were unpredictable and he had no desire to get caught. Grumpy demons had sent the last unlucky eavesdropper home in a soup bowl.

At first he could only see two figures talking, but a quick shake of the ball fixed the audio.

"What do you mean, you were summoned?" asked the taller of the two in a scholarly accent. He was dressed in a well-tailored suit, his head bald and his black beard neatly clipped. He would have looked at home in any metropolitan city except for the claws, pointy teeth and yellow eyes slitted like a goat's. Merlin knew this demon's name was Tenebrius. They'd had uneasy dealings before.

"I know," replied the other demon, who called himself Gorm. He was small, about the size of a large cat or a smallish monkey, and his leathery skin reminded Merlin of an old shoe. "In these days of computers and binge television, who bothers to summon a demon? But there I was in a chalk circle just like the old days. Talk about retro."

"Don't try to be funny," said Tenebrius, narrowing his eyes. "Who was it?"

"LaFaye. You know, the Queen of Faery?"

The image of Tenebrius stiffened. So did Merlin. Morgan LaFaye had caused most of Camelot's headaches until she'd been imprisoned. She shouldn't have been able to summon so much as pizza delivery from inside her enchanted jail.

"What does *she* want?" asked Tenebrius with obvious caution. He was staring at Gorm with something between suspicion and—was that envy?

Gorm shrugged. "Power. Freedom. King Arthur's head on a platter."

Tenebrius looked down his nose and clasped his hands behind his back, resembling a supercilious butler. "The usual, you mean."

"She is a queen locked up and separated from her people."

Tenebrius snorted, releasing a cloud of smoke from his nostrils. "She rose to power by trading on the fae's grievance against Camelot. I'd hardly call that a good qualification for a leader. They're better off without her, even if they have lost their souls."

And that summed up the damage caused by the spell Merlin had used to banish the demons. Gone was the fae's love of beauty, their laughter, their art. Now they were emotionless automatons sworn to take vengeance on Camelot and feast on the life energy of mortals. Old, familiar guilt gnawed inside him, no less sharp for all the centuries that had passed.

Gorm frowned. "Her Majesty has a grievance."

"Don't we all?" Tenebrius examined his claws. "Do you trust her?"

"Would you trust someone who summoned one of us?"

Tenebrius rolled his slitted eyes. "But why *you*? Was her magic so weakened by prison that she was forced to grab the first demon she came to?"

"Uh—" Gorm started to look up, as if sensing Merlin's intense interest in the conversation, but was distracted a moment later.

"Who's grabbing whom?" came a third and very female voice.

Merlin all but dropped the ball, his mouth suddenly desert dry. The image warped and churned until he forced it back into focus—and then wished he hadn't. Vivian swam into view. She looked as good as she had the last time they'd wrestled between her silken sheets. Scholars claimed demons were made of energy and therefore had no true physical form, yet there was no question that Vivian was exquisite. She was tall and slender but curvaceous in ways that were hard to achieve except as a fantasy art centerfold. A thick river of blue-black hair hung to her knees and framed a heart-shaped face set with enormous violet eyes. Warm toffee skin—bountifully visible despite her glittering armor—stirred dangerous, even disturbing, memories. Beyond Vivian's inhuman loveliness, her demon ancestry showed in the long, black, feline tail that twitched behind her.

Ex-lovers were tricky things. Demon ex-lovers were a whole new level of dangerous. Merlin still wanted to devour her one lick at a time. *Merlin the very, very Unwise.* He closed his eyes, hoping she'd disappear. Unfortunately, when he looked again, she was still there. Then he cursed the loss of those two seconds when he might have been gazing at her. Vivian had been *his*, his pleasure and poison and his personal drug of choice. He'd moved on, but she'd never completely left his bloodstream.

"Gorm got himself summoned," said Tenebrius.

"Who was the lucky enchanter?" Vivian asked. She gave a lush smile with dainty, feline fangs.

"The Queen of Faery."

"Oh," said Vivian, quickly losing the grin, "her. It's almost tempting to give the fae their souls again. Then they'd get rid of LaFaye themselves."

Tenebrius gave her a sly look. "You don't think the situation presents some interesting opportunities?"

Merlin wondered what he meant by that, but Gorm interrupted. "Is it even possible to restore their souls?"

"Theoretically," said Vivian. "Everything's possible with us."

"But we could do it?" Gorm persisted.

Tenebrius shrugged. "The spell came from a demon to begin with. Therefore, demon magic could reverse it."

By all the riches of the goblin kings! Merlin sat frozen. Hope rose, wild and shattering, and he squeezed the ball so that his hands would not shake. He had searched and searched for a means to fix the fae, but had found nothing. Then again, he'd been searching among healers and wielders of the Light, not hellspawn. Demons corrupted and destroyed. They did not improve.

And yet Tenebrius had just said that the demons could provide a cure. Impossible. Brilliant. Amazing. Merlin struggled to control his breath. How was he going to get his hands on a demon-crafted cure? Because it was immediately, solidly obvious that he had to, whatever the cost.

His gaze went from Tenebrius back to the she-demon again. At the sight of her sumptuous body, things—possibly his survival instincts—shriveled in terror while other bits and pieces heated with a toxic mix of panic and desire. Any involvement with demons was an appallingly bad move. Sex was beyond stupid, but he'd been there and done that and insanely lusted for more.

Vivian wanted him dead, and some of her reasons were justified. To begin with, he'd stolen from her. The battle spell that had gone so horribly wrong had come from her grimoire—the great and horrible book of magic that rested on a bone pedestal in her chambers. Maybe she had the power to help the fae—but that would mean facing her again. Now, there was a terrifying idea.

The door behind Merlin banged open with a loud crack. "Hey, you busy?"

Startled out of deep concentration, Merlin jumped, dropping the globe. With a curse, he snatched it up.

"Oops. Sorry, dude." The new voice seemed to ring in the rafters, blaringly loud against the profound silence of the magical circle. A corner of Merlin's brain identified the speaker as his student, Clary Greene, but the rest of him was teetering on the edge of panic. When he righted the globe, the swirling clouds parted inside the stone once more. He peered until the image of the room grew crisp. Three demon faces stared back at him with murderous expressions.

Merlin said something much stronger than "oops."

Vivian's eyes began to glow. "Merlin!" she snarled, his name trailing into a feline hiss that spoke of unfinished business.

Merlin quickly set the agate ball on the floor and sprang away, colliding with Clary's slight form. His student's pixie-like features crumpled in confusion. "What's going on?"

"Duck!" he ordered, grabbing her shoulder and pushing her to the floor.

Bolts of power blasted from the agate globe in rainbow colors, arcing in jagged lightning all through the room. With three demons firing at once, it looked like an otherworldly octopus, its tentacles grabbing objects and zapping them to showers of ash. Merlin's bookshelf exploded, burning pages filling the air as if he was trapped in an apocalyptic snow globe.

"Making friends again?" Clary asked, flicking ash from her shaggy blond head. Her words were flippant, but her face was tense.

"Stay low. They're demons."

Clary's witch-green eyes went wide. She was Vivian's

opposite—a lean, fair tomboy with more attitude than magical talent. She was also everything that Vivian was not—honest, kind, thoughtful and far too good to be in Merlin's life. She was a drink of clean water to a man parched by his own excesses, an innocent despite what she believed about herself. Everything about her had beckoned, woman to man, but he'd kept their relationship professional. It was bad enough that she had begged him to teach her magic. He should have refused. Nothing good came to anyone who lingered near him.

And right now lingering was not an option.

"Move," he snapped, forcing her to creep backward one step at a time. The slow pace was nerve-racking, but it gave him a moment to weave a protective spell around them both.

He was just in time. Lightning fried his worktable, shattering a row of orderly glass vials, and then his bicycle sizzled and warped into a piece of futuristic sculpture. Merlin scowled as the seat burst into flame. Maybe he should rethink the slow and steady approach.

Vivian's clear voice rang from the agate globe. "Curse you, Merlin Ambrosius. I vow that you shall not escape me, but shall suffer due vengeance for what you have done!"

"What did you do?" Clary whispered. "She's really mad."

"Not now," Merlin muttered. Not ever, if he had a choice.

He sprang at the agate ball, intending to break the connection between his workshop and the demon realm with a well-placed bolt of his own. Before he was halfway there, a purple tentacle of energy lashed out and fastened on his chest. A blaze of pain sang through him, fierce as a sword stroke. He thrust out a hand, warping the stream of power away before his heart stopped.

Then Clary cast her own counter spell, just the way

he'd taught her. The blow struck, but only clipped the edge of the stone ball, rolling it outside the containment of the ritual circle. Merlin pounced, but the damage was done. Once outside the circle, the demons were free to cross over into his world. As he groped on the floor for the agate, Vivian's armored boots appeared in his field of view. He looked up and up her long legs to her shapely body and finally to her furious eyes.

"Who is this witch?" Vivian pointed a claw-tipped finger at Clary. Her long black tail swished back and forth, leaving an arc in the ashes coating the floor.

"Darling. Sweetheart. She's my student," he said in calming tones as he got to his feet, still clutching the stone. The agate sparked with the demons' power, as if he held a heavy ball of pure electricity.

"Does she know what you really are?" Anger twisted Vivian's beautiful face. "Or should I say, does she have any idea how low you will stoop for power?"

Clearly, the demon was still mad that he'd stolen her spell. Or, more likely, she was furious that he'd left their bed without a word—but there had been no choice, under the circumstances. It was that or hand Camelot and everybody else over to the hellspawn.

Vivian's furious form was just a projection of energy—half in her own world and half in his—and yet Merlin took a cautious step back. "Clary is only a student, Vivian. I can promise you that much."

"I'm standing right here," Clary snapped.

It was the wrong tone to take with an angry demon. Vivian flicked a bolt of power from her fingertips that hurled Clary against the wall. To Merlin's horror, the young witch stuck there, suspended above the floor like a butterfly on a pin. Clary grabbed at her chest, tearing at the zipper of her leather jacket as if she needed air.

"Enough!" Merlin roared. "She is nothing to you."

"But she is something to you. I can smell it!"

"She's under my protection." He lashed out, breaking Vivian's hold.

The demoness rounded on him, fixing him with those hypnotic violet eyes. Her predatory beauty held him for a split second too long. As Clary crumpled to the floor, Vivian's claws slashed at the girl, leaving long, red tracks soaking through the sleeve of thin burgundy leather. Vivian snarled, showing fangs. In moments, Clary would be dead—and for no reason other than because she'd interrupted his ritual.

Desperation knotted Merlin's chest. He lifted the agate globe, infusing it with his power. Part of him screamed to stop, to guard his own interests, but the fever of his grief and guilt was too strong. With a howl, he smashed the globe to the floor. It exploded into a thousand shards, taking most of his earthly wealth with it. Vivian shrieked—a high, pained banshee wail—and vanished with a pop of air pressure that left his ears ringing. A heavy stink of burning amber hung in the air, borne on wisps of purple smoke. Clary began to cough, a racking, bubbling gasp of sound.

Merlin fell to his knees at her side. "It's over."

He put an arm around the young woman, helping her to sit up. The warm, slender weight of her seemed painfully fragile. Witches were mortal, as easily broken as ordinary humans, and Clary's face had drained of color. He touched her cheek with the back of his hand to find her skin was cold.

His stomach clenched with panic. "How badly are you hurt?"

She didn't answer. She wasn't breathing anymore.

Chapter 2

Clary jolted awake. Power surged through her body, painful and suffocating. Her spine arched into it—or maybe away from it, she wasn't sure. Merlin had one hand on her side and the other on her chest, using his magic like a defibrillator. The sensation hammered her from the inside while every hair on her body stood straight up. When he released her, she sagged in relief. A drifting sensation took over, as if she were a feather in an updraft.

Merlin's fingers went to her neck, checking for a pulse. His hands were hot from working spells, the touch firm yet gentle. In her weakened state, Clary shivered slightly, wanting to bare her throat in surrender. She was a sucker for dark, broody masculinity, and he projected it like a beacon. All the same, Clary sucked in a breath before he got any big ideas about mouth-to-mouth. If Merlin was going to kiss her, she wanted wine and soft music, not blood and the dirty workshop floor.

Another bolt of power, more pain, another pulse check. Clary managed a moan, and she heard the sharp intake of Merlin's breath. His hand withdrew from her pulse point as she forced her eyes open. He was staring down at her with his peculiar amber eyes, dark brows furrowed in concern. She was used to him prickly, arrogant or sarcastic, but not this. She'd never seen that oddly vulnerable expression before—but it quickly fled as their gazes met.

"You're alive." He said it like a fact, any softness gone.

"Yup." Clary pushed herself up on her elbows. She hurt all over. "What was that?"

"A demon."

"I got that much." Clary held up her arm, peering through the rents in her jacket where the demon's claws had slashed. Merlin's zap of power had stopped the bleeding, but the deep scratches were red, puffy and hurt like blazes.

"Demon claws are toxic."

"Got that, too."

"I can put a salve on the wound, but you'd be smart to have Tamsin look at it," Merlin said. "Your sister is a better healer than I am."

"She's better than anybody." Clary said it with the automatic loyalty of a little sister, but it was true. "She's got a better bedside manner, too."

Merlin raised a brow, his natural arrogance back in place. "Just be glad you're alive."

She studied Merlin, acutely aware of how much magic he'd used to shut Vivian down. He looked like a man in his early thirties, but there was no telling how old he actually was. He was lean-faced with permanent stubble and dark hair that curled at his collar. At first glance, he looked like a radical arts professor or dot-com squillionaire contemplating his next disruptive innovation. It took a second look to notice the muscular physique hidden by the comfortable clothes. Merlin had a way of sliding under most radars, but Clary never underestimated the power he could pluck out of thin air. She was witch born, a member of the Shadowring Coven, but he was light-years beyond their strongest warlocks.

That strength was like catnip to her—although she'd never, ever admit that out loud. "What were you doing?" she demanded, struggling the rest of the way to a sitting position.

"A surveillance ritual." His face tensed as if afraid to

reveal too much. "There've been rumors of demon activity in the Forest Sauvage."

The forest lay at the junction of several supernatural realms. "Demons show up there anyway, don't they?"

"One or two of the strongest hellspawn can leave the Abyss, but only for brief periods. It's not a regular occurrence. Yet Arthur's spies report a demon has been meeting with the fae generals on multiple occasions."

"You want to know what they're up to," she murmured, a horrible awareness of what she'd interrupted settling in. Gawd, how stupid was she? It was a wonder Merlin hadn't kicked her out of his workshop after her first lesson. He would have to now.

"I was summoning information through a scrying portal. The conversation was growing interesting when you arrived." His tone was precise and growing colder with every syllable. Now that the crisis was over, he was getting angry.

Clary pressed a hand to her pounding head. "They heard me come in?"

"Yes."

She cringed inwardly, but lifted her head, refusing to let her mortification show. "Then Babe-a-licious with the tail showed up."

"Yes." There was no mistaking the frost in his tone now. "Vivian. Do you have any idea how dangerous she is?"

"She tried to kill me." Clary's insides hollowed as the words sank home. *Dear goddess, she did kill me!* And Merlin had brought her back before a second had passed—but it had happened. Her witch's senses had felt it happen. The realization left her light-headed.

"She doesn't get to have you," he said in a low voice.

Their gazes locked, and something twisted in Clary's chest. She'd been hurt on Merlin's watch, and he was furious. No, what she saw in his eyes was more than icy anger.

It was a heated, primal possessiveness that came from a far different Merlin than she knew. Clary's breath stopped. Surely she was misreading the situation. Death and zapping had scrambled her thoughts. "What happened when you smashed the stone?"

"The demon returned to where she came from."

"Will she come back?"

"If she does, it will be for me. She won't bother you. You were incidental."

Clary might have been insulted, but she was barely listening now. The events of the past few minutes fell over her like a shadow, pushing everything else, even Merlin, aside. She'd felt death coming like a cold, black vortex. She began to shake, her mind scrambling to get away from a memory of gathering darkness. She drew her knees into her chest, hugging them. "I shouldn't have walked in on you."

"No, you shouldn't have," he said in a voice filled with the same mix of ice and fire. "You'd be a better student of magic if you paid attention to the world around you. That would include door wards."

Tears stung behind her eyelids. Trust Merlin to use death as a teachable moment. "You could be sympathetic. At least a little."

He made a noise that wasn't quite a snort. "You asked me to teach you proper magic and not the baby food the covens use. If you want warm and fuzzy, get a rabbit. Real magic is deadly."

Clary took a shuddering breath. "No kidding."

He was relentless. "Today your carelessness cost me a valuable tool."

She sighed her resentment. "I'll get you a new stone."

"You can't. There was only one like it, and now I'm blind to what the demons are doing."

Abruptly, he stood and crossed the room to kick a shard of agate against the wall. It bounced with a savage clatter.

Clary got to her feet, her knees wobbling. Merlin was right about her needing Tamsin's medical help. She braced her hand against the wall so she'd stop weaving. "I'm sorry."

He spun and stormed back to her in one motion, moving so fast she barely knew what was happening. He took her by the shoulders, the grip rough. "Don't *ever* do that again!"

And then his mouth crushed hers in a hard, angry kiss. Clary gasped in surprise, but there was no air, only him, and only his need. She rose slowly onto her toes, the gesture both surrender and a desire to hold her own. She'd been kissed many times before, but never consumed this way. His lips were greedy and hot with that same confusing array of emotions she'd seen a moment ago. Anger. Fear. Possession. Protectiveness.

Volatile. That was the word she'd so often used in her own head when thinking about him. Volatile, though he kept himself on a very short chain. Right now that chain had slipped.

And she liked it. Head spinning, she leaned back against the wall, trapped between the plaster and the hard muscle of his chest. Now that the first shock was past, she moved her mouth under his, returning the kiss. Hot breath fanned against her cheek, sending tingles down her spine. She'd never understood the stories about danger sparking desire until this moment, but now she was soaring, lust a hot wire lighting up her whole frame. Being alive was very, very good.

Merlin had braced his hands on either side of her head, but now he stroked them down her body in a long, slow caress. It was a languid movement as if he was measuring and memorizing her every curve. Clary let her arms drift up to link behind his neck.

"I think I'll skip the fuzzy bunny and keep you instead," she murmured.

The effect of her words was electric. He stepped out of her embrace as unexpectedly as he'd entered it, pushing a hand through his hair. "We can't do this." He turned away as if he needed to regain control.

After being killed, revived, scolded and ravished, Clary was getting whiplash. "Why not?" she asked through clenched teeth.

"Vivian."

"She was angry," Clary conceded. "Did you and she have a, um, thing?"

He made a noise like a strangling bear. "She is everything unholy."

Yup, Viv was an ex. For some reason, that sparked her temper in a way nothing else had. Clary wiped her mouth on her sleeve.

"I said you were incidental to her." His voice had gone cold again. "Let's keep it that way. Touching you was a mistake."

"A mistake?"

Merlin faced her, frowning at her sarcastic tone. "Yes."

"So Vivian is a jealous mean girl," Clary snapped. "That's not my problem, and I'm not a mistake. I don't deserve that kind of disrespect."

And yet she did. She was a screwup, a talentless hack of a witch and not much better with her personal life. She'd just proven it all over again by bursting in where she wasn't wanted. The knowledge scalded her, but it also raised her defenses. It was one thing to reject her as a magician, but he'd just rejected her as a woman.

"Don't be difficult," he replied.

"Don't be an idiot. I'm a person, not an error." She'd never spoken to Merlin like this, but she'd never been this upset. She didn't care if he had a point.

Clary pushed away from the wall. Merlin took a step forward as if to support her, but she wasn't dizzy now.

Anger had cleared her head and set her pulse speeding at a quick march. Her whole body sang with pain, but she stalked toward the door on perfectly steady feet.

"Clary!" Merlin said, his tone thick with irritation. "Come back here."

"Don't talk to me right now. And don't come after me." Clary slammed the workshop door behind her, taking the steps down to the main level of the warehouse at a run. She didn't look back.

When she reached the street a minute later, the late May sunshine seemed strange. There was no darkness, no storms and certainly no demons. Sparrows flitted through the last blossoms of the cherry trees lining the streets, and a senior couple walked matching Scottie dogs in the leaf-dappled shade. It was the perfect day for a cross-country bike ride, the kind that might take her fifty or sixty miles. Clary shook her head, feeling as if she was suddenly in the wrong movie.

She started walking, the residue of her anger still hot in her veins. Merlin's workshop was at the edge of Carlyle's bustling downtown and a twenty-minute walk from her sister's apartment. If Clary went for a visit, she could get her throbbing arm checked and complain to Tamsin about men at the same time.

Tamsin would be sympathetic for sure. Clary was the baby of the family and her uncertain talent upset a cart-load of familial expectations, but she was an accomplished computer programmer and was making a new career as a social media consultant for Medievaland. Tamsin would tell her she was doing fine, which was exactly what she needed right now.

The social media job had been a stroke of luck, something she'd pitched to Camelot when she'd moved across the country to study with Merlin. In fact, she was his first student in a hundred years because she'd refused to take no for an answer the moment she'd found out her big sister had met the man. In her imagination he'd been the ultimate enchanter, a rebel prince of the magical world. He'd turned out to be short-tempered and demanding, arrogant and aloof. She'd been crushed.

It wasn't that Merlin was a bad teacher—he was fabulous. He drilled her remorselessly, showing her three or four ways to launch a spell until they found one that worked for her. Fighting spells, spying spells, portals, wards—he taught far more practical application than theory and approached every lesson with resolute patience. Her skills had leaped forward. It was just that he was so very *Merlin*.

Clary swore under her breath. You'd think he could have put a sign on the door to keep visitors out. Sure, she'd dropped by unexpectedly with a question about the homework he'd given her and, yes, there had been a ward she disarmed to walk in, but he *always* had a ward on the door. Sometimes he put them there just to test her. How was she to know he'd be chatting with hellspawn?

And as for the rest, why was she surprised? It had been a kiss in the moment, a rare moment of compassion from a very dark horse. Merlin was the greatest enchanter in written history. She was so far down the food chain she wasn't even on the menu. There would never be anything more between them, however much that one embrace made her imagination explode.

She ground her teeth. Maybe she should have stuck with computers. At least software didn't have claws. At least it didn't kiss her and then shut down the moment with a wall of ice.

Clary's thoughts scattered as she neared Tamsin's street. This block was lined with low-rise storefronts featuring a drugstore, a used-clothing exchange and a place that still sold vinyl records. The neighborhood was like a small town where shopkeepers greeted their customers by name and residents knew which child belonged to which mother. Normally, she enjoyed the relaxed atmosphere, but she was starting to feel sick again. Whatever fury she'd been running on was draining fast. There was a café with a few outdoor tables, and she sat down on one of the ornate metal chairs. She rested her head on her good hand and cradled her injured arm in her lap. *I should call Tamsin*, she thought, but the pocket with her phone seemed miles away.

Her heart was hammering, perspiration clammy on her skin. It took her a moment to recognize the sensation as raw, primal fear. But why? She was out of danger now, wasn't she? Hadn't Merlin said Clary herself was of no interest to the demons? And yet, it felt as if something was looking over her shoulder. She jerked around, but saw nothing except a passerby startled by Clary's frown.

The sudden motion sent spikes of pain up her arm. She pushed up the torn sleeve of her jacket to see the scratches were swelling now. She touched the pink skin and discovered it was hot. Infection. Wonderful. No wonder she felt queasy. She slumped in the chair, aware of the clatter and bustle of the coffee shop though it seemed far, far in the distance.

She fished her phone out and set it on the table, realizing she'd have to dial it left-handed because the fingers of her injured hand had gone numb. Clary had managed to punch the code that unlocked it when a wave of pain struck her. It was like the shock of power Merlin had administered, but on steroids.

Clary hunched over the table, robbed of the breath even to cry out. A white haze swallowed the world around her, turning everything to static. Sound vanished, a high, thin hum filling her brain. She began to shake—not a ladylike trembling, either. Her head lolled back as her jerking knees rattled the table. All at once she was on the ground, her cheek pressed to the gritty sidewalk.

Blackness.

Hands gathered her up. Voices distant and muffled as if she was underwater. She was in the chair again, the cold metal beneath the seat of her jeans. Hard to stay in the chair because her limbs were like spaghetti.

"Miss? Miss?"

There was a sound like a bubble popping, and she could see and hear again.

"By the Abyss!" Clary gasped as the world smacked her like cold water. Sounds, colors, smells all seemed out of control. Clary blinked, wiping her eyes with the back of her good hand.

"Can we call someone for you?" asked a voice.

Clary squinted, recognizing the square, pleasant face of the woman who ran the coffee shop. She searched for the woman's name, but it was gone. "Huh?"

"You passed out," the woman said slowly and carefully. "You might have had a seizure."

Goddess! She should probably be in the hospital, but then she'd have to explain the claw marks. Clary looked around. Her phone was still on the table. "Tamsin," she said but couldn't manage more. A wave of disorientation swamped her. Her voice sounded wrong, but she wasn't sure why.

"Tamsin who lives in the apartment building down the street?" the woman asked.

Clary nodded, afraid to speak again.

"She ordered a birthday cake for the weekend. I have her number." The woman bustled back inside.

Clary closed her eyes. Whose birthday was it? The name bobbed just out of reach of her thoughts. Facts and memories receded, as if her consciousness was a balloon that had come untethered. When she opened her eyes again, she caught sight of her reflection in the café window and froze.

Her face was familiar, and it was not. *So this is what it's like to be human.*

Clary's thoughts swerved. *What the blazes?*

She'd recognized the voice in her head. Cold needles of fear crept up her body, turning her fingers and nose so cold it felt like January. Something had been watching her, and now she knew it was Vivian.

Or what's left of me after Merlin smashed his precious globe. Immortals are hard to kill, but I was vulnerable when he did that. I needed a safe harbor and your body was empty for a split second before he brought you back. Hope you don't mind a roomie.

Clary sat up straight, fighting a sudden urge to scream. Her head, seemingly of its own accord, turned back to her reflection. She took in the mop of shaggy blond hair, the ragged, bloody clothes and her wide, frightened eyes.

It's not the body I'm used to, but beggars can't be choosers. Still, we need to do something about the wardrobe.

Chapter 3

Surely it had all been a horrible hallucination. The next morning found Clary sitting at her sister's kitchen table, a cup of black coffee before her. Everything seemed normal, and Clary felt as loved and cared for as Tamsin could manage. She'd slept in her sister's tiny second bedroom and still had a crick in her spine from the lumpy futon.

"How are you feeling?" Tamsin asked, putting a hand over Clary's. Gawain, Tamsin's soon-to-be husband, had already left for the day and the two women were alone. Normally, Clary would have been disappointed. She liked Gawain, and he'd spent almost as much time teaching her self-defense as Merlin had spent teaching her magic—if there was to be a fight with the fae, she needed to be ready. But today she wanted alone time with her sister.

Clary looked up from staring into her cup. Like Clary, Tamsin was green-eyed and fair-haired, her long locks pinned up in a messy bun. The similarity in coloring was deceptive. Tamsin was actually a stepsister who had joined the family when Clary's mom had married a second time. They had all been lucky—Stacy, the eldest, and Clary, the youngest, had readily accepted their new middle sister. Tamsin was easy to love and Clary adored her. She'd been the gentle hand that had led Clary through a rebellious adolescence when their mother had all but given up in despair.

"My wound feels better," Clary answered, pulling up her sleeve.

Tamsin angled Clary's arm for a better look. Besides

working as Medievaland's historian, Tamsin's magical specialty was healing. After a round of smelly ointments and ritual, the wounds on Clary's arm were now just scratches, as if Clary had lost an argument with an alley cat.

"I've met demons, but I've never treated any injuries they caused before now. I never knew they had poisoned claws," Tamsin said, releasing Clary's arm.

"Do you think that's what caused the seizure?" Clary sipped her coffee, welcoming the caffeine as it hit her bloodstream. She hadn't said anything about the hallucinations. She'd stopped hearing that voice in her head by the time Tamsin had finished doctoring her, and decided to keep the crazy to herself. "Maybe the infection was messing with my brain?"

She could hear the pleading in her voice. She felt okay now, and desperately wanted to put yesterday behind her.

"I'd bet the two are connected." Tamsin picked up Clary's hand again. It was a comforting gesture, but Clary could feel the faint tingle of Tamsin's magic course through her. Tamsin leaned forward and kissed her forehead as if Clary was a little girl again. The gesture salved Clary's hurts the way no medicine could.

"You're still not a hundred percent," Tamsin said, "but I don't detect any lingering damage. Take it easy for a few days."

"I'm supposed to be at Medievaland today."

"In the office?"

It was a reasonable assumption. Clary handled pretty much all of Medievaland's online presence. Since King Arthur and a handful of his knights had awakened to join the modern world, they'd become famous for the mock tourneys hosted by the theme park. The knights now had a rapidly expanding fan base, which Clary fed with judicious tidbits of insider knowledge—none of which included the fact that they were born centuries ago and had returned to save humanity from soul-sucking fae monsters. She tried to keep things upbeat.

However, today's activities weren't about posts and blogs. "Merlin's doing the special effects at today's show and he wants a second pair of hands."

Tamsin frowned. "You should call in sick. Obviously, he'd understand."

"Maybe, maybe not. I broke his ball."

Tamsin arched an eyebrow. "Just one of them?"

Clary grimaced. "Crystal—stone—ball. His spy camera to the demon realms. He had to smash it to save me from Vivian." She was feeling more than a little guilty about that.

"Yeah," Tamsin replied, drawing the word out. "Those stones are expensive and rare."

"He said it was one of a kind."

"Are you sure you're still his student?"

Clary pulled her smartphone from the pocket of the boho-style dress Tamsin had loaned her to replace her bloodstained clothes. It was pink and flowery and nothing like what she usually wore. She held the phone up as if it was evidence. "I'm scheduled to be there at noon. He sent a text to confirm."

"That's probably his way of checking on you. You had a near death by demon, then a seizure." Tamsin had that frozen look that said she wasn't happy but was trying to be polite about it. "I think you can skip a session."

"Normally, I'd welcome a day off, but as you say, I cost him a piece of expensive equipment. Showing up is the least I can do."

"You feel guilty."

"Pretty much."

Clary's mind immediately went to the kiss. Her cheeks heated at the memory, and she looked away from her sister. Merlin's behavior was just one more strange thing to add to the list of yesterday's weirdness.

"What else happened besides the demon who attacked you?" Tamsin asked. She'd always been able to read Clary's expressions.

Clary rose from the table. "I need to get ready to go." She suddenly didn't want to talk anymore.

Tamsin—still protesting—drove her to Medievaland. They parked and passed a long line at the gate that proved the summer tourist rush was beginning. The weather promised to be warm, so the steady stream of paying customers would only increase as midday approached. And why not? Medievaland, with its jousts and feasts and rides and games, was good family fun.

Clary and Tamsin passed the turnstile and pushed through the knot of visitors milling at the information booth. A herald rode by on a milk-white mare, shouting directions to Friar Ambrose's delicatessen and the noon show at the bandstand. To the right was the market area crowded with merchants selling all manner of handcrafts and snack foods; to the left the traditional arcade that led off to the rides, where the Dragon's Tail—a roller coaster that challenged even Clary's daredevil instincts —swirled high above the crowds. Tamsin's destination was the Church of the Holy Well, the one truly medieval structure in the park. It had been moved, along with the stone knights, from the south of England and turned into the museum where Tamsin worked.

The two women stopped when they reached a fork in the path. "You're absolutely sure you feel up to this?" asked Tamsin. "No headaches or weakness?"

"I feel fine," Clary protested, and that much was almost true. "As if there was anything on the planet that could withstand your healing!"

"Then, be brave, little witchling." Tamsin gave her a hug. "I'll check on you in a few hours."

Clary laughed at her childhood nickname. "You're such a big sister."

Tamsin made a face and left, heading toward the ancient church ahead. Feeling content for the first time since before barging into Merlin's workshop, Clary took the path to the tourney grounds.

Jousting and other events took place in an amphitheater, where the audience could get a good view of the armored horsemen doing battle. Behind the large structure were the stables, changing rooms and other service buildings. As Clary hurried in that direction, she could hear the stampede of hooves and the crash of lance on shield. The crowd roared and applauded, which meant someone had scored a good hit. After a glance at her phone to check the time, she picked up her pace, ignoring the hawkers selling T-shirts and ball caps.

When she reached the change rooms, she grabbed a long blue gown out of her locker and quickly put it on. All the employees at Medievaland dressed the part, and by the time she was done, she'd added a long belt of glittering—if fake—jewels and pinned her hair under a fluttering white veil. Then she headed for the amphitheater, where she was to meet the enchanter in one of the high boxes that overlooked the field.

Nerves made Clary's breath come faster. She was here because, despite yesterday, she still wanted Merlin as her teacher. She wanted to be an effective witch, ready to fight fae or demons or whatever threat darkened Camelot's door. She wanted to belong here like Tamsin did. Still, she had to admit she'd come for other reasons, too. She needed to bury the anger between her and Merlin. He'd been a jerk, but she'd burst in on him. He could have handled everything better, but she'd resorted to a tantrum. Neither had been at their best with dying and exes and all.

And—here, she mentally shied away just a little—they had kissed. She had to face him with her head held high and not reveal how much more she desired. Sometimes attitude was all a person had.

When she saw Merlin, her step slowed so she could take in the sight. He wore long robes of deep blue and carried a tall staff of knobby wood. With his lean face and unusual amber eyes, he carried the fantasy-wizard costume well. Very well, and with the kind of brooding intensity that teased something low in her belly. He was gazing at the tourney ground, a thoughtful frown on his face.

"Hi," she said.

He looked up, his expression startled for an instant before it settled into his habitual reserve. "How are you feeling?"

"Fine," she said, sounding as defensive as she suddenly felt. "I can work."

A long moment passed in which Merlin studied her, his expression closed. "Do you remember what you're supposed to do?" he asked.

If he was trying to keep her at a distance, it was working. All at once, Clary felt exposed in her feminine dress, the light breeze tugging and touching in ways that didn't happen with her usual denim and leather. She wanted to say again how sorry she was for yesterday's mistake, but the words died under his cool stare. His mood felt like punishment, but whether it was for himself or for her, she couldn't say. It took a moment to get her lips to move. "Yes, I know what to do."

"Good." He turned back to the amphitheater. The packed dirt field had been cleared, ready for the next event. "Keep to the script, regardless of what else you might see. I'm raising the bar a notch for today's show."

Clary swallowed. The show would be grunt work for Merlin, but for her it would be tricky. She tried not to think about the time she'd accidentally teleported a moose into her hotel room. *Be brave, little witchling.* "I'm ready."

Merlin gave a signal, and the voice of the announcer boomed through the public address system. "Lords and ladies, honored guests of Medievaland, welcome to this afternoon's main event. This is the moment of dread, the true test of bravery and the battle you've all been waiting for—Medievaland's courageous knights versus the enchanter Merlin's monsters!"

The audience roared its approval. The gates at the far end of the amphitheater swung open, and the knights rode in two by two—Gawain and Hector, then Beaumains and Percival, and finally Owen and Palomedes. They parted, each pair splitting left and right to form a colorful double line. The last to appear was King Arthur, resplendent in blue and gold and riding a huge bay stallion. The amphitheater rumbled with enthusiastically stamping feet as the knights took up their position flanking the king.

Two musicians with long golden trumpets blew a fanfare, silencing the crowd. Merlin turned to Clary and gave a nod. She braced herself. She'd practiced this spell hundreds of times and now she recited the words of the spell exactly as he'd taught her. Then she released her power. With relief, she felt the magic shape itself, swirling until it solidified into an enormous black wolf. It bounded toward Palomedes, jaws open to reveal a lot of drool and fangs.

"Nice," said Merlin.

He didn't give praise often, so Clary felt her cheeks warm with pleasure. Far below, Palomedes did battle with the illusion to the obvious pleasure of the paying guests. But that was only the first of many monsters, and Clary set about creating the next. A quick sideways glance showed Merlin had begun an incantation of his own. Clary wondered what it would be, but quickly pushed the thought away. She couldn't get distracted.

With exquisite care, she wove the next spell bit by bit, checking and double-checking each element she added.

Seriously? said the voice in her head—the same voice that had plagued her at the café. *This isn't brain surgery.*

Startled, Clary released her power an instant too early and it bobbled wildly. Then—without knowing how she did it—she reached out and patted it back into shape. Except it was the wrong shape. She'd planned on one over-size lion. Instead, two flightless raptors straight out of the Jurassic era popped into existence and began charging the knights at lightning speed. Clary stared at them in dismay. *What did you make me do?*

I upped your game. You should be grateful.

Stop it! Go away! You're a hallucination! At least she'd hoped Vivian's voice had been the product of her infected wound.

The voice in her head gave a wry snort. *Do you feel feverish?*

No, Clary felt physically fine. Better than ever, in fact—which meant even worse trouble. "Why are you doing this?"

She didn't realize she'd spoken out loud until Merlin gave her a quick glance. "Keep going." Then he turned back to his long, intricate spell.

The show must go on. With a flick of Clary's wrist, the demon summoned not one lion, but a whole pride. All at once, the knights were extremely busy.

Vivian! Clary protested. She wanted to round on the demon, glare at her, maybe punch her. Except it was impossible when the opposition was inside her head. *What do you want?*

Vivian's gaze—in the form of Clary's eyeballs—turned to Merlin. *He took something from me and walked away.*

An ominous feeling gripped Clary as if she'd just stumbled upon an unquiet grave. *What?*

Vivian didn't answer. She was watching Merlin work, and Clary had a front-row seat to the demon's emotions. They weren't as deep or complicated as human feelings, but they were uncomfortably frank. Vivian liked everything about Merlin, from the straight line of his nose to the angle of his jaw. There was also distinct disappointment about how much of his body the robes concealed.

An image of Merlin, his hair longer and his clothes absent, flicked across Clary's mental screen. The vignette revealed a lot of long, lean muscle and tanned limbs. Clary's skin heated, suddenly too tight as her own desire melded with the demon's.

I know his secrets, the demon mused. *You wouldn't worship him half so much if you knew the truth.*

Clary struggled, now barely aware of the spectacle below. *It's none of my business.*

He's your flawed hero, your rebel prince. Of course you're curious.

With horror, she realized Vivian was quoting her own thoughts. Fury pounded against Clary's temples. This hopeless attraction was her own affair, buried where it couldn't embarrass her.

Don't bother, said Vivian. *He thinks you belong to him, but that is a far cry from passion.*

Clary's nails bit into her palms. *And what's he to you?*

Another sweep of eyes, another rush of need. It was all Clary could do to keep her hands at her sides and not reach out to touch the enchanter's warm skin. *Merlin Ambrosius was my soul mate, the one who filled the empty places in my heart.*

Was the demon lovesick? Clary wondered with astonishment. She shifted uncomfortably, suddenly hot and weak with their mingled need.

No. Vivian flexed her power—which Clary felt in a sudden head rush. *I'm here to take my revenge.*

He'll stop you. Clary dug her nails into her palms, using the pain to focus. *I'll stop you. I'll tell him you're here.*

Really? And you think there would be no consequences?

I don't care what he does to me as long as he stops you.

Vivian laughed, a low, husky sound that belonged on a phone sex hotline. *Oh, very good, but I'm not done with you yet. On the other hand, I have no use for your sister.*

Clary's lungs stopped working. Tamsin! She didn't need the demon to say more. If Clary gave Vivian away, Tamsin would suffer.

Sorry it has to be her, Vivian drawled, *but you don't have a vast selection of loved ones to choose from.*

That stung more than Clary liked. *Leave her out of this!*

But this is revenge, remember? Before I'm done, Merlin will wish he were dead. And if you don't do exactly as I say, little witchling, so will you.

Chapter 4

Merlin's lips moved over silent words as he worked his spell. A faint glimmer sparked in the cloudless sky above the auditorium. It would look like nothing to one of the cheering spectators that crammed the seats, just a random flash of light, but to Merlin it was hard-won success. He'd practiced the spell the way a musician learned a piece from memory, going over and over each element until they formed part of his instincts. It was the way he taught Clary: ritual, rinse, repeat. The drill wasn't just for the sake of perfectionism—it was as much for safety. With this amount of powerful magic in play, he couldn't afford to stumble.

Which was why he couldn't think about Clary, for all he felt her gaze on him. Her attention was like the heat of the sun, and all the more tangible because of his own disquiet. If only he hadn't kissed her, because now he could not deny how she made him feel. He might have immense skill, knowledge and power beyond the fantasies of mortal men, but he was still flesh and blood. She was a happiness he wanted but could not have—and for an instant, he'd forgotten that last part.

His control had slipped after witnessing her death and revival. Still, that was no excuse. His enemies were too dangerous for a junior witch who was just beginning to master her talents. He had no right to draw their attention to Clary. At the very least, he had to be careful until he was sure Vivian was safely locked back in the Abyss. The demoness was definitely the jealous type.

So he ignored his student, keeping his focus on the spell. It was tricky but, unlike women, it followed a pattern of logic he understood. With the force of one driving a spike deep into bedrock, he fixed the silver glimmer to the canopy of the sky. From there it spun, growing larger and larger into a disk of shimmering light. If his thrust had been too great or too feeble, the swirl would have wobbled and collapsed, but this was as perfect as a whirling top. The momentum of the magic formed a tunnel between worlds, splitting open a passage between the mortal realm and the enchanted worlds beyond.

The perfection of the spell eased Merlin's temper. The silver bled to a blue deeper than the surrounding sky. The audience cheered in anticipation, believing they watched a special effect none of Medievaland's competition could copy. In a way they did, because no other theme park could boast a guest appearance by a real live dragon.

With a lazy flap of wings, Rukon Shadow Wing floated through Merlin's portal. A smile split Merlin's face at the sight and he allowed the pleasant tiredness that followed a well-cast spell to claim him. Portals took a lot of energy, but they were worth the effort for a sight like this.

The great male dragon flew low enough that Merlin caught the scent of musk and cinders as the wings blotted out the sun. The dragon's green head was long and narrow, the sinuous neck twisting to survey the ground below. As it turned, the light caught the bony ridge of spikes that traced its spine to the tip of its snakelike tail.

Rukon's head bobbed toward Merlin in acknowledgment. The dragon's visits were made in exchange for Camelot's assistance last autumn, when Arthur and Guinevere had freed Rukon's mate. Plus, preening before a crowd of unsuspecting humans seemed to amuse the beast no end.

It was only then, with the spell complete, that he could risk a good look at Clary. Her face was flushed with effort, her eyes wide with what looked like shock. Stomach tense, he followed her gaze to the field below.

Clary's illusions sometimes had a mind of their own, but normally they were forms without substance, as dangerous as a puff of smoke. As long as they showed off the knights and their shiny swords, what else mattered? So he hadn't paid much attention when triple the number of required monsters appeared from thin air. Apparently, that had been a mistake.

A lion raked its claws across the flank of Sir Palomedes's steed. The horse screamed, rearing up to reveal a bloody gash. Surprised, the knight struggled to keep his seat, but the terrified horse threw him and bolted for the stables. Horror gut-punched Merlin, and he grabbed the cold metal railing before him. Illusions didn't draw blood. Something was very wrong, and now the lions were circling Palomedes.

Merlin shot a glance at Clary, who had raised her hands and seemed poised to begin another spell. He grabbed her wrist. "Stop!"

She rounded on him. "I can't!"

Her voice held a sharp edge of panic that clutched at Merlin's instincts. She'd gone from flushed to bone-white, her lips trembling with panic. Normally, he made students fix their own problems—it was the best way to learn—but lives were at stake. Right now he had to take charge. He pointed to the bench at the back of the space. "Sit down!"

"I need to make it stop!" Tears stood in her green eyes. Her distress tugged at him, sharp as any beast's fang, but until everyone was safe, he couldn't afford pity. Not even for her.

He thrust her toward the seat. "Sit down and don't touch anything. Whatever you do, don't use magic."

She collapsed so hard the bench squeaked against the concrete. "It's not my fault."

"I don't care." Blame could come later. He needed solutions now.

Merlin turned back to the chaos below. The wolf Clary had conjured was gone, the magic of the illusion spent. That was what was supposed to happen—and it was the only normal thing that *had* happened. The far-too-real lions were only part of the problem. There were a pair of prehistoric creatures straight from nightmare, and one of them had Beaumains cornered. The knight's blade ran red with blood, and so did his sword arm. Merlin's thoughts scrambled in confusion. What the blazes had Clary done?

The audience sensed something was wrong. A strained silence had fallen over the amphitheater, as if every spectator held his breath. The show was supposed to be make-believe, but the fearful whinnies of the horses were all too real. Then shadow fell over the field once again as the dragon flew another loop in the sky. Merlin looked up to see Rukon peering back, the slitted pupils of the huge topaz eyes wide with interest.

The lioness crouched, the motion of her hindquarters making it plain she was about to spring at Palomedes's throat. The sight jerked Merlin back to life. He summoned a shimmering ball of lightning to his hand and hurled it. It struck the lioness square in the back with a flash of pure white brilliance. Air rushed in a thunderclap as the creature burst into a cloud of tiny black scraps that looked like bats. They arrowed upward in a chorus of shrill cries.

Merlin's breath stuck in his chest. The cloud of flying darkness said this was demon magic. Rukon recognized it, too, for the dragon released a stream of blinding, blue-white fire that wiped the flapping shadows from the sky. The spectacle of a fire-breathing dragon changed the somber mood in an instant. The crowd erupted in a collective gasp of wonder and glee. Cries of "Whoa!" and "Go, Merlin!" drowned out the sounds of battle.

But Merlin was just getting started. He scanned the field, giving an involuntary wince at the sight of the dinosaurs. The raptors pranced around Beaumains like naked chickens sizing up a worm. One bled but seemed oblivious to the wound, a primitive need to kill stronger even than pain. Merlin's chest tightened with apprehension as Beaumains stumbled, his own injuries obvious.

Merlin's next fire bolt split in midair to target the two raptors. The fireballs struck the earth with a *thwump* and crackle that fried both monsters to ash. This time nothing flew out of the smoldering ruins. Demons were hard to kill, but enough raw power did the trick. Without sparing the time or energy for satisfaction, he turned his attention back to Palomedes and the circling lions.

Clary—ignoring his orders as usual—was back at Merlin's elbow in time to see Palomedes swing his blade at a shaggy-maned beast. The knight's sword sliced into the lion's hide, driving deep into the massive shoulder. The great cat roared, but the sound twisted into an unholy shriek as the beast dissolved into a flurry of blackness. Merlin flinched, every reflex recoiling at the sight.

"What just happened?" Clary demanded, her voice rising as she pointed at the sight. "Are those crows? Bats?"

"Demon magic does that," Merlin replied, giving her a hard look. "The filth break apart and reform as some other monster."

Her expression raised the hair along his arms, though he couldn't say why. The scowl was Clary's—he'd seen it often enough during their lessons—but there was something else, too. And then the look was gone, leaving him wondering if the battle with Vivian had left him paranoid.

Above, Rukon banked and turned to pass over the field once more. The wind in his huge wings rumbled like rippling thunder. Merlin gathered himself, every movement deliberate, and returned his attention to the lions. He hurled another ball of lightning that smashed into the pride and sent dirt fountaining into the air. One by one, the great cats burst into flurries of squeaking shreds of blackness. They swirled upward in a spiral, no doubt preparing to meld into some other, more horrific creature. Merlin searched for a fresh spell, something powerful enough to prevent a demonic attack on the crowd of innocent humans. Was this what the hellspawn had wanted all along? A means to infect this world with their evil?

If so, they had forgotten about dragons. A blast from Rukon's flame scoured the bats from the sky. Merlin felt the clean heat on his upturned face, fanned by the stroke of Rukon's wings. The stink of charcoal tickled his nose, but not before he caught a distinctive whiff of spice and sulfur. *Vivian.*

Then every thought was driven from his head by the roar of the crowd. They were on their feet, stamping and howling appreciation as the unprecedented spectacle wound to a new close. As if on cue, Rukon looped upward, climbing toward the open portal with another flourish of flame. The dragon rose with seemingly weightless ease and was soon swallowed by the azure sky of the Crystal Mountains. But his long neck curved backward for a last glance at Merlin. It didn't take magic to read the message written in Rukon's topaz eyes: *be careful.* And then the portal sealed with the efficiency of an invisible zipper, and the dragon was gone.

Merlin gripped Clary's arm, holding her at his side while they stepped forward to take their bow. He was carefully blind to the knights below, acting as if their wounds and bewildered fury were all part of the entertainment. They'd finished the show. No one was dead and the demon magic dispelled. The audience was none the wiser. The only thing left was to exit the stage—and then he could start asking hard questions.

After three standing ovations, the audience finally let them leave. By then, Merlin's temper was at a new peak. He dragged Clary into the corridor that led to the locker room, striding at top speed.

"Slow down!" Digging in her heels, she tried to wrench free of his grip.

He stopped, but didn't let go as he turned to face her. The harsh overhead lights bleached the color from her face, adding to the shadows beneath her eyes. He crushed a rising panic that told him she was in trouble. "Very well."

She blew out a long breath, but otherwise seemed tongue-tied.

He let his voice drop to something near a growl. "Let's take this slowly. Start talking."

She was shuddering as if plunged into Arctic waters. "I don't know what to say."

"Velociraptors? Really?"

"I didn't mean to! I—" She broke off, her face flushed with confusion. She looked as if she couldn't decide what to say.

Merlin's chest tightened with foreboding. "If you didn't mean it, then why did it happen?"

Clary sucked in a breath as if he'd struck her. The sound was loud in the echoing corridor.

Her expression gut-punched him. "What did Tamsin say about your wound?"

"She thinks it's okay." She pulled up her sleeve to show her arm. "It doesn't look like much now. She fixed it."

And yet Clary had started casting random spells far beyond her level of skill. That didn't say *fixed* to him. Her gaze turned to him, now empty of everything but fear and pleading. The look broke him.

Like a man in a dream, Merlin reached out, stroking

her cheek with his fingertips. They came away wet with her frightened tears. For that, he would have cheerfully sent every demon back to the Abyss all over again. As the pounding of his heart slowed, anger caught up with him, along with a profound sense of awe. Something had given Clary immense, even stunning, power. Demons were the obvious answer, but how?

Clary was the least talented student he'd ever taught. Could a mere scratch have changed everything? He really didn't know. Demon magic followed different rules—if you could apply rules to its chaotic nature—and not even Merlin the Wise understood every last nuance. A hard knot of worry gathered in his chest. He could not resist the urge to touch her, brushing back a wisp of hair that was falling in her eyes.

Somehow that innocent gesture turned into an embrace. He'd sworn to himself that wouldn't happen again, but her lips were against his, soft and uncertain. The first kiss ended, her breath warm and a little too fast against his face. It had been a long time since he'd allowed himself this kind of intimacy—not just physical need, but with emotion attached. Everything around him—the concrete walls, the dull roar of the crowd—fell away, leaving only this woman and her haunted gaze. It was plain she was seeking reassurance, someone to catch her and put her on her feet again. If he was a better man, he'd be a little less literal about the catching part, but he couldn't seem to take his hands from her waist.

Her fingers curled in the fabric of his costume. "What are you doing?"

This unguarded, vulnerable side of her destroyed his equilibrium. "Making certain you're well."

He pushed back the veil of her costume and tangled his fingers in her shaggy blond hair. She tilted her head, studying him from beneath her lashes. "You can't tell anything by kissing me." And yet she looked afraid that he might find something.

He released her, but didn't back away. Her eyes were their usual color, like new leaves in the golden light of May. Her skin glowed the same delicate cream, her mouth still invited him—and yet something was different. It prickled against a sense that had no name.

She put one hand on his sleeve, the lines of her face going tight. "Tell me what I should do."

He couldn't answer. He didn't know how to put his uneasiness into words.

The moment ended when a door slammed behind him. Heavy footsteps marched their way. Clary took a short, sharp breath.

"Merlin!" came a booming voice that rang against the concrete walls.

Merlin turned to see Arthur Pendragon, still in full armor, closing the distance between them. The king's russet hair was brushed back from a face dominated by pale blue and furious eyes. He came to a stop just feet away, chain mail rattling with the sudden halt. His fingers tapped once on the helmet clutched under his arm. "What happened? My knights were injured, two of them badly."

Arthur's gaze went from Merlin to Clary, demanding answers.

Silently, Merlin stepped between them, blocking the king's view.

Chapter 5

Merlin never protected me that way, Vivian commented inside Clary's head, her tone haughty. *I never needed it.*

No doubt the comment was meant as an insult, but Clary didn't care. One look at Arthur's scowl said she needed all the protection she could get, and one of the few people who could face Arthur down was Merlin. The king and the enchanter had a long, if sometimes volatile, friendship.

"How are Beaumains and Palomedes?" Merlin asked.

"They will survive," the king replied. "Fortunately, Tamsin was working at the church today and could come in minutes."

"That's good news," said Merlin.

Clary literally gulped, wondering how bad the wounds might be. Her stomach felt like ice.

Don't worry, said Vivian. *Those wounds are clean. I don't bother with poison when simple fangs and claws will do.*

Why do it at all? Clary shrieked inside her head, but as she peered around Merlin's straight back at the king, she understood. Arthur was furious. Of the hundred and fifty knights of the Round Table, only a handful had awakened in the modern era. They were his friends, the only familiar faces from his old life, and they were all he had to fight the armies of the fae. What better way to pit Arthur against Merlin than threatening his men?

"You put my knights in danger," said the king in a low, rasping voice.

"That was not our intent." Merlin shifted, blotting out her view of Arthur's flushed face.

"Perhaps it was not yours, but I know the script of the show." The king's tone rose, sharp with anger. "Your student was responsible."

Again, people were talking as if Clary wasn't there. Her temper stirred, but she didn't dare protest when this was her fault.

"There was a mistake," said Merlin with icy calm.

"A mistake?" Arthur snarled. "If it was not for Tamsin, Beaumains would never hold a sword again!"

Clary squeezed her eyes shut, heartsick. Beaumains was a good friend—cheerful, kind and almost like a brother. He *would* be an in-law once Gawain and Tamsin married, since he was Gawain's youngest sibling. And her hands had cast the spell that had nearly killed him. The knowledge made her stomach roll.

"I want answers." Arthur's demand gave no room to refuse.

"We all do," Merlin said evenly. "I will find the cause of what happened."

Clary fell back a step. Answers were the one thing she needed and the last thing she could ask for. The demon inside her was still, and yet she could almost hear it snicker. Clary took another step, this time toward the exit to the locker rooms. The distance gave her a view of the two men. Arthur had one finger planted on Merlin's chest. The king's expression was thunderous, but Merlin's was like stone.

Merlin looked at her, moving only his head. "Go get changed and I'll meet you at the concession stand. Don't leave until we've talked."

Cringing with guilt, Clary wasted no time making her retreat. She'd put Merlin at odds with his king. She'd put the knights in danger. If that wasn't bad enough, she was hiding the vengeful demon behind it all. She was a coward—but

Vivian had threatened her sister. What was she supposed to do?

Frustration made her move quickly. It took less than five minutes to change and walk to the concession stand, where happy throngs of tourists were buying Knightly Nachos and Jalapeño Dragon Fries by the bucket. Clary stood beside the booth with the straws and napkins, watching the path for Merlin's approach. Normally, she'd be tweeting or posting pictures from the afternoon's show, but she wanted to hide instead. Even the smell of the food, usually so tempting, turned her stomach.

The familiarity of the place oppressed her, too, as if Medievaland itself knew what she'd done. So many of her hopes and dreams were tied up in the place. She'd spilled blood on this earth during her endless sparring matches with Gawain. There had been countless midnight practices with Merlin on the tourney ground, throwing balls of energy until she hit the target. He'd drilled her mercilessly, not just in illusions but in portals and farseeing, summoning and casting. The big empty grounds had been perfect for the messes she'd inevitably made. Merlin never seemed to care, but just made her do the spells over and over and over...

She didn't notice the couple approach until it was too late. They were both in their teens, the boy tall and rangy and the girl with a short afro and ebony skin. "Are you Clary Greene?" the boy asked with an infectious smile.

Clary managed to nod.

"We saw you with the wizard today. That show rocked."

"Would you?" the girl asked, handing her a program and a pen decorated with moons and stars.

"Sure." Clary took the pen and paper and managed what she hoped was a friendly smile. She didn't want to celebrate her role in the show, much less take a bow for something that was actually a disaster. Still, she couldn't confess to launching homicidal demon constructs. Those conversations never ended well, even with other witches.

Vivian's amusement hit her like heartburn. Grinding her teeth, Clary braced the program against the side of the booth and started to write, then blinked. Rather than her own name, she'd scrawled an elaborate rune. *Well,* sighed the demon, *you can't blame me. No one's ever asked for my autograph before.*

That's not a spell that will harm the girl? Clary demanded.

And injure my first human fan? Goodness me, no. I haven't had this kind of adoration since I was revered as a goddess, and that was simply ages ago. I'm feeling generous.

After a moment of confusion, Clary scrawled her name beside the rune and handed the pen and paper back to the girl.

"Cool!" the girl said, peering at the scribble. "Thanks a lot!"

Clary barely noticed them leave, directing her thoughts inward instead. *Don't do things like that! You'll give us away.*

Do you care that much for my safety? The words dripped with sarcasm.

Don't play games. Clary shifted, finding a patch of deeper shade. *You've already threatened to harm Tamsin if you're found out.*

Do you think I'd blame you for something I did?

You're a demon. Isn't that the kind of thing demons do? I care for my sister too much to risk it.

You do care for your sister. I can feel it like a warm fire in your soul. The sarcasm was gone. *And you care for Merlin, though that is a very different fire.*

Merlin had kissed Clary right after the show—she hadn't had time to take that in before now, and the memory made her palms grow damp. It hadn't been the angry, frustrated kiss he'd demanded from her after the ritual—this time his touch had been gentle, as if meant to comfort. She'd never seen that side of him before, and it left her a little shaken, almost humbled. Merlin the Wise never dropped his guard.

Oh, for pity's sake, haven't you ever had a lover before? Vivian sounded irritated.

Sure. Clary stiffened. *Lots.*

Why aren't you with one of them? Vivian's curiosity was a tangible thing. *Surely there is a better fit for the likes of you.*

Yeah, well, the witches have an expression. They didn't waft my wand.

There was a beat of blessed silence where Clary was free to watch the hot dog–munching public come and go. A warm breeze rippled through the maple trees, promising a pleasant evening. Then Vivian broke into her thoughts again. *Why not? Why weren't they enough?*

Clary's temper stirred. *None of your business. You're not my BFF.*

To her surprise, Vivian fell quiet again without a fight. Still, Clary could feel her presence like a dull toothache. There was something wistful about her mood, as if beneath her contempt was a childlike confusion about human relationships. That didn't make Vivian any less dangerous or passionate. Rather, it was more like being trapped in an elevator with a toddler—a toddler armed with a flame-thrower.

She saw Merlin striding toward her. He was still wearing his enchanter's robes and drawing stares from the crowd. His face was stony.

"Come with me," he said, grabbing her arm and pulling her into the stream of pedestrians.

"What's going on?" she asked, tension swarming

through her. "Is everyone okay? How mad is the king? Am I fired?"

"You're not fired yet, but unless we get out of sight that may change." As he spoke, patches of color flushed his high cheekbones. "The only reason you're not in the king's custody is because I've promised to investigate this afternoon's events. If I don't find satisfactory answers, we're both in trouble."

He was putting himself on the line for her. Clary felt Vivian's twinge of satisfaction, followed by the image of Tamsin's face. A plain warning.

Clary pulled out of Merlin's grasp. "You don't need to do this for me."

"You're my student. I know what you're capable of, and none of that should have happened." He glared down at her. "It doesn't make sense."

"Sorry that offends you." She wanted to get away, to put as much distance between Merlin and Vivian's revenge as she could. And yet one look at his face said he wasn't letting her leave his sight.

"You put everyone, especially yourself, at risk." He put an arm around her shoulder, propelling through the exit and into the parking lot. It might look like an affectionate gesture, but Clary felt the steel in his arm. "I can't let this slide."

He led her to a four-door black SUV, one of Camelot's vehicles. Merlin himself didn't own a car, more often using magic to travel, but after a show he often drove to conserve energy. He pulled the robes over his head and threw the costume in the backseat. He was left wearing jeans and a black T-shirt.

Clary folded her arms. "So what do you intend to do?"

"Go for coffee." He opened the passenger door, releasing warm air that smelled vaguely horsey. One of the knights must have driven the car right after jousting practice. "You and I need to talk."

He drove to Mandala Books, which had a coffee shop and bakery in the back. The merger of the two businesses—and of the old Victorian houses that contained them—had been recently completed and the scent of new paint and sawdust still lingered in the air. Nimueh, the fae Lady of the Lake, was still a silent partner in the business, but she and Sir Lancelot du Lac rarely visited anymore. Most of their time was spent in the Forest Sauvage, keeping watch on the prison of Morgan LaFaye.

Merlin chose a table far in the back of the café, where they had some privacy. A server brought black coffee and a cinnamon bun before Merlin had to ask, which said something about how often he went there. Clary ordered a London Fog and looked around the place. It had wooden floors and pine tables with checkered cloths, geraniums in the window boxes and chandeliers made from old mason jars. An enticing view of the bookstore peeped through the archway that joined the two buildings. It was homey and simple.

"This doesn't seem like your kind of place," she said to Merlin as the waitress set the vanilla tea latté before her.

He shrugged. "Nimueh placed powerful protections around it, which makes it safe. Plus, they have an excellent bakery."

She watched him take a huge bite of the cinnamon bun. She'd never pegged Merlin as having a sweet tooth. Usually he was all about vitamins and lean protein. "That thing has enough calories to feed a small village."

He shrugged. "I burned it off during the show. Fireballs take energy."

She looked away, her mind's eye fixed on memories of lightning and dragon fire. "Why did you protect me from Arthur?"

"I need to understand what happened." He washed the pastry down with coffee, his shoulders easing a little. "Tell me what you experienced when you cast those spells."

She could feel Vivian come alert inside her, and so she chose her words with care. "The show started okay. The spell that made the wolf worked normally. Then the next one had a mind of its own and then—I can barely remember."

He studied her through critical eyes. "You're holding something back."

"So are you," Clary retorted. It was a random strike, but the fleeting alarm in his expression said she'd struck home. She sucked in a breath. "Trust works both ways, doesn't it? There was more to that ritual you did than you're saying."

"I told you already. I was conducting surveillance on the demons, which you interrupted." He made a face. "A demon has been sighted in the Forest Sauvage in the company of the fae. The king and I wish to know why."

"Did you learn anything?" Clary sensed Vivian's interest and wished she hadn't asked.

"Perhaps."

"What?"

"Nothing that concerns you."

"I got hurt. That makes it my concern." Clary pushed her tea away. More than anything, she wanted to demand he evict the demon from inside her head. Despite Vivian's threats, the need for privacy was like a maddening itch.

Don't, warned Vivian. *If he knows I'm here, he will do his best to destroy me. Your mortal form is too fragile to withstand such an assault.*

How long are you going to keep this up? Clary demanded.

As I said, you are too weak a vessel for an open fight. I will have to take him by surprise. Therefore, I need you until that moment.

Clary's lips parted in surprise. She had to say something—this was unbearable.

Remember your sister.

Clary let loose a sob, but covered her mouth. Merlin was looking at her, a furrow creasing his brow.

But the demon chose to drive her point home. Paralysis crept from Clary's tongue all the way to her lungs. When she tried to inhale, nothing happened. A fiery pain spread through her chest. Clary strained, starting to choke. *Please! Please let me go!* Fear clawed at her insides until Vivian suddenly released her. Clary dissolved into a spluttering fit of coughing. Merlin jumped up, making the dishes rattle. He bent over her, patting her back until she stopped. "Did you choke?"

She nodded, mopping her eyes with a napkin. "Something stuck in my throat."

"Perhaps an explanation you aren't telling me?" he asked, sliding back into his chair. Now that the crisis was over, he was once again cool and professional. "You have a secret and I want an answer. I suspect they are exactly the same thing."

And Clary was almost certain whatever he wasn't telling her contained the answers to her predicament. They were in a deadlock. Merlin had dirty laundry—dirty, demonic laundry.

"If you hate demons so much, why did you have one as a girlfriend?"

Merlin's face was like stone. And now, the one time Clary wanted the demon to chime in, Vivian was mute. Okay, then. Apparently, there was a juicy story there.

He leaned forward, fixing her with his amber eyes. "Are you going to help me?" he asked softly.

Clary had to tell him something, so she gave him the merest sliver of truth. "What if Tamsin didn't cure everything? What if there is a lingering demon poison that affected my magic?"

She felt Vivian's claws prick the inside of her mind, threatening to shred her from the inside out, but Clary stood her ground. The demon needed her alive for the moment, and she hadn't given away the whole truth. They had to compromise to get through this.

Merlin's face remained still, but his eyes closed as if in thanks. "That's possible."

"Can you test for something like that?"

"Sort of." His face fell as he put money for their coffee on the table.

"Just sort of?"

"There are one or two methods that do not harm the subject." He looked uncomfortable.

"You're such a romantic," Clary said, and then gripped the edge of the table, blackness nibbling at the edge of her vision. Her heart drummed in her ears, leaving her hot and weak.

Merlin circled the table, kneeling beside her. "What's wrong? You've gone pale."

Clary struggled to answer, and this time it wasn't the demon who froze her tongue. It was the horrific realization it hadn't been her that had spoken. *You're such a romantic.* That had been Vivian's thought, Vivian's words. She was losing control to the demon.

Clary met Merlin's eyes, holding his gaze and willing him to understand all the things she couldn't say. A crease formed between his brows, and he put a hand to her cheek, his palm cool against her fevered skin. Slowly, his thumb stroked her cheekbone, the gesture offering her a shred of comfort.

"Help me," she begged.

Chapter 6

Merlin's hand covered hers. "Of course."

Clary closed her eyes, not able to meet his gaze any longer. She concentrated on the feel of his touch and the long, strong fingers wrapping around hers. She was being split in two, but he was a solid anchor. "Okay," she whispered.

"Come." Merlin's hands were gentle as he pulled her to her feet. "Let's take care of this."

Clary followed him to the car. "Where are we going?"

"To your sister's."

"Tamsin's?" she asked in horror. The last thing she wanted was to put Vivian and her sister in the same room.

Merlin shot her a curious look as they got into the SUV. He started the engine. "Is there a problem with that?"

Vivian's claws dug into Clary's mind, sharp as any physical pain but far more frightening. Somehow she knew whatever injuries the demoness might cause to her mind and soul would never heal. She cleared her throat. "Tamsin's done what she can already."

Merlin pulled away from the curb into Carlyle's afternoon rush. "Maybe, maybe not. I have an idea she can help me with."

"She won't have time. She'll still be at Medievaland, healing the knights."

"I already asked her to meet us at her place when she's finished." He gave her an inscrutable glance. "We talked before I met you at the concession stand."

Defeated, Clary sank back into the leather seat of the

SUV. How was she going to keep Vivian in check? Even if there was a cure for her demon problem, surely Vivian would fight back.

You're quite right, little witch, but let's not get ahead of ourselves. Your lovely sister hasn't had a patient quite like you and me before.

And she'd failed to detect Vivian's presence once. There was every chance she'd miss it again.

Just so. If Merlin trusts her healing skills to find me, her failure will work in my favor.

Clary understood. After all, Vivian wanted to catch Merlin by surprise. However, if Tamsin made a correct diagnosis… Clary dropped that train of thought, already feeling a wave of nausea clog her throat. There was no way to win. She stared at the passing streets, scrambling for an answer where no one got hurt.

When they arrived at Tamsin's door, the smell of tomato sauce filled the apartment hallway. Her sister answered Merlin's knock, a wooden spoon in her hand.

"It's Gawain's favorite dinner," Tamsin said in explanation. "He'll be home soon and after today, we all want comfort food."

"Aren't you tired?" Clary asked, noting the dark circles under her sister's eyes. "You must have just got home."

She followed her into the kitchen. Tamsin moved the pot of sauce and turned off the burner, her movements brisk. "Of course I'm tired, but I just did the cleanup. I didn't fight."

Then she turned to face Clary, fear tightening her jaw. "I've seen demon-born monsters before. What were you doing?"

Clary took a step back. She could see the picture forming in Tamsin's head—Gawain, brave knight and love of her life, perishing in the jaws of Clary's creation. Tamsin's future destroyed by her hapless kid sister. The scene wasn't far off the mark.

"I'm sorry," Clary said softly. "In perfect honesty, I don't know exactly how that happened." *And for all our sakes,* she willed her sister, *don't look deeper.*

Emotions cycled through Tamsin's expression. Anger. Fear. Compassion. The last was the worst because it was so familiar. Once again, Clary was the weak magical link in the family. The only difference now was that her incompetence had hurt their friends.

Tamsin licked her lips, seeming to come to a decision. "Go have a seat in the living room. Send Merlin in here so I can talk to him."

Clary's first instinct was to object on principle. As the youngest child, she'd been shut out of adult conversations too often. This time, though, she'd be keeping Vivian out of earshot. Clary did as she was told and turned on the TV to make eavesdropping impossible.

You think you're being clever, Vivian sneered.

Yes. Clary changed the channel to a home renovation show. She didn't care about fascia boards and roof tiles, but the shirtless construction guys were cute.

Vivian snorted, but her attention drifted to the show. *Do humans truly have to rely on teams of physical workers to keep the rain off their heads?*

Clary rolled her eyes at the demon's appalled tone. *Pretty much. When you don't have magic powers, you need helping hands. That's how this world works.*

And sometimes the magically gifted needed help, too. When Tamsin and Merlin reappeared, her sister was holding a clay goblet filled with steaming brew. Clary turned off the TV and accepted the cup. The mixture smelled of woodlands and flowers, more like a herbal tea than a strong medicinal. Nevertheless, Vivian's interest zeroed in on it with laser focus.

"What is it?" Clary asked.

With a weary sigh, Tamsin sank into Gawain's oversize leather chair. "Just drink it."

Merlin sat on the sofa to Clary's left, putting her between the two of them. His expression was, as usual, guarded and cool. "It will stimulate the body's natural healing and help the infection pass from your system."

Clary took another sniff. "There are raspberry leaves in here."

Raspberry? Vivian scoffed. *That's supposed to stop me?*

Clary looked up at her sister, who folded her arms. "Drink up," Tamsin said.

Clary lifted the goblet, feeling the steam against her cheeks.

Wait! Vivian demanded. *There has to be something else in there. Something she's not saying.*

Clary—and the demoness—studied Tamsin for answers, but her sister's expression gave nothing away. And, concentrating as she was, Clary didn't feel the needle Merlin stabbed into her thigh until it was too late. Brew splashed as she dropped the goblet in surprise. It thunked to the carpet and rolled to Tamsin's feet.

What was that? Vivian shrieked. Clary felt the slash of claws, but they were already blunted, rendered harmless by whatever had been in the needle.

With a shaking hand, her sister picked up the goblet and set it on the coffee table. "I'm sorry, little witchling. We had to do it."

Clary watched her sister with an open mouth, too surprised for any deeper emotion, then spun to face Merlin, who still held the hypodermic. He glanced at it, and it dissolved into smoke.

"You tricked me!" she said, accusing them both.

"Apologies," he said. "We had no way of knowing if this lingering infection of yours might try something."

Bewildered, Clary glanced down at the stain on the carpet.

"It was just Pixie Forest blend from the local tea shop," said Tamsin, not meeting Clary's eyes. "The most it was going to do was make you sleepy."

Betrayal stung almost as much as the fiery sensation crawling up her leg. They didn't trust her to take whatever cure they offered. Worse, they saw her as a genuine threat that had to be managed. Her mind understood, but her heart hurt.

"Then what was in the shot?" she asked, her voice gone rough.

The pain had reached her belly. Vivian howled—or maybe it was her. Clary doubled over, clutching her middle. Merlin steadied her with firm hands, easing her back onto the couch. "It will put whatever you have to sleep. It might interfere with your powers for a time, but the tradeoff in safety will be worthwhile."

Merlin the Wise always knows what's best, said Vivian in a sarcastic snarl.

But he spoke the truth. Clary could feel Vivian draining away, disappearing to somewhere too deep inside for Clary to detect. She wanted to test for the demon's presence, poking around as she would for a sore tooth, but her thoughts scattered. The pain rippling through her was like wave after wave of fire.

At the same time, that feeling of being watched was finally gone. "There was a demon's voice talking in my head," she gasped. "It was Vivian."

"I suspected something like that." His face unreadable, Merlin stroked a hand over her bowed head just once, more apology in his gesture than his words. "Demon essence leaves echoes behind. Demons are energy and Vivian was caught between worlds. It's not surprising that a bit of her touched you during the ritual."

Sure, during the part where she blew into messy demon bits as the portal closed. Clearly, those bits had tried to re-assemble themselves inside Clary.

"Witches are vulnerable because demons can attach themselves to another person's magic." Despite Merlin's closed expression, his voice was gentle. "It's serious, Clary. It can drive people mad."

"How long will this cure last?"

Tamsin knelt before her, pressing a damp cloth to Clary's face. It was wonderfully cool. "It's hard to say, but it should hold until the infection leaves your system."

"She'll come back. She's more than just an echo."

"Hush," Tamsin murmured, putting a hand to Clary's face. "We don't know that yet."

Clary wanted to argue, but her head was pounding now. A tide of sickness rose up, swamping every other consideration. She jumped up, pushing past her sister, and ran for the bathroom.

The only good thing was that she hadn't had much to eat. Too bad whatever drug Merlin had given her didn't care if her stomach was empty. At some point, she locked the door to keep Tamsin out. Her sister might be a healer, but Clary needed privacy more than soothing words. After a while, Tamsin's anxious voice faded and Clary slumped on the cold tile in peace.

What was she going to do? If the cure wasn't permanent, she'd be back in the same hopeless place the moment Vivian woke up. Except it would be worse. Vivian would be furious, and Tamsin would be in even more danger. Merlin would be vulnerable, because now he believed Clary was, if not cured, at least inert.

She needed to get away, far away, to someplace where Tamsin and Merlin would be safe. Her own Shadowring Coven was on the opposite coast of the continent. Better yet, she could go to a circle of witches where she didn't know anyone and there would be no friends or family Vivian could use as hostages. The moment she formed that thought, it became her plan. It was clear, simple and the right thing to do.

Clary already hated the idea. It made sense, but she craved emotional comfort, too. She'd always been the independent misfit, whistling her way through scrape after scrape, and yet home had always been there. So had her sisters. Cutting herself off wouldn't be easy.

She heard Merlin's voice, muffled by the door and distance to the next room. Tamsin replied. The words weren't clear, but her sister's concern was evident. Clary didn't have much time before someone was knocking on the door again. If they stopped her before she got away, it would be twice as hard to leave them behind.

Eventually, Clary got to her feet. Pain made her knees wobble as she stood. She drank some water, then stole some mouthwash to get the vile taste out of her mouth. Finally, she looked in the mirror, confirming she looked as awful as she felt.

Slowly, she opened the bathroom door. Merlin and her sister were in the living room down the hall, their view of her blocked by the angle of the wall. To Clary's left, just a few steps away, was the apartment door. A glance told her that Tamsin hadn't locked it when they'd come in.

Years of teenage misbehavior had made her an expert at sneaking out. Clary slipped away, silently shutting the door behind her. Since she didn't carry a purse, she still had her keys, wallet and phone in her pockets. Nothing was left behind at her sister's place. All she had to do was make it home to pack a suitcase, and she'd leave town. A quick mental check told her Vivian was still gone.

Clary ran down the apartment stairs, not bothering with the elevator. The exit emptied into the parking lot, and she strode across the sunny pavement with renewed confidence. And nearly ended up a speedbump for Gawain's motorcycle.

Oh, hell! She jumped back, plastering a smile on her face and waving brightly. The Scottish knight waved back, used to her coming and going. That would only buy her minutes at best. The instant he opened the door and mentioned that he'd seen her, the search would be on.

Clary slipped out of sight and ran. Now going straight home wasn't an option. In fact, all the places she knew—Tamsin's, her own apartment, Medievaland, Merlin's place—were bound to be under Merlin's magical surveillance. She wasn't sure what to do. Maybe head to the bus station and catch a ride out of town?

She entered an alley that crept between a gas station and a pub. It was smelly and narrow, the brickwork on either side black with age and dirt. Patches of straggling grass grew under rusted downspouts. Clary looked over her shoulder even though she'd barely taken two steps into the confined space. But that was stupid. She was a witch with a demon on board. That made her like a bomb in an action-adventure movie, one that had to be dumped in an ocean or shot into outer space before it nuked the free world. She could blast any mugger to smithereens.

Squaring her shoulders, Clary pushed on. It was broad daylight, and she could tell this alley was a shortcut to the main road ahead. Going this way would put distance between herself and well-meaning friends.

Halfway across, she heard music from a window above. It was an ordinary pop tune, barely worth remembering, but someone with an exceptional voice was singing along with the words. *That* was special.

The sound vanished as quickly as it had come, but Clary paused just long enough to look up. There were curtains and knickknacks in the second-floor windows, and the sash of one was pushed up. That had to be where the voice had come from. There was only one kind of being that could sing so beautifully—a fae.

Despite the lovely song, Clary drew back. The soul-sucking monsters found witches especially tasty. She spun on her heel, ready to run, but a figure dropped from the window right into her path. The male rose from his crouch as if this was a perfectly normal way to say hello. He was tall and slender, casually dressed but for an elaborately tooled belt of green leather. A long, silver-handed knife hung at his hip. He sniffed the air, as if confirming it was she who had smelled so tasty.

"Great," Clary muttered under her breath.

"Where are you going, my girl?" asked the fae. He had dark olive skin that showed off the bright green of his eyes. His long, white hair was pulled back to reveal a fine-boned face that would have put him on the front of any fashion magazine.

"I'm going past you." Clary raised her hands, ready to weave a spell that would hurl the fae into the next block. Except no power flowed through her body, ready to shape to her will.

She was helpless. Merlin had warned her that the injection might mess with her magic, but she hadn't expected this.

The fae must have seen her confusion, because he burst into a cruel laugh.

Chapter 7

Panic made Clary stagger back. Her magic had never been brilliant, but it was as much a part of her as sight or hearing. She clenched her fists, fighting a need to scream. Her struggle seemed to amuse the fae even more. Or maybe amusement was the wrong word. While fae had no feelings, they still seemed to enjoy tormenting their prey.

"Who are you, pretty boy?" Clary demanded, mostly to make him stop sniggering.

"I am Laren of the Green Towers." He waved a hand at the alley. "Or perhaps I should say the back streets. The hunting is far better here."

By hunting, he meant stealing the life essence of mortals. Drinking mortal souls restored a fae's emotions, their love of beauty and ability to create—but only for a short while. Those addicted to the rush left a trail of dead or mindless victims in their wake. At least Laren appeared physically healthy, which meant he hadn't been a soul-eater for long.

"What happened to your witch's tricks?" he taunted.

"I'm on a cleanse." She shifted her feet, bracing to run. Fae were incredibly strong despite their slight appearance. Unless Clary found a weapon, she'd lose the fight before it began.

"Afraid to face me, wench?" Laren glided forward, his steps silent. His intent, predatory posture reminded her of the velociraptor's.

"The name's Clary. I'd stay and brawl, but my calendar's full."

She spun and ran, pumping her legs for all she was worth. She'd made it past a row of garbage cans before Laren tackled her to the ground, his arms wrapped around her waist. Apparently, the fae were as fast as they were strong.

Clary's knees exploded with pain as she fell, the fae's weight driving her into the ground. She raised her arms to protect her face, but not before a blur of gravel and straggling weeds filled her view. Her lungs emptied in a rush. Stunned, she lay helpless as Laren flipped her over and straddled her waist.

It was then she met his eyes. They were green like her own, but a vibrant shade unlike any mortal's. And they were utterly, chillingly void of feeling. The loss of his soul had turned him into something alien. She might as well have been pinned by a shark.

Terror flooded her, robbing the last shreds of her strength. She had no magic and no weapon. She drew in a shaking breath, fighting down the urge to wail.

His lips drew back from his teeth in a mockery of a smile. "What a pretty thing you are." He placed a fingertip between her eyes and traced downward, over the tip of her nose and the bow of her lips. "You will be delicious."

Clary shuddered at the naked hunger in his face. It promised a brutal end, and a primitive instinct to live took over. She twisted beneath him, arching her back against his weight. Laren pushed her down again, but not before the knife in his belt caught her eye, its silver hilt gleaming in the alley's muted sunlight. A fae hunter would need such a thing to finish his victims. It taunted her, promising death or just maybe deliverance.

She widened her eyes, letting all her fear show. Laren's nostrils flared as if scenting her distress. His knees tightened against her hips and he grabbed her jaw, using one hand to pin her head in place. That was all he needed to control her. Compared with his strength, her arms might have been helplessly beating wings.

Or not. Clary plucked the knife from its scabbard with a quick hiss of steel on leather and drove it toward his ribs. It would have worked, if not for fae reflexes. He twisted with the agility of a cat, his free hand clamping around her wrist in an iron grip.

A chilling sound of regret escaped his lips. "Very good. I see I'm growing careless." He peeled the knife from her fingers and tossed it just out of reach. Clary heard it fall with a ping of metal on stone. Clearly, he wasn't a warrior obsessed with keeping his blades in perfect condition.

Then he bent over her again, the smell of his skin and sweat far too intimate. He grabbed her jaw once more, forcing her mouth open with bruising insistence. "Give yourself to me," he whispered. "Give me your joy and tears and hope." His lips sealed over hers.

The assault on her soul was far, far worse than she had ever imagined. It felt as if her insides were being torn through her throat, leaving an icy vacuum behind. She pushed against his chest, but he was solid as granite. Her hands fumbled to his face, poking and clawing and finally to his hair, but nothing made him flinch. Sight and sound vanished, leaving only an unholy pain. Finally, Clary screamed, but Laren drank that down along with everything else.

Then something hurled him back. Clary collapsed backward, hitting her head on a sharp rock. The universe swam for an instant before she rolled to her side to see Merlin standing over Laren. She expected Merlin to pound the fae into a pulp, shock him with thunderbolts—something— but the enchanter stood poised and unmoving, a look of naked curiosity on his face.

Then she realized that the fae writhed on the ground in agony, his grinding moans like nothing she'd ever heard. Taking no chances, Clary fumbled for the knife he'd thrown aside and staggered to her feet, using the filthy wall for support. Slowly she approached, the long blade gripped in one hand.

Laren's eyes had rolled back into his head until only the whites showed. Foam coated his lips and he trembled with long, violent spasms. Merlin's face was grim as he took her by the shoulders and turned her to face him, scanning her slowly from head to the scuffed toes of her shoes. He squeezed her gently, angling his arms as if for a reckless moment he might decide to pull her close. After an odd hesitation, he let his hands fall away. "Thank the gods you're all right," he said quietly.

For an instant, she saw possessive anger storm over Merlin's face, lighting his odd amber eyes. The primitive heat stirred an answering call deep in her core. Her response was as inevitable as the autumn flight of birds—or perhaps the rage of earthquakes. It was that deep and mesmerizing.

And then the heat in Merlin's eyes was gone, buried again—but this time she saw the effort it took him to hide it, as if it was growing harder to smother. *But why does he care about me, especially after the trouble I've caused?* Not that she'd let him see her doubt. That would leave her cracked open like an egg dropped from its nest to the pavement below. And this wasn't the time for confessions, anyway. She'd just about had her soul snatched. After a long moment, she stepped back, heaving a long breath. She was grateful he'd come and angry he'd stolen her power, and she didn't have the strength to deal with either of those things right then.

Instead, she pointed at the fae writhing at their feet. "What happened to him?"

"I'm not certain, but my first guess would be indigestion," Merlin replied drily.

A slightly hysterical laugh escaped Clary. Her world wavered and she gripped Merlin's arm. Humor aside, the enchanter's remark made no sense, but the evidence was before her eyes. Still, how could her life energy be toxic to a fae? It was ludicrous, and just a little embarrassing.

She opened her mouth to say so just as she passed out.

Clary woke up in an unfamiliar bedroom. After jerking into a sitting position, she pressed a hand to her aching head and found a lump where she'd hit the pavement. An involuntary groan escaped her as she blinked the room into focus. She was clothed and lying on a king-size bed. One wall of the room was exposed brick, the floor wide planks of hardwood sanded to a soft sheen. Another wall was a balcony with a view of the sun fading over the distant hills. This had to be one of those trendy lofts in the downtown's converted warehouses. The furniture was plain but top quality, the bed linens definitely not from a big box store. Whose place was this?

She swung her feet off the bed and took a second look around. The room was nice, but the clutter said a real person lived there. A bookshelf spawned stacks of books around it, like seedlings around a tree. Unfolded laundry was heaped in a chair and spilled over onto the floor.

Slowly, Clary bent and pulled on her shoes, which someone had removed and left beside the bed. Her head throbbed with the change in angle, but it was manageable. When she stood, she caught sight of the T-shirt on the floor by the closet. It was black with a faded logo of a metal rock band, and she'd last seen it stretched over Merlin's chest. Was this his place? It looked too—she searched for the word—normal.

She left the bedroom, curiosity in full flood. The room

opened directly into the main living area, and she caught an impression of more wood, brick and large windows hung with plants. "Anybody home?" Clary called.

Merlin appeared around the corner. "Ah, you're up." His usual mask was firmly in place—cool and slightly amused, as if the world were a movie and he'd already seen the credits. The only clue to his mood was the vertical pleat between his brows.

"Do you live here?" she asked.

He nodded, sipping from a glass of something green. "How are you feeling?"

"Not sure yet." She wrinkled her nose. His drink smelled like lawn clippings. "Is that brew from the Fabrien Spell Scrolls?"

One corner of his mouth quirked. "It's wheat grass from my juicer. Want some?"

Clary shuddered. "Not unless we're going for a true exorcism. Why am I here?"

"Medical observation. You've been through a lot in the past few days." His eyes were thoughtful as he sipped his disgusting drink. "Why did you run from your sister's place? Imagine my surprise when Gawain lumbered in to announce he'd seen you crossing the parking lot."

She looked away. "I'm putting everyone in danger."

"The danger won't vanish with a change in location. You'll just take it somewhere else."

Clary heaved a breath. "Vivian wants revenge on you, and she threatened Tamsin so I would cooperate. We're dealing with more than a slight touch of possession." There, she'd said it. She watched Merlin's face for a reaction.

To her disappointment, he just shrugged, hard to read as ever. "That's Vivian."

"I'm serious."

"I know." For an instant, his composure slipped and she saw lines of tension bracket his mouth. "I suspected as much about halfway through the show at Medievaland. Not even demons are typically that skilled at conjuring, but she is."

"Why didn't you say something?" Her tone grew sharp.

He tossed back the rest of the wheat grass, making a face as he swallowed. "What would Vivian have done if I'd confronted her?"

Clary swallowed, not liking the truth. "She'd have lashed out."

"And that would not have ended well for anybody, especially you."

Clary buried her face in her hands. Of course Merlin had figured it out. He'd just kept his cards hidden from his ex-lover. She hated him for it, but knew her life depended on his skills. "Vivian will come back, you know."

Merlin put a hand on her shoulder and gave it a gentle squeeze. "Yes, but now we have time to figure out a solution."

Clary caught the scent of him: clean soap and cotton and the faint spice of herbs. She realized how familiar it had become to her and how badly she'd come to crave it. She was as addicted as the soul-craving fae. She turned her face away, needing to keep her wits about her. Nothing had changed just because he'd rescued her again. "I can't stay here."

"You're too vulnerable to leave. Your magic doesn't even work."

Her stomach tightened as she struggled between needing Merlin and wanting to punch him. "You took it!" She pulled away from his touch. "You could have asked permission."

"And what would Vivian have said? We've already had that conversation."

Clary all but growled. "You're right."

"Of course I am, which is why you're staying here. Tamsin is getting some things from your apartment." Merlin waved a hand. "Shall I show you around?"

Reluctantly, Clary nodded. She wanted to know what Merlin's home said about him. The kitchen was large and sunny, the dining room dominated by a farm table big enough to seat a dozen people. Instead of dishes, it was covered by a scatter of books and an expensive-looking laptop. In the corner was a telescope with a stand. Another balcony ran on this side of the suite, this time with a view of the downtown. They stepped out to watch the purpling dusk and leaned on the black iron rail, side by side.

"Are you working on a project?" Clary asked with a backward glance at the books on the table.

"Always."

The reply didn't give her much to work with, but she persevered. "What?"

Merlin looked up at the dusky sky. "I'm searching for a cure for the fae. It's my one goal. You saw up close what they've become."

"Yes." She shuddered, feeling again the fae's power draining her soul.

He waited a moment as if to let the memory take full effect. "That's my doing."

The simple statement said so much. Everyone knew the story of how Merlin defeated the demons at the expense of the fae. His battle spell had broken the magic of the witches, too, but at least they had eventually recovered. The accident, in truth an unexpected side effect, had defined him. Many still hated him for it, saying the disaster was a punishment for his pride.

He turned so his back was to the view. He frowned. "Did I tell you that during the ritual one of the demons said their magic could cure the fae?"

The revelation was so unexpected, Clary's mouth dropped open. "Really?"

"I will find out how."

There was no conceit in him now, just a quiet determination. He had vast power, the ear of a king and centuries of wisdom. None of it had helped him until this one thread of hope had come his way. She reached out, brushing his arm with her fingertips. He finally met her gaze, and she finally understood the deep sense of responsibility he carried. It left no room for anything else. No joy, no plans of his own. All those emotions he locked away.

"If you find the cure," she said slowly, "it will erase what happened."

"No," he said, sounding tired now. "It won't erase the past, but it will make the future something I can live with."

His words had brought an ache to the back of her throat. She let her hand drop, suddenly overwhelmed with the need to touch more of him, but uncertain if that would be welcome. "How are you going to get this cure?"

"Come with me." He pushed away from the balcony, leading the way back inside.

The rest of the condominium consisted of a small library, the usual storage closets and a guest bedroom. He paused at the door to the bedroom, holding up a hand to indicate Clary should stay where she was. He opened the door slowly, revealing a small chamber with the bed pushed against the far wall. An elaborate spell circle was chalked on the remainder of the floor. She'd been Merlin's student long enough to recognize the containment spell that would keep just about anything within the boundary of the chalked lines.

Laren of the Green Towers hunched in the middle of spell circle. The fae had his knees drawn up to his chest as if cold, his expression pure misery. Clary didn't care if he wasn't happy about captivity. This was the creature who had tried to devour her soul.

She rounded on Merlin. "What's he doing here?"

Chapter 8

Laren cowered at the sound of Clary's voice, curling in on himself like a frightened child. Nothing about his posture reminded her of the fae who'd attacked her in the alley, and she glared at Merlin, silently demanding an explanation.

"He is not who he was," Merlin replied, his voice almost colorless. "Or perhaps I should say he's someone he hasn't been for a long time."

"No." Laren began to rock, lowering his forehead to his knees. "I cannot be what I was. I remember it all and there is no hope of going back."

Clary was utterly mystified. "I don't get it."

"He tasted your life essence," said Merlin. "Not a lot, but enough that it reversed the spell."

She swore under her breath. "Demon essence to reverse a demon spell."

And it was in her, whether Vivian was contained by Merlin's potion or not. Apparently, it was mixing with her own life force sufficiently to roofie a hungry fae. If Clary needed more proof that she was in trouble, this was it. Her temples throbbed. "Is he okay?"

"Laren's soul has returned to him," said Merlin. "But as he says, he remembers everything."

She closed her eyes, only able to guess at what a fae might have done after a thousand years without a conscience. With no sense of beauty, no joy or natural desire, novelty was everything to his kind. That typically involved bloodshed, or a taste for mortal souls. Now he had to face what he had done.

He began to softly sob. It was the sound of a heart breaking.

Clary's breath was jagged. She looked up into Merlin's face. For once, his mask had slipped and Laren's pain was mirrored in the lines around his eyes and mouth. She could hear his words once more: *You saw up close what the fae have become. That's my doing.*

This was Merlin's nightmare, almost as bad for him as it was for the fae. It didn't take magic to know he blamed himself for every crime, every ounce of suffering his spell had unleashed.

Laren raised his head, his green eyes fierce with grief. He knelt facing Clary and beat a fist to his chest, a gesture of anger turned inward. "My offense against you cannot be forgiven."

She heard Merlin's intake of breath, a sharp, painful rasp. As terrible as it was, the sound freed something inside her. She took a step toward the circle.

"Clary!" Merlin's warning was sharp.

She held up a hand, palm out. "I'm fine."

She hoped that was true. Laren was still kneeling, head bowed and arms loose at his sides. He made her think of a prisoner awaiting execution. She walked up to the edge of the circle, her toes almost touching the chalk lines. The fae lifted his head. His long, white hair had come loose and hid most of his face, but she could see the tracks of tears down his cheeks. The sight hurt something deep inside her.

"None of this should have happened to you," she said. "You didn't deserve it. Nobody did."

He blinked, his mouth drawn tight. "But I…"

"I know," she said. She couldn't ignore what he'd done, but then, she couldn't blame him, either. Judging him was beyond any wisdom she had, so she didn't try.

He hung his head again, releasing his breath as if speech deserted him. Clary bit her lip. The chalk circle was there to keep Laren contained, but every instinct told her there was no need for that now. The fae was no longer a danger. She stepped across, ignoring Merlin's noise of protest, and knelt to face Laren. She took his hands. They were unresisting and almost lifeless. She squeezed them gently. "If you need forgiveness for what you did to me, I forgive you. I'm not sure it shouldn't be the other way around, though, for bringing you such anguish when you tasted my soul."

His head came up, seemingly startled. Their eyes met, and this time she saw how beautiful his were, filled with warmth and energy. He had a soul now, and in that moment she fully understood what the faery people had lost. A throb of grief ached in her chest.

"I am infinitely grateful to you for walking across my path," he said softly. "The miracle you brought demands a price, but I gladly pay it. You have saved me from doing more harm in this world."

Warm wetness touched her face, and she realized she'd begun to cry. With a tentative smile, Laren brushed them away. "Be at peace. I am whole again, thanks to you."

Without thinking what she did, Clary embraced him. "Welcome back, Laren."

Merlin cleared his throat. Clary looked up to see him leaning against the doorframe, arms crossed over his chest. His expression was neutral except when he turned to Laren. Then his eyes narrowed the slightest degree. "I hate to end this touching scene, but there are practical matters to discuss."

Laren rose and bowed deeply to the enchanter. "I am in your debt for sparing my life. Ask whatever service I may perform in your name."

Merlin frowned. "You owe me nothing." He gestured

toward the chalk circle, and Clary felt the spell that bound it drop away.

"Come sit with us, Laren of the Green Towers," Merlin asked formally. "Will you accept food and drink?"

"I shall, with thanks."

The rituals of hospitality had power among the fae, and sharing a meal was an act of friendship. As long as Laren was under Merlin's roof, neither would harm the other. Clary got to her feet, following them out of the room.

"Do you know if any of the fae are in communication with the queen?" Merlin asked.

"Queen Morgan LaFaye is held prisoner by the Lady of the Lake, deep in the Forest Sauvage," Laren replied. "How could any of my people contact the queen?"

It was a good question, Clary thought as they settled in Merlin's living room. The comfortable chairs were a deep forest green that complemented the natural wood floor and fieldstone fireplace.

"I have it on good authority that LaFaye is summoning demons to her prison," Merlin announced. "In addition, one of the hellspawn is meeting with generals among the fae army. She could be directing her lieutenants that way."

Laren sat up, surprise sharpening his features. "That explains many rumors I have heard."

"What rumors?"

"That there is an alliance between the demons and fae against Camelot. I gave it no credit until now. It seems utterly unnatural."

"That may not matter," said Merlin. "Not if there is greed. LaFaye was always lavish with her promises."

Laren lowered his gaze, not meeting Merlin's eyes. "There is another rumor that says time alone should have healed the fae. Why didn't that happen?"

Clary answered, because this was one fun fact she knew. "LaFaye kept the wounds fresh with her own magic."

Fury lit his face. "Is this true? How do you know?"

"There is a small contingent of fae who are friends of Camelot," said Merlin. "They healed or escaped the spell's effects altogether. They know the truth."

"Why would the queen do such a thing?" Laren demanded.

"Tell me this: What does she promise her armies of fae when she asks them to invade the human world?" asked Merlin.

Laren turned pale, his fingers curling into fists. "An abundance of mortal souls for the taking. If we were cured, her promise would have no power."

"Exactly."

"Perhaps you are to blame for the original spell that injured us, Merlin Ambrosius, but our queen has made herself our jailer." Laren rose, pacing the room. "Where are these other fae you speak of? Surely they work to free our kin?"

"They have formed an alliance." Merlin rose, as well. "I'll make a call and let them know you're here, if you wish to join with them."

Laren's face filled with a defiant hope. "Please."

Despite Merlin's confident tone, the business of introducing a stranger to the close-knit resistance was hardly simple. Many of the fae had tragic histories, and the risk of betrayal was too great. However, in the end, a meeting was arranged and Merlin took Laren to meet his contact. Clary remained behind at Merlin's insistence, under observation even if she was the only one in the condominium.

After saying a heartfelt goodbye to Laren, she took a shower, stole a clean T-shirt from Merlin's drift of unfolded laundry and settled at the dining room table. With the beginnings of a plan, she opened the laptop and hacked through Merlin's password—Wiz123—in less than ten minutes. He might be light-years ahead in magic, but she knew math and computers, not to mention basic internet security.

She ignored Merlin's files and opened a blank spreadsheet, typing in the rudiments of a formula. If a taste of demon essence cured one fae, how much would it take to cure all the fae? In their natural form—that is, not muddled up inside Clary—demons were raw energy, so how would one begin to disperse that energy? Could it be converted into a beam of light? Sent over Wi-Fi? Atomized and spritzed? Clary fiddled with mathematical models, but there were too many unknowns to get very far. She was still heads-down with the problem when Merlin returned.

"I see you've made yourself at home." He dropped his keys on the table and raised an eyebrow.

"How did the meeting go?" she asked, still intent on the laptop's screen.

"Perfectly. Laren is among friends. You needn't worry on his account."

A knot of tension unwound under Clary's ribs. "Good."

"That's my computer."

"Your password sucks," she said, wishing her complexion didn't show every blush. "I'm trying to figure out a way to rain demon essence on the Kingdom of Faery. I'll donate it myself if I can figure out a way to do it."

His lips curled into the shadow of a smile. "A generous offer, but I doubt one demon, even Vivian, would go far enough. We need to think bigger."

He'd said *we*. Relieved, Clary stopped typing and turned in her chair to face him. "How?"

The slight smile faded. "I don't know." He put one hand on the table and leaned down, brushing his lips against her cheek. "But I'm infinitely grateful that you tried."

She froze, surprised by his gesture. For once, he'd reached out without something incredibly bad—death, monsters, murderous fae—having crossed their path moments before. Her pulse pounded double time.

He began to rise, but Clary caught his arm, pulling him closer. "You're not in this alone anymore. You know that, right?"

As soon as she said it, the words felt ridiculous. Why would he care if his student—one whose failures were bound to get him in trouble—was in his corner? She hadn't even come up with a good theory for the cure on paper, and that was stuff she was good at. Clary let go of his arm, folding her hands in her lap. She was so far out of her depth, she'd lost sight of the shore.

"Clary," he said softly. He was looking at her intently, his expression speculative as if he was seeing her for the first time.

Heat burned up her neck, over her ears and flamed across her cheeks. There was no hope of pretending she didn't care what he thought of her, and yet she tried. She turned her face away. "Yeah?"

He put two fingers under her chin and turned her face toward him. "I work alone for a reason."

"I know," she said quickly, still avoiding his eyes.

"It's not always a very good reason, but I've lived a long time and it's not always easy to change."

She had to look at him then. His expression was serious, but something had shifted beneath it, the way a pond thawed under the surface layer of ice. It gave her back a little of her swagger. "So?"

He nodded to the computer. "You have skills I don't. I may need your help before this is over."

Her face went numb with shock. He was actually letting her a step closer into his world. "I know there was a compliment somewhere in that statement."

He leaned closer. "You were a model of compassion

with your would-be murderer. You could try giving me a break."

"Will you forgive me for breaking your crystal ball?"

"Agate."

"Whatever."

"Is there a good reason why I should?" Merlin's voice was hoarse, but it wasn't with anger or his usual arrogance. All at once, the mood shifted to something far more risky.

Clary curled her fingers in the front of his shirt and pulled him closer until their lips were a hairbreadth apart. His breath fanned her face as she tilted her head slightly, finding the best angle to kiss. He tasted like coffee and chocolate as if he'd had refreshments at the meeting. Clary suddenly realized she hadn't eaten for hours, but it was a fleeting thought. She was hungry in a lot of different ways.

She kissed him again, and this time he responded. Nervous energy pulsed through her. What was she doing? She never let anyone get this close, not when it mattered. That was why all those past boyfriends had never worked out. So why was she throwing herself at Merlin? He terrified her. He didn't just *matter*; she'd crossed the continent to be near him, even if it was as a lowly student.

There was no denying the need burning low in her belly. It was her own desire, but the volume was cranked to a pitch she'd never experienced before. Their lips were locked, but her hands were in motion, trailing down his back and over the curve of his jeans.

Merlin broke the kiss, but did not pull away. His amber eyes were just visible under the sweep of his lashes, but she could feel him studying her. He was breathing hard, almost panting. "What are you doing?" he asked.

"Shall I draw you a map?"

A shudder ran through him, and it was a moment before she realized he was laughing. "I think I can find my way."

"Men never want maps."

"It ruins the process of discovery."

Then Merlin took charge of the kiss, teasing the seam of her lips until they parted. His hands curved around her cheeks, holding her with firm gentleness as if she were a piece of precious sculpture. Then they brushed her neck as he traced her jaw with kisses. It was a slow exploration, but it was not tentative. He simply refused to be rushed.

Fear suddenly blanked Clary's mind as if she'd unwittingly stepped off a cliff. She hadn't imagined this, hadn't expected it. And then, as if an updraft caught her, she surrendered to joy. This was a turning point, and it was good. She'd wanted Merlin for so long, and now here he was in her arms. In the midst of so much bad luck, it was a surprising gift. Heat climbed up her cheeks all over again, a sign of her excitement and an unexpected bashfulness.

Clary's blood thundered so hard in her ears, it took a moment before she realized there was a steady pounding on the door.

"Merlin!" bellowed the angry voice of King Arthur. "Answer me! I know you're in there."

Chapter 9

Morgan LaFaye, Queen of Faery, felt Laren of the Green Towers slip from her grasp. It was a slight sensation, barely a tickle, but the predatory part of her mind was ever on the alert for threats. The fae were hers. *Hers.* She'd seized their throne in the aftermath of Merlin's ridiculous blunder and had guarded it since. Morgan had used her magic to keep the fae damaged, hungry, obedient as long as she supplied them with mortal souls. She'd found an easy road to power—why not make it last?

Especially when *easy* was in short supply. She rose from her throne in the white tower that imprisoned her— it was really just a chair, but it was a throne if she said it was—and swept to the window. The view of mountains and lakes was stunning, but it gave the queen no pleasure. *I lost something of mine this day.*

Every time one of the fae regained his or her soul, it stole a tiny bit of Morgan's queenship. Worst of all had been the loss of her jailer, Nimueh, the famous Lady of the Lake. The fae enchantress had rediscovered her soul and her extra-shiny knight, Sir Lancelot du Lac, right before locking Morgan up. The two lovebirds were still camped outside the tower, making certain their prisoner remained secure. The tower's magic ensured she never lacked for the necessities of life, but she was bored, lonely and helpless.

She hadn't felt this way for a very long time, but it wasn't the first occasion. Just before the demon wars, when she had still been part of Camelot's court, Arthur had commanded there be a winter feast, and all the guests wore white. Morgan knew she was beautiful, and that night she'd shone like the evening star. Merlin had been there, too, handsome and laughing and for once dressed in all the finery his rank decreed. They were rivals, Morgan and Merlin, each proud of their magic and forever vying to outdo the other. Merlin did it to win Arthur's regard and she did it to spite them both, but that night had been different. They had flirted—or she thought they had. At the very least, they had danced and drank and exchanged quips like sparring lovers, right up until Arthur had invited them to play a game.

"I say we play a kissing game," she'd said to Merlin. "I dare you to tell us the name of the lady you love, or else kiss me in forfeit. I warn you, I'll invoke a charm to make sure you tell the truth."

Merlin had bowed. "Madam, I do not play games that might touch on a lady's reputation."

In hindsight, she should have left the matter there, but her pride had been wounded.

"Don't be a cold-blooded codfish," she'd said, giving his arm a playful slap. "Are you sure it's not me, and you're simply embarrassed to draw attention to a hopeless *amour*?"

That brought the laughter of the courtiers, and even Arthur.

Merlin had bowed again. "I will shovel the stables, kiss the lowliest chambermaid and ply my magic in the village square before engaging in a game that will only bring dishonor."

The courtiers had applauded his arrogant, insulting words, saying that he won the match by adhering to the rules of chivalry. Which meant Morgan had not. The wretched magic-monger had embarrassed her in front of the entire court of Camelot, and she had been teased without mercy for weeks thereafter. She felt then as she did now, cast adrift by those who were lesser than she.

If Morgan had been attracted to Merlin that night, it was for the very last time. Their rivalry had turned to something worse until finally he'd helped the Lady of the Lake put her in this tower prison. He would pay for that.

And her revenge would come soon. She'd struggled against Nimueh's enchantments, finally punching a hole just big enough to work her summoning circle. Demons were scum, but they could be very useful messengers.

She felt her visitor arrive before she saw him. His presence was like a pressure between her shoulder blades. Fear tingled. Demons might be scum, but they were also deadly. Nevertheless, she turned to face the new arrival with a gracious smile.

"To what do I owe this pleasure?" she asked. "It must be important since I didn't invite you."

Tenebrius regarded her with his yellow, goat-slitted eyes. Today he was dressed in scarlet robes, his claws crusted with tiny gemstones that winked as he wiggled his fingers in a tiny wave. "But you would have eventually. I just saved you the trouble."

He never used her title as queen, so she also dispensed with false courtesy. Why bother? They'd never liked each other one bit. "What do you want today, hellspawn?"

"We have a deal. I assist in your escape and you free me and my followers from the bonds of the Abyss."

"I know this," she said, growing irritable. "I offered you the deal, if you recall."

He shifted his weight, but did not move. He might have invited himself in, but he couldn't step outside the summoning circle she'd drawn on the floor. Morgan folded her hands, doing her best to look regal. It was hard when one had been wearing the same gown for so many months. The dark folds had gone ragged, like the feathers of a storm-tossed crow.

When she said nothing more, his brows flexed downward into an inky V. "Then why are you dealing with that pustule, Gorm?"

"Ah." She waved a careless hand. "I'm surprised you heard about that."

"He is less than discreet."

That was a problem—one she might need Tenebrius to solve. She spoke a word and the summoning circle released the demon. Morgan indicated a pair of chairs that sat before an empty fireplace. "Sit. Tell me all."

The demon reclined in a majestic sprawl of red silk. "What can Gorm do that I cannot?"

"His involvement bothers you." The temptation to needle Tenebrius until he bled—figuratively, of course—brought Morgan to the edge of her seat.

He stroked his long, black mustaches with glittering claws. "Please answer my question."

She bridled, but she wasn't stupid. Nothing could jeopardize her endgame. "I've known Gorm for many years. He invented spells to make horses lose their shoes, and carts their wheels. When foundries and factories covered the lands, he devised ways to foul their gears. Even from exile in the Abyss, he delights in making the works of humanity crumble."

"So?"

"So, I wanted to know what he was working on these days," she said, doing her best to sound reasonable. "Now that Arthur is in the modern world, he is vulnerable to Gorm's brand of chaos in new and interesting ways."

"Arthur." Tenebrius sighed and rubbed his forehead. "It is always Arthur with you. Retribution, magic swords, blah, blah. Isn't the crown of Faery good enough for you?"

She clenched her teeth in aggravation, but was forced

to loosen them to speak. "I should have been Queen of Camelot. The crown rightfully belonged to my kin. He stole it with the help of that interfering mountebank, Merlin. In truth, I think I hate Merlin worse than the king."

The demon nodded in a way that said he'd heard it all before. "Right. So you asked Gorm over for tea."

Morgan sat back, her temper simmering. She hated having to explain herself. She also hated the shabby room, her aching boredom and the fact that the only creatures who would talk to her had to be summoned from the Abyss. But then, no one said conquering the world was a popularity contest.

"Gorm promises a unique means of attack," she said. "One that will cripple Camelot while opening the door for demons to return to the mortal realms."

Tenebrius sat forward, his strange eyes lighting with interest. "Really? What is it?"

"Something technical," she said dismissively. "Something very Gorm. I don't understand the specifics, but it's modern and he promises that it will work."

"And why did I not know of this?"

"You would have been informed the moment construction began on his spell. He said there are ingredients he needs that are in your keeping. He will also need both our powers to fuel it. The three of us will need to work together."

She hated the notion of working with demons, of her magic touching theirs. It was a fall from grace, but she told herself it was also a means of recovering her power.

The demon crossed his legs. "And how does this escapade of Gorm's coincide with your plans for escape from this tower?"

"There will be a test run," she said with a shrug. "If it succeeds in providing a safe means of escape from the Abyss, you will take it at once and free me."

Even if the demons abandoned Morgan then and there, she'd escape in the resulting confusion. Besides, she was certain Arthur and his flunkies would perish trying to defend their precious humans. It was a perfect plan.

"Interesting," Tenebrius mused.

Morgan could see the conflict behind the demon's languid pose. It was no secret that he preferred Arthur to Morgan, at least on a personal level. But she was offering him freedom while Arthur's war—and Arthur's enchanter—had banished the demons from the mortal realms. She watched his face, seeing the moment self-interest conquered his personal inclinations.

"There is a complication," he said.

Her stomach dropped. "What?"

"Gorm was prattling to me about his visit to you. We were overheard."

"By whom?" Her voice was shrill. She had too much riding on this plan to risk interference.

"Vivian. She is a friend, but she has a history with Merlin, who was listening, as well."

As he spoke, Morgan rose and began to pace. Her steps grew quicker as he explained what had happened with the ritual and the scrying ball and Merlin's foolish student.

"Vivian is gravely injured," he finally said. "Trapped between realms."

The Queen of Faery spun to face the demon. "If she knows anything she should not…"

"Don't fret," he said with a wicked smile. "Who but Vivian is better positioned to be our informant inside Camelot's court?"

"Very well," Morgan said. "But make certain she's on our side. If she's not, you know what to do."

Clary jumped at the pounding on the door, her green eyes widening at the sound of Arthur's voice. "Why is he here?"

Merlin clenched his jaw, his mind still fixed on the taste of Clary's lips. They reminded him of sun-warmed cherries, ripe and sweet and begging to be devoured. It took an act of will to shift his attention to the rattling door.

"Give me a minute!" he shouted, the angry snap in his words unmistakable.

The pounding stopped, but he could still feel Arthur's impatience like a physical pressure. Though he didn't want to admit it, he'd put off another encounter with Arthur. The king had legitimate concerns, but Merlin loathed explaining himself to someone who barely understood magic.

He'd rather be interrogating—or whatever he was doing with Clary. His actions had something to do with the scene with Laren, the sight of her holding him, her forgiveness, her generosity and the trust she'd shown the moment she'd crossed into the circle that held the fae. He'd never seen the likes of that before in all the centuries of his life. Clary was special.

He finally released his grip on her waist and stepped back, still holding one of her hands. The absence of her body against his made him annoyed all over again.

"What does the king want now?" Clary whispered, clearly nervous.

Merlin frowned, aware that he hadn't been able to protect her from Vivian—not well enough to keep her out of this bizarre situation. The very least he could do was keep her safe from Arthur's temper. "Go to the bedroom and close the door. Don't come out until I give you the all clear."

She nodded solemnly, but neither of them moved. He heard Arthur's impatient shuffling outside. That wasn't due so much to supersonic wizard ears as to Arthur making a point. Monarchs didn't enjoy waiting.

Merlin took a reluctant step back, finally releasing her slim palm. With contact finally broken, they both regained their wits a little. Clary shook herself and went to the bedroom, but kept her gaze locked with his until she shut the door. Slightly dazed, Merlin went to answer the knock. When he opened the door, a small green suitcase sat in the hall. No doubt it contained the clothes Tamsin had packed for Clary. Merlin set it inside, wishing the delivery was the only reason for Arthur's visit but knowing he wouldn't be so lucky.

He stepped into the hall, folded his arms and looked around. Arthur had wandered down the corridor toward the elevator and was now pacing from one wall to the other like an agitated cat.

Merlin frowned. He'd been on the cusp of something wonderful with Clary. From the first moment she'd burst into his world, with her wayward magic and smart mouth, he'd wanted her. He'd meant to teach her, protect her and launch her career as a witch, but never to give in to desire. Not with an innocent—and yet he yearned to break his own rules. For all her attitude, she was a loving, forgiving woman and much, much more than he deserved. Her generous heart had saved Laren as much as any cure.

Merlin took a deep breath and let it out slowly. As for him, how often had he said nothing good came of knowing Merlin the Wise? Maybe this interruption had saved both of them from a step they'd regret. Surely it had.

Or had it? He couldn't tell at the moment, and he wouldn't get peace and quiet to figure it out for a while. Right now he had to deal with an angry king.

Arthur leaned against the wall next to the elevators. "Well?" he demanded. "What have you discovered?"

Merlin's thoughts flashed to Clary's lips, her smooth, slender neck and the promising softness of her curves. "Many things, Your Majesty."

Chapter 10

Arthur's eyebrows rose in question.

"Perhaps this is not the place to discuss them," Merlin suggested. "It would be helpful to have the queen present and a few of your closest advisers."

"What of Clary?"

Merlin pulled the door closed behind him, letting the lock click into place. "She is safely confined for the moment. Tamsin and I leashed her magic as a precaution."

Arthur visibly relaxed. "Good."

"None of this is her fault, you know," Merlin said.

"You don't need to defend her."

"I do." Merlin's voice was flat.

"I realize she's your student."

"She is also Tamsin's sister, your dedicated employee and a faithful member of your court." Merlin struggled to keep his tone quiet, but it was a losing battle. All at once, he'd lost the capacity to hide what he felt.

Arthur held up his hands in a placating gesture. "Fair enough. She's Gwen's friend, too, but after what I saw today, I want assurances it's safe to let her near my wife."

That much, Merlin could accept. After literally centuries of waiting, the queen carried Camelot's heir. Her term was near, and everyone was on baby watch.

"Where shall we go?" Merlin asked, mostly to change the topic.

"My place, if you care to take us there," Arthur suggested. "Perceval drove me here, but I sent him on his

way. The lad cannot distinguish city traffic from a battlefield melee."

"No wonder you look green."

"He attempted to parallel park. Please return me to my
home, where I can pour myself a drink."

Merlin allowed himself a smile. With one hand, he
sketched an arc in the air before them. White light trailed
behind his fingers, showing the gesture's path and the outline of a door in space and time. The glow brightened, rays
of blue and green flowing into the arc's center. When it
was filled, the light growing almost solid, the brightness
changed course and began to dissipate like a morning mist.
What was left behind was a window into Arthur's apartment. The two men stepped through and Merlin closed the
portal with a wave of his hand. The spell allowed them to
enter silently and unobserved, and for a moment he paused
to take in the scene.

Queen Guinevere sat in an easy chair with her feet
propped on a stool. Her hands rested protectively over her
burgeoning stomach, but she'd lost none of the lively energy that made the queen the beating heart of Camelot's
court. Beaumains, his arm in a sling, sat next to Gawain
on the couch. All three were watching baseball.

"Where did you come from?" Gwen asked.

"Just passing by," Merlin returned with a smile. "How
are you feeling?"

She grinned. "Like a beached whale. Cheer me up."

He summoned a carnation from thin air and presented it
to her with a flourish. The queen took it and held it to her
nose. "Thank you. You are gallant as always. Have some
birthday cake. Tamsin brought it over for Beaumains. I
think he's finally reached drinking age."

That brought a general laugh. Gawain's youngest
brother was in his early twenties, but had a melting smile

that would make him look boyish forever. Merlin accepted a slice of cake, which was chocolate and very good.

"How fares Palomedes?" Merlin asked.

"Resting," Gawain replied as he switched off the TV. "He will fight again, but he will carry the scars from that encounter with the lions."

Merlin heard the edge in the knight's words and didn't blame him. As one of the senior knights, Gawain's job was to protect his own.

Arthur sat on the stool and gathered the queen's feet in his lap. He set about gently massaging them. "Merlin says he has news."

Gwen's blue eyes turned his way. "About Clary?"

"In part."

Her gaze grew troubled. "I'm counting on you to look after her."

Merlin gave her a nod, not able to find the right words. He had failed Clary the moment Vivian put one demonic toe in this world. He put down his plate of cake, his appetite gone. "There are rumors that the hellspawn are in league with the fae."

"Which hellspawn?" asked Gawain.

"Tenebrius, for one," Merlin replied.

"That makes no sense," Arthur said. "When LaFaye challenged us to a tourney just before she was imprisoned, Tenebrius clearly disliked her. He judged in our favor and awarded the prize to me."

"You never claimed the prize," said Gawain. "Can you use that to your advantage?"

"If it were only that simple," Arthur muttered under his breath. "We are speaking of hellspawn."

The knights fell deathly silent, their faces drawn. These men had fought in the first demon wars, and all remembered the horrors. But as little as he wanted to darken the shadows already gathering around them, Merlin had to tell the truth. So he did, relaying everything he'd learned from the ritual to the discovery of an unexpected cure to the information Laren had provided. The only thing he glossed over was the growing heat between himself and Clary. That was nobody's business but theirs.

Beaumains was the first to speak. "Of all of this, the news of Morgan LaFaye's involvement worries me the most."

"If there is a danger she might escape," Arthur replied, "we should send word to the goblins to gather their armies."

"And the Charmed Beasts of the Forest Sauvage," Gwen added. "They are our eyes and ears."

Merlin listened with growing unease. All the suggestions were sensible, but no countermeasure would be enough if Morgan truly slipped her leash. Merlin's spell to bring the Round Table forward in time hadn't worked as well as he'd hoped, and only a handful of knights had awakened from their stone effigies. Modern humans didn't believe in magic, and even if they did, there was no reason to believe they'd follow a king who earned his living in an amusement park. And if that was not discouraging enough, every accord with the hidden world, including the goblins, pixies, witches and even the fae who still retained their souls agreed that the magical realm had to stay hidden. Humans had a bad habit of burning things and people they didn't understand, and breaking the accords meant war with the few allies Camelot had left.

The only real answer was to turn the fae armies against Morgan, and that meant a widespread cure that would restore their souls. But although he had found the beginnings of a solution, Merlin—even with Clary's help—had a long way to go.

"I have a question." Gwen's soft voice interrupted his

thoughts. "Who is more powerful—the demons or La-Faye?"

"In the magical realms, demons are the darkness where fae are the light," Merlin said. "They should be in balance, except LaFaye has changed the equilibrium of magic by bargaining with the hellspawn. She risks much by trusting in that pact."

"Good riddance," Beaumains said hopefully.

Merlin frowned. "Don't be so quick to hope she is the loser. Once the demons demanded all earthly powers to kneel before them."

"We would not," Arthur said simply. "But that refusal began the war."

Merlin remembered how it had started. He'd been standing on the balcony of his tower at Camelot, a shiver up his spine telling him magic was afoot. The morning had taken on an unearthly quiet as if the land held its breath. The first visible sign of what was to come was his pet raven flapping against the iron-gray sky. The bird had been arrowing toward him, its panicked caw a warning of approaching doom.

Then Merlin had caught the scent of rain. That would have been innocent enough, but the cold March sky had seemed to crumple, going from the flat gray of early spring to billowing charcoal clouds in the span of a heartbeat. Thunder ground through the heavens like an avalanche, and then the deluge had begun. Suddenly, rain danced on the edge of the stone balcony, on the slate roofs and the cobbled courtyard. In an instant Merlin was drenched, with the sodden raven landing in a heap in his arms. No birds flew in that rain—the force of it was too hard.

It churned the fields and the forest for months on end, and then the summer came with brutal heat. No crops were harvested that year. The winter took what supplies remained. Disease and hunger cut like twin scythes. The mortals had to surrender, or they had to fight and win. Failure would mean the certain death of thousands upon thousands of innocents. That was when Arthur had asked Merlin to lend his battle magic, whatever the cost.

In the face of the destruction of the land and its people, what could Merlin do but agree?

Vivian opened her eyes and then squinted as a bright light flared in her face.

"Ah, you're awake," said Tenebrius, allowing the flame at his fingertip to go out. "I was beginning to wonder if you were already snuffed."

His goat-slitted eyes were impatient as if she'd delayed mealtime. Vivian frowned and sat up, taking in her own opulent bedchamber. Demons might be made of energy, but they all chose a physical form and concrete environment to dwell in. This month she'd chosen the Hollywood interpretation of an exotic pleasure palace just in case she got the chance to drag Merlin back to her lair. For all his cool swagger, he could be flustered if one knew how.

She swung her legs over the edge of her scarlet silk bed. "How did you bring me back? I was stuck inside that pathetically incompetent witch, and then Merlin knocked me cold."

"I know," Tenebrius said drily. "As demonic possessions go, that was a poor effort. You barely qualified as a guilty conscience."

Vivian rose, her feline tail swishing with temper. "I was injured. It was a dreadful experience, trapped in all those complicated human emotions." She drew the last word out for effect.

She stomped to and fro for a moment. "I felt like a spider swimming in syrup. I was about to come down with a case of stomach ulcers. Or poetry."

"My, but you had a narrow escape."

She ignored his sarcasm, focusing on that ridiculous fae, Laren. She'd been paralyzed inside Clary, but she'd heard every weepy word of his tale. She turned to the other demon. "Is it true some of our leaders are working with LaFaye? Are you?"

His smile was sly, which was as good as an emphatic yes. "If I told you, I would have to kill you."

Her hands fisted. "I thought you hated LaFaye."

"Arthur and your ex-lover cast us out of the mortal realms."

"So? Everyone would have, given half a chance."

"The Queen of Faery is willing to help us return to our former glory."

"And you believe her?"

He waggled a hand in a so-so gesture.

"How will she do it from inside a prison?"

"A plan of Gorm's. I'm not sure if it will work yet, though from what I hear the modern age offers some interesting opportunities. It will release us from the Abyss."

Vivian rolled her eyes. "If you'd mentioned this before, I might have kept my eyes open while I was in the mortal realms. Now I'm back here, as stuck as I was before."

There was a beat of uncomfortable silence that raised the hair on her neck. If she didn't know better, she'd think Tenebrius was embarrassed.

"You're still trapped," he finally said. "You're there, and you're here. You split when Merlin broke his scrying ball."

"What?" Vivian stilled, only the tip of her tail tap-tapping against the floor. "How do you know?"

"I saw it happen."

"I feel fine."

"You're numb. You can't feel it because the energetic bond between your two halves is nearly severed."

"How? That should not have happened. The bond should be strong."

He shrugged. "An accident, I suppose. You won't last like this, Vivian."

She slumped down on the edge of the bed, her normal grace lost. Horror crawled through her, bushing her tail. She looked up at the other demon's pinched expression. "But I'm immortal."

"Not like this, you aren't." Sadness filled his eyes, but like everything else with demons, it was hardly trustworthy. "The only thing keeping you alive is the witch's natural strength."

It was a death sentence. It was impossible. It was unfair.

"Then get the rest of me back," she said, her voice quiet. "Make me whole."

Once upon a time, Merlin would have hugged her and tried to soothe her distress. Even Clary seemed to weep for her would-be assassins. Why was no one here for her? Vivian slammed down on her sudden yearning to return to the mortal world. She didn't need mortal sympathy. Weakness wasn't the demon way.

"I can't make you whole again," said Tenebrius. "The most I could do was to summon your consciousness for a brief period. You will wake up inside your witch. There is no coming home, Vivian."

Her chin jerked up. Her mind scrambled with the idea of a finite life, of actually dying.

"Is that the truth?" she whispered. "Do not play tricks with me. Not about this."

"I am sorry." This time he did look genuinely regretful.

The first shock past, her temper flared. "So, you brought me here to pronounce my death sentence. Anything else?"

"Help me wreak havoc on his precious Camelot. Make the most of the time you have left."

"How?" Vivian narrowed her eyes.

"Be my informant. You have a front-row seat to Arthur's court."

Vivian considered. "I want vengeance on Merlin."

"You can't kill him yet. He's your source of information."

"Your source, you mean." She watched Tenebrius's goat-slitted eyes go cold and knew she was courting trouble.

"LaFaye ordered me to kill you. I told her you'd work for her instead."

That would happen about the same time Vivian took up crochet. "Very well," she lied. "I'll be your spy. Then I'll kill him."

"A good choice. I'll be in touch." Tenebrius reached out one clawed hand and touched her forehead.

Vivian woke for a second time, but in a different bed. She had a fuzzy recollection of lying down for a nap when Merlin left with Arthur, and then a bizarre dream about...

That wasn't a dream.

Groggy, Vivian pushed herself upright and dragged a hand through her hair—short, fair hair and not her thick cascade of blue-black locks. She was back in Clary's body, but their positions had been reversed. Now she was completely in control, and the witch's consciousness was a tiny spark buried deep inside. Triumph swelled inside her. Her newfound freedom was undoubtedly Tenebrius's handiwork. A parting gift, perhaps?

She closed her eyes, shutting out the room around her. Dying? It made no sense. She felt strong, clearheaded and filled with purpose. Could he have been mistaken? She didn't think so—Tenebrius might lie to her, but not about this. All the same, his information might not be complete. He didn't say how long her demise would take. Months? Years? A mortal lifetime?

And yet now every second was made precious just because their number could be measured. Tears pricked at the backs of her eyes. Demons didn't cry, but a death sentence was a good excuse to make an exception.

Vivian rose, in sole control of this body for the first time. She stretched out one arm, then the other, feeling the delicacy of the bones and muscles. By mortal standards, the witch was fit, but Vivian would need to be careful. Such bodies were easily broken.

And now she was stuck in one. Who was responsible for this? Merlin. Always Merlin. She'd shared her treasury of scrolls and grimoires, which was why he knew about that cursed battle spell. She'd shown him the many realms of the known world, from the Crystal Mountains to the grim wonder of the Abyss and its silent, barren lakes. She had unlocked his magic and made him a great enchanter. Most significant, at least to her, they had lain together.

Still, he'd betrayed her. He would pay for that, and she wasn't going to let the opportunity slip, whatever Tenebrius wanted. What was he going to do, kill her?

The first step in her plan was to clean herself up. The little witch needed a lesson in style. After a long, hot shower, Vivian contemplated her clothing options. She had a vague memory of a suitcase arriving. Once she located it, she undid the zipper and stared inside. A rising sensation of dismay brought heat to her checks. Most of the clothes looked as if they belonged on a boy. She'd seen pictures of current fashion—the Abyss was far away, but advertising had an astonishing reach. Clary could have done so much better, with a splash of red and some body-conscious styling. She knew the girl was savvy about clothes and had all but dressed Queen Guinevere during her first weeks in the modern age. She was just too self-conscious to take her own advice.

Vivian snorted and tipped the suitcase upside down, rummaging through the piles Tamsin had carefully folded. A handful of dog-eared paperbacks fell out, and she pushed them out of the way to better see the fashion options. She finally selected slim-legged black slacks and a spaghetti-strapped top in white. It had a low-cut back that showed off a bit of skin. Vivian dressed and stood in front of the mirror on the back of the bedroom door. Clary's figure was far less dramatic than what she was used to, but she could work with it.

Vivian reached out, touching her reflection fingertip to fingertip. For an instant the image in the glass wavered, showing her own dark-haired features before breaking apart like a mirage. Vivian gave a superstitious shudder and turned back to Clary's clothes.

The only interesting shoes were high-heeled sandals, but walking in them would take practice. The girl had no tail, and that ruined Vivian's sense of balance. She opted instead to paint Clary's toenails a vivid scarlet called The Devil Made Me Do It. Who said demons had no sense of humor?

With her toes still wet, she padded to Merlin's expansive kitchen to see what she could cook up. For a man who lived alone—and ate a lot of home delivery, judging by the menus on top of the microwave—he had a lot of pots and pans. Vivian quickly figured out why. One set was for cooking food, the nicer one with copper bottoms was for cooking spells. She selected a double boiler and set it on the stove.

A trip to the pantry revealed row upon row of glass jars filled with herbs, ground minerals and dried bits of things most humans would never willingly touch. She gathered what she wanted and began to measure out ingredients. It was a painstaking, exacting process but she only needed enough to make a single dose.

Once everything was measured and sifted, she added a generous splash of Chardonnay she found in the fridge.

Then she began heating it all gently, stirring as she began a lilting chant. The trick was never to let the mixture overheat.

As Vivian had told Clary, she had to take Merlin by surprise. He had to be vulnerable, unguarded and unsuspecting—essentially opposite to his default mood. This potion would put him in the right condition for her plan to work.

As the chant ended, she lifted the mixture from the heat and poured it into a mug to cool. For the final ingredient, Vivian pricked her finger with a kitchen knife and let a drop fall into the brew. She stirred it in, wrinkling her nose at the scent of the steam. Love potions were powerful, but they tasted like swamp water. How was she going to get him to drink it?

Vivian's gaze fell on the unwashed dishes in the sink. Among the usual mugs and plates were the cast metal pieces of the wheatgrass juicer. A tray of the bright green grass sat on the wide windowsill, looking like a misplaced fragment of a meadow. Vivian found Clary's memory of the pungent juice Merlin had been drinking. That would cover the smell and taste of just about anything.

She rinsed off the juicer and, after a few false starts, reassembled it. It was a hand-cranked model that clamped to the wooden butcher's block that topped the island counter. A few minutes later the apartment smelled of freshly mown lawn. Now all she needed was to make it appealing to someone besides a sheep.

Fortunately, there was a fully stocked bar and a cupboard dedicated to organic juices. She mixed a selection in a glass pitcher, added the wheat grass and poured herself a glass. Then she added her love potion to what remained and mixed it thoroughly with a wooden spoon. By the time Merlin had unlocked the front door, she was washing the dishes while sipping the frothy green concoction.

"I didn't mean to take so long," he said, leaning against

the archway that led to the kitchen. "What do you have there?"

Vivian leaned on the counter, careful to mimic the way Clary moved—a little bit awkward, a little bit defiant. The mortal had a way of leading with her chin as if expecting a fight. "I got bored waiting. I've been experimenting to see if there's a way to make that stuff drinkable."

She nodded at the flat of grass, which was missing a few more tufts than it had been twenty minutes ago. Merlin followed her gaze, oblivious to who she truly was. He was thinking like a mortal, mistaking the physical body for the person who lived inside it. Unless she made an obvious blunder, he'd never guess that she wasn't Clary.

Merlin picked up the glass pitcher and sniffed it. "What's in this?"

"Call it a smoothie," she said lightly. "There's strawberry and apple juice, coconut milk, a few other things. Try it if you like."

She sipped her glass as he poured an inch into another tumbler and tasted it with the air of someone being polite. Then he paused, glass at his lips. Vivian tensed when he raised his eyebrows.

Then he smiled. "This is actually pretty good."

"Then help yourself," she said, turning back to the sink and rinsing plates. It was good to keep her hands busy and her face hidden so she didn't accidentally give herself away. She heard him top up his glass as she scrubbed the last of the cereal bowls. "So, what did Arthur have to say?"

He told her, eventually grabbing a towel to dry. Vivian's chest tightened as she listened, imagining the war that would devastate the mortal realms. It was not as if she had a fondness for humans, much less for Arthur and his court. It was just that it was nice in the kitchen, with the soap suds and companionable conversation. She'd missed having Merlin around and wanted the moment to last a little while longer.

"Is that everything that needs a wash?" she asked, looking around.

"Don't forget this," he said, holding up the empty pitcher. There was nothing left in it but green scum.

"You drank all that?" she asked in genuine surprise. The drink was okay, but not exactly ambrosia.

"Arguing with Arthur is thirsty work. Sorry, I didn't mean to hog it."

"That's okay." She sank the pitcher in the dishpan, doing a quick mental calculation. The normal dose of that potion was a few spoonfuls, not the whole batch. How long would it be before it took effect?

Chapter 11

Vivian had barely finished the thought before his hands snaked around her waist from behind. He pulled her tight to his chest, fitting his body to the curve of her spine. "That pitcher needs to soak," he murmured in her ear.

She couldn't help herself. She shivered as if they were the most erotic words in any mortal tongue. It was his voice—low and rough with intent—or the sudden nervous tension in his hands.

He turned her around with slow, careful movements. She complied, ending up with her back to the sink and her soapy hands pressed against the wall of his chest. The room was suddenly silent except for the sound of bubbles popping in the sink.

Merlin cradled her face, his thumbs stroking over her cheekbones with an urgent gentleness she remembered with piercing clarity. He'd done that to her, but not this way. Back then he'd been fascinated but his touch had possessed none of this protective tenderness.

He truly cared for the little witch, then. Jealousy tore at Vivian's insides. She'd inspired many things—fear, adoration and even terror—but never love. In the end Merlin had stolen her spell and left her behind.

He moved one hand, trailing his fingertips over her lips. Vivian's fists clenched in his shirt, leaving dark, wet handprints in their wake. She had come here for revenge, and the unusual softness in his amber eyes—softness he felt for another woman, but never her—would make it oh, so easy.

His lips touched hers, startling a gasp from deep in her core. She hadn't taken the potion but her limbs trembled almost as much as his. Anticipation hammered like a second pulse, demanding satisfaction.

The next kiss was almost brutal, a taking that left no doubt what he wanted. The edge of the counter dug into her back, damp puddles of water soaking into her shirt. But the only thing that mattered was his hunger. The potion was taking full effect, blotting out reason and conscience. Vivian knew how to mix it well—every demon did. There were few more effective tools for sowing trouble among unsuspecting victims.

Except his desire stirred hers, especially in this frail human body. Clary had wanted this, and so nothing lingered to block the need crackling through her. Vivian's core throbbed, making her rise on her toes to meet his embrace. He hitched her up to sit on the counter and spread her knees so he could stand even closer. She dug her fingers into his dark hair, bending over to take charge of the kiss. His short beard prickled just as she remembered it, but now the memory was clouded with want. This might be her revenge, but nothing said she couldn't enjoy it.

His mouth was hot and velvety, tasting of the drink she'd made. He captured her tongue, teasing with his teeth as she sucked and nibbled in turn. Warm breath fanned her skin, bringing every nerve ending to life. Her hand slid down his front, finding his jeans and the hard evidence that her potion had worked.

All at once there were too many clothes between them. He was so close, his body pressed against hers. She locked her legs around his waist, shifting so that he bore her weight. "Take me to the bedroom," she murmured in his ear.

He needed no urging. Moments later they were both on the bed. He pulled off his shirt, the gesture showing off the muscles of his chest. Most forgot that Merlin was skilled with sword and spear, but it showed now in the flow and curve of solid flesh. Vivian swallowed, realizing that she was actually drooling.

She fell back against the pillows and spread her arms. "Come get me."

Merlin's chest rose and fell with quick, shallow gasps. He grabbed the front of her shirt and tore it in a single, swift wrench. Vivian squeaked and then chuckled, amused and gratified by his eagerness. The pupils of his eyes were huge as he bent to run his tongue along her breastbone in a long, warm line that cooled with his breath. She arched into it, luxuriating in his attention. This body couldn't purr, but she wanted to.

With a deft twist of his fingers, he undid the front clasp of Clary's bra. It sprang apart, letting the weight of her breasts fall free. He moaned, the sound wrenching her core. His mouth fell to one nipple while his hand closed over the other, and all at once Vivian's senses were swamped. Sparks of electricity seemed to shoot from the heat of Merlin's mouth straight to her belly, firing her need as he sucked. Her nails—pathetic, short, human nails—dug into his shoulders, clawing her response into his skin.

Having sex with him was every bit as good as she remembered, and every bit as immediate. Her teeth found his shoulder, and she bit down, claiming him until she tasted the copper salt of blood. He did no more than flinch, the urgency of the potion riding him hard.

She did not notice when her pants disappeared, but she heard the growl of relief when Merlin let loose his zipper. He was full and ready, the sight of him making her slick with need and a little afraid. She drew up her knees but he pinned her down, caging her limbs with his.

Merlin's amber gaze held her, his pupils blown to twice their normal size. They had always reminded Vivian of a hawk's steady gaze, the predator in him plain in this one feature. Yes, he was loyal and loving to those he claimed, but he could be equally cold, and even more lethal. Vivian had seen and recognized that trait as one of her own. What would he do if he caught her hiding here, inside his lovely little protégée? What would he do once the potion wore off?

Would Vivian let him live long enough to find out? She held his gaze a little longer, counting down the moments until that decision had to be made. It was a thrill to teeter on this knife's edge, the throb of her body answering the merciless lust in his eyes.

He used his knee to part her legs, then thrust a hand against her core. She jumped at the pressure. She was already slick and throbbing, protected only by the flimsy fabric of her panties. Heat flared beneath her skin, raising a pink flush across her pale flesh. Her breasts ached with every beat of her pulse, the nipples tight, burning nubs. His thumb flicked at her cleft, nearly making her come.

With a word of magic, he tore away the last scrap of fabric that covered her. She was naked and entirely his. His next kiss bruised her with its heat but Vivian didn't care. It said something about Merlin's strength of will that he had not taken her with simple brute force, even if the potion left little room for anything but blunt desire.

He drove into her with slow precision, the length and breadth of him drawing a moan from her. All at once, there was nothing but the sensation of fullness, stretching, of surrendering to a pulse that had suddenly gone wild. For an instant Vivian quailed. Sex had never been like this before. The fragility of this body, its deep vulnerability, thrilled her. She felt naked in ways that had no words.

It also left her without a single defense.

When Merlin drew back, even halfway, she was bereft, digging her fingers into his shoulders to make him stay.

And then he was back, thrusting deep. And again. And again. Sensation fluttered and exploded, winding her belly tighter and tighter with need. She began to whimper, her head pressed deep into the pillow.

There were some rewards for being a puny, helpless human. Vivian closed her eyes as deep pulses of desire tore through her. Her mouth fell open on a cry as the pulses turned into a shattering cataclysm inside her. She cried out, cresting again as she felt the hot explosion of Merlin's seed inside her. It should have ended there, but he thrust on and on, her body shuddering with pleasure at each push as the power of the spell she'd woven into the potion spun its own climax. It had been a robust work of craftsmanship.

Finally, everything went still as if they'd rung a perfect, pure note.

Vivian panted, hot tears sliding from the corners of her eyes. The savage gnawing of desire had ceased, but a different kind of ache had settled into her. She'd always understood simple, mindless need and had been prepared for it, but this mortal lovemaking had transformed lust into complicated emotions. She'd come for revenge. Now she was tangled in doubt.

Merlin rolled to the side in a profound slumber, his limbs settling in perfect relaxation. Within seconds a soft snore escaped him. An irrational stab of fury shot through her. How dare he sleep, when she was here to be adored?

Wait—why did that matter? She needed to settle down and focus on her plan. Enjoying the effects of the potion was one thing—demons enjoyed pleasure as much as the next sentient entity—but she was there for a reason. Slowly, Vivian stretched, waking her limbs one by one. Despite her roiling thoughts, satisfaction sang through her. Her body was sore and still slightly aroused, but she couldn't remember ever feeling this relaxed. No wonder humans bred like rabbits.

She rose to her elbow, looking down on Merlin's sleeping face. He looked younger this way, relaxed and peaceful. With one finger, she lightly traced the straight line of his nose, the bow of his upper lip and the fullness of the lower.

Vivian smiled to herself. Merlin had his tribe's dark hair and even features. They had lived in the ancient kingdom of Mercia, fending off the invading Romans with spear and spell. They'd lost, of course. Merlin's mother —matriarch, warrior and druidess, had charged her son with saving the land for her people. Eventually, Merlin had found Arthur and tried to fulfill that promise through Camelot's king.

Vivian had watched it all, year after year, wondering where the story would end. It had been fun right up until Merlin had betrayed her trust. Vivian lifted her finger from his lips, her mood suddenly somber.

This deeply unconscious, his enchanter's powers could not alert him to danger. Vivian had achieved what she wanted with the potion—he was finally at his most vulnerable. She had only to pluck a knife from the block in the kitchen, or one of the blades she'd seen among the heap of Merlin's clothes. He wore such things the way a woman wore jewelry, selecting each one to suit his mood that day. Weapons would be easy to find. Or she could choose poison, or suffocation or even another spell.

She'd expected this moment to feel triumphant, but instead a gray sadness filled her like poisonous fog. She sank down on the bed, Merlin's warmth against her side. She sighed, then her own breathing quieted, leaving only his light snore to fill the room.

I'm dying. She'd managed to put it out of her mind for hours, but now the idea pressed in again, blackening what was left of her serenity. Even a demon could grasp the irony of a death sentence on the same day she'd discovered this kind of pleasurable intimacy. Was this the mortal state? How did they survive the strain of it? Well, clearly they didn't, which was the point. Vivian pressed a hand to her forehead, wondering if she was about to experience her first headache.

I just had mortal sex. And it rocked my world. It had reached inside her to places she rarely noticed. There had been unfamiliar nuances of emotion involved, but she hadn't minded that so much. They had made the event memorable, maybe even meaningful. Absurdly, she was glad her first time as a mortal had been with Merlin. Someone important to her. Someone who had changed the course of her life, even if she loathed him for it.

It certainly made the prospect of ending his life seem less satisfying. She sighed again, rolling over so that she could rest her head on his shoulder. They fit together well. If she killed him, they would never lie together like this again, and that seemed a shame.

Vivian stared up at the ceiling, more confused than she had ever been in her long existence. Should she simply spy for Tenebrius and LaFaye instead?

Merlin awoke with a jolt, sitting upright before he was fully conscious. He was vaguely aware of a warm body in the bed, but his first thought was for the magical residue clouding his brain. It was like a hangover, the bad kind that came from mixing drinks on a hot day that involved too much greasy food and no sleep. The light made his eyeballs burn and he squeezed them shut as he groped for some clue as to what had led to this moment.

He rewound his memory. Arthur. Talking to the knights. Returning home. Clary and the jug of wheatgrass. Soapy water. *Oh.* There was a reason he was completely naked. He forced his eyes open and turned to look at the other person in the bed. Clary looked deliciously tousled. She had a blanket pulled up to her chin, but he could see the slope of a pale shoulder that promised a garden of delights below. Random snatches of memory told him what they'd done and that he'd enjoyed it very much. In fact, he hadn't had so much fun since… That thought stopped him cold. *By the ashes of the ancient gods!*

Her green eyes were wide and cautious, searching his face for clues to what he was thinking. Fury began crawling through him, but he reined it in. He'd already lost what little dignity he had that day. "You drugged me." He kept the words neutral, just a statement of fact, and watched her reaction.

She bit her lip, but it looked more like laughter than contrition. "What makes you say that?"

"Love potions are nothing new. I know the aftertaste. I got that recipe from an old girlfriend." The urge to rage and scream surged through him, but tantrums would get him nowhere. Neither would magic, if his suspicions were correct. He'd learned long ago to never start a spell battle he wasn't guaranteed to win.

Now that he was angry, his thoughts were clearing fast. He studied Clary's expression, her eyes, the way she held her hands, and they were familiar. But they were not Clary. His stomach dropped, dread certainty rising. "Under ordinary circumstances, you wouldn't need a potion to get me into your bed. But neither the circumstances nor the people are what they seem."

"Oh?" She rose to her knees, her expression still intent. There was no bashfulness, no embarrassment. Just concern about what he'd do next. It was the kind of poise Clary had never possessed.

Until someone else possessed her. His hand snapped out, catching her wrist. "Why did you do it?"

"Why do you think?" After a moment's hesitation, the mask dropped and Merlin's skin pebbled with a sudden chill. The bones and flesh were the same, but the spirit behind the eyes transformed. A fierce, proud fire lit her face as she dropped the blanket, abandoning all modesty. It took every ounce of Merlin's will not to savor the sight she offered.

His fingers closed tighter around her wrist until she winced and he remembered whose body this was. He released her and she sank back on her heels, amusement lurking at the corners of her lips.

"I don't believe you merely wanted the pleasure of my company," he said drily.

"Are you certain?" Her gaze raked him up and down, at once appreciative and mocking. "You have certain, uh, attributes that I remembered fondly all these years."

Merlin swore under his breath. He'd already tried the best treatment he knew for possession by a powerful demon. At least it was the one cure that wouldn't kill the host. "We both know very well that you want me dead. You weren't exactly restrained about telling the world."

Her gaze went dagger-sharp. "And yet you gave me such an enthusiastic welcome."

Despite a rush of chagrin, Merlin's scalp prickled with dread.

"Hello, Vivian." He gave an unfriendly smile. "What have you done with Clary?"

Chapter 12

"Your little witch is safe," Vivian said. "She's slumbering the same way you put me to sleep. We simply changed places."

Relief unclenched Merlin's fists, but only for a moment. He wondered how the demon had managed the switch, but then, this was Vivian. She was every bit his equal in power, not to mention cunning. He gave a reluctant nod. "And then you slipped me the potion, knowing that I would trust Clary."

"Mmm-hmm." Vivian lay back on the thick pillows, slowly stretching. "She was the perfect Trojan filly."

And he had been so besotted with her that he, the greatest enchanter in the human realms, hadn't bothered to check his drink for potions. Lust had made a fool of him. "Why do it?"

"Revenge. I swore to kill you, remember?" She cast him a sidelong look, a glint of emerald from under her long lashes.

"And I won't kill you?"

The threat would have carried more weight if they hadn't just made love. Merlin tried to convince his body that the luscious, naked female mere feet away was a monster, but it wasn't easy. Parts of him refused to be convinced. He jumped off the bed and snatched a pair of pants out of the laundry basket. Her amused chuckle brought unwelcome heat to his ears.

"Hide, o mighty wizard," Vivian drawled. "You can't kill this body without snuffing your pet witch."

He pulled on a shirt, unsuccessfully ignoring the naked woman lolling on his bed. She'd turned on her stomach and was facing his way now, chin in her hands and feet kicking in the air. As good as she looked, the gleam in her eyes was more predatory than flirtatious.

Merlin shrugged, striving for casual. "Speaking of snuffing, why didn't you murder me when you finally had the chance?"

"I like to play with my food."

Her smile was slow, a good imitation of her usual feline grin, but it lacked conviction. There were few beings in any realm—mortal, fae or the demonic Abyss—who would see that crack in her armor, but Merlin knew Vivian too well. He made careful note of it. There would be precious few weaknesses he could use against her.

He tucked in his shirt, feeling slightly better now that he wasn't on display. "Let Clary go, Vivian. Go home and leave us alone."

Her chin jerked up. "Are you sure that's what you want? If I leave, you'll never see me again."

"Since you're here to kill me, it's hard to see the downside to your absence."

"Oh, really?" The heat in her stare nearly unraveled his self-possession. "I doubt you've enjoyed yourself so much since you ran away from my bed."

"I didn't run. I left."

"Once you've gone hellspawn, the rest is like cold oatmeal." Her grin spread wider this time. "Admit it, Merlin. You missed me."

"Oatmeal is rarely homicidal." He leaned against the dresser, crossing his bare feet at the ankles. He was outwardly calm, but inside his guts were in a knot. She was right about one thing—demons understood lust like no one else. Memories of their potion-induced gymnastics, however confused, made his pulse jump.

She chuckled low in her throat, no doubt sensing his discomfort. "You thought you had me, didn't you? You thought a mere injection could put me in chains?"

Merlin said nothing, hating her so deeply that he tasted it like bile. How was he going to make her leave without harming Clary?

"Oh, my poor little half-druid monster, how long have you been watching your sweet student and wanting this?" Vivian rose to her knees and spread her arms wide, displaying her body. "A bit skinny, don't you think? But then, not everyone can be me."

Fury jerked him from his slouch. He grabbed a clean shirt and threw it at her. "Put some clothes on!"

Vivian snatched it from the air. "Have you turned prudish, grandfather?"

She chuckled as she pulled the shirt over her head. The sound seemed to crawl over his skin, reviving memories of a different bed and Vivian in a different body. Merlin shifted, his nerves on alert.

"Is that better?" Vivian asked in mocking tone. The shirt fell halfway down her thighs and bore a faded logo of pouting lips and a lolling tongue.

"Whatever." Soft shadows had stolen over the room as daylight failed. What should have been intimate was suddenly claustrophobic. He made a move for the door, but her voice stopped him in his tracks.

"You can't be so proper if you're lusting after your students. Just like I seduced you, or have you forgotten?"

Not likely. "Don't go there, Vivian."

"Why not?" she purred. "Guilty conscience?"

Maybe. He'd wanted Clary since they'd first met, but he'd resisted an entanglement. At least he had right up until she'd been all but dying in his arms. He hadn't kissed her until then, but that had opened a floodgate of emotion he hadn't been able to close.

He glared at the impostor in his bed. "You're right that I want her. That's why your potion worked so well."

Vivian's face scrunched as if she smelled something bad. "Why her? She's weak."

That was where Vivian was wrong. Clary had nearly died at Laren's hands, but she'd held the fae while he wept in shame and grief. "You'd never understand."

The dying light blurred Vivian's features, making her look impossibly young in that oversize shirt. "Explain it to me," she asked softly, sliding off the bed and padding toward him.

"You'll take whatever I say and make it a weapon."

"But say I don't." There was a hint of uncertainty in her eyes that gave him pause. Vivian was never uncertain.

"If I tell you, will you leave?" he asked.

"No." She stepped closer, putting both palms against his chest. "But I do want to know."

The pressure of her hands felt completely ordinary, but his skin still crept at the touch. His first instinct was to back away, but rejecting her out of hand would not be wise. She was too proud to accept another rebuff, even from him, and wounded pride meant payback.

Her fingertips dug into his shirt, reminding him they should be claws. "We used to have lots of discussions. We would talk for hours," she said softly. It nearly sounded like a plea. "Remember?"

Of course he remembered those conversations. For all their intelligence and prodigious powers, demons were almost childlike when it came to matters of the heart. Complex emotions baffled and repelled them, but unlike most demons, Vivian was curious. Merlin had found himself trying to explain why guilt and rage could be confused in the mortal mind, or how anger at another could become hatred of oneself, or a thousand other conundrums. In the end he'd become just as confused and fascinated by the vagaries of the human heart.

Vivian searched his face through Clary's witch-green eyes. By her expression, she saw the truth. He didn't want to speak that way with her ever again. Not after the way their affair had ended, and not now that Vivian held the woman he wanted hostage in her own body.

"Did you ever care for me?" she asked, a faint smile playing on her lips.

Trust Vivian to wonder. "In my own way," he said, knowing it was a poor answer.

She pulled her hands from his chest and took a step back. "If I asked what that meant, would you tell me?"

Merlin hesitated, unsure what to say because there was no single answer. He'd begun his time with her as a student, then as a lover and then as a thief and traitor. During that time he'd learned what demons truly were, and they'd shown him the darkness inside his soul. How could he love that? And yet there had been a time…

It began in a town that clung to the towering cliffs above the white-capped Mediterranean Sea. He'd been far from his birthplace, wandering in search of knowledge, pleasure and easy money. The fledgling Roman Empire had seemed like the place for a strapping young man to find all three. Sadly, all he'd gotten for his trouble so far was sore feet and bruises from a dozen tavern brawls. But that, he'd told himself, was all part of the adventure.

One hot summer day he came upon a shady olive grove and stretched out in the long, cool grass. The blades tickled his cheek as the breeze ruffled through it, and he closed his eyes and wished for a jug of wine to ease his dry throat. Then he let his thoughts drift away like early morning mist. The sun was much lower in the sky when he woke again to find restless fingers combing through his hair. Merlin sat up with a start to find a hooded figure crouched beside him. He put a hand to his brow, still feeling the brush of what had been decidedly feminine fingertips.

"Who are you?" he asked, unsure if his visitor would answer. The soft gray robes looked like something a priestess would wear, and he'd heard of virgins sworn to shun the company of men. He'd just started to spin an interesting fantasy when she spoke.

"I am called Vivian." Her low, throaty voice seemed to smoke with sensuality. Though her features were hidden, he was certain she was a carnal goddess, figuratively speaking. "You are sleeping in my grove."

"Yours?" He looked around, but there were none of the fine stone villas he'd seen in these parts. There wasn't even a shepherd's hut. "Where is your dwelling?"

"It is both near and far, Merlin Ambrosius."

He sucked in a breath, surprise banishing his pleasant daydreams. "How do you know my name?"

"I know your name and the name of Brida the Druidess, who gave you life."

The odds of anyone knowing him this far from home were infinitesimal unless, of course, there was magic involved. Suspicion cramped his shoulders. He was new to the ways of enchantment, but he already recognized how little of it was innocent. This woman—whoever she was—could not be trusted. Merlin slowly rose to his feet, watching the hooded form as he might a wild animal. No sudden movements. No taking his eyes from her. Ready to run.

She rose with him, proving to be almost his height. "My knowledge troubles you."

"What do you want?"

"I can give you much," she said with a casual wave of her hand.

A long staff appeared in her hand. At the top was an intricate cap of metalwork that held a frosted white stone in filigreed claws. Merlin eyed it, knowing it was a true wizard's staff worth more than his entire village back home. Such objects held immense power, enough to launch him from obscurity to the right hand of kings. He itched to grip the polished rosewood and fold it to his chest the way a young girl clutched her doll. But even an obscure bumpkin of a hedge wizard knew nothing so precious came without a price.

"Why?" he asked, so shocked that his voice was nearly lifeless.

"We've been watching you from the cradle. We've been watching for signs of greatness."

A surprised laugh burst from his lips. "Any luck?"

She went very still. It was impossible to see her face beneath the hood, but he got the impression she wasn't pleased by his laugh. Fear prickled along his skin, responding to an instinct he only half understood.

"You are a disappointment to your people," she said. "Your mother trained you well to follow in her tradition, but your magic is weak. You have not led your tribe to greatness, or even safety. Invaders will come from this faraway land and crush your people into the dust of history."

Her words burned, as had his mother's, but he knew the simple truth. "I'm not a war leader. I'm not even as good a magician as my mother."

"No, you're not. You are barely wizard enough to amuse children at the midsummer festival. You ran away to find your fortune because of the disappointment you saw in every eye, from the chieftain down to the lowest goatherd."

Shame itched along every nerve, begging to be soothed by some spark of promise—but that would never come. He simply wasn't that talented. She rested the butt of the staff in the thick grass, clearly tired of holding it out to a fool who wouldn't take it. Merlin clenched his fists, straining not to grab it and rewrite his future.

The robes shifted as if their occupant was casually leaning on one hip. "I know what's holding you back, young Merlin. You have more power than all the Druids in the western islands, but your magic works a different way. They cannot teach you the way I can."

His mouth went dry. He worked his throat a moment before words would form. "What are you saying?"

"Let me teach you. I understand you. I can make you fulfill the promise of your birth."

He'd been born to the greatest Druidess in all the kingdoms of Britain and yet his power produced as much bang as a soggy drum skin. Her promise wasn't so much temptation as an offer of survival—or so his pride told him. A thousand clamoring needs brushed aside all his caution.

She understood him. No one at home had ever done so much.

And then she pushed back the hood. Her hair was a lustrous blue-black and her eyes a violet he'd never seen before. It was the shade of dusk just before the night. Merlin swallowed hard. He'd been a favorite of the ladies all the way across Gaul and Germania, and now here in these sun-baked lands. He'd seen his share of feminine beauty, and yet he could not stop staring at her face. Vivian wasn't pretty or even beautiful—she was a true goddess.

She held out a hand. "Come with me."

Some shred of sanity reared up. "I still don't understand why."

"Let's just say I took an interest because of your father."

Merlin stilled. "No one knows who my father was."

She wiggled her fingers, urging him to follow. "I'll tell you someday."

It was more than anyone else could offer. He finally took her hand, finding comfort in the soft, warm press of her palm. He should have known it would go horribly wrong in the end. Nothing came without a price.

Merlin stared down at her now, recognizing the same glint in her eyes. It didn't matter that they were green, or a different shape, or that she was fair instead of dark. Vivian was what she was. A change of form wouldn't alter her essential nature. Better to ask a crow to sing like a canary.

But she had changed his life. Nothing had been the same since that day in the south of Italy. Vivian had taken a foolish youth and made him wise. Along the way she'd set the stage for Camelot's destruction and pointed him toward the precipice. He'd done the rest himself because, all else aside, she was an excellent teacher. After all, she'd made him understand his true nature—as little as he'd wanted those answers. But now? She was inhabiting the body of the woman he loved and threatening his life.

So why ask if he cared for her? She had never asked such a thing before.

Merlin narrowed his eyes. "Get out of her, Vivian."

Her grin was carnivorous. "What if I said I wanted to stay with you?"

"You, of anyone, should know that nothing good comes of being with me."

"Ah, you blame yourself for that spell in ways no one but me can guess. Before you take me back, you will have to forgive yourself."

"That day will never come."

With that, he turned and left the bedroom, desperate for air and even more desperate for a plan.

Chapter 13

Of course, Vivian followed Merlin from the bedroom like a lethal shadow. Even without looking, he was aware of how her steps glided like a cat's. It was the opposite of Clary's brisk tread.

Clary. The thought of her made him frantic, but he couldn't let Vivian see that. Dismay was catnip to a demon.

He stopped in the living room, bowing his head in thought. Resentment twisted inside him. Revenge he could understand—he'd wronged Vivian in ways that were hard to forgive—but by taking a body, she was hurting an innocent woman.

"Your residence is charming," the demon said from behind him. Her voice was casual as if she'd dropped by for coffee. "The light reminds me of the place we first met. Perhaps it has something to do with being near the ocean."

Merlin felt the heat rise to his face as rage scattered his thoughts. She had to go. Vivian had taught him a lot, but he'd had a few centuries to find tricks of his own. He turned to face her, bracing his feet on the pine floor. The natural decor—bare wood, plants and stone—was more than a decorating choice. Druid magic came from life energy, and he could feel the traces of that force through his bare soles. He began to draw it into his core.

One corner of her mouth quirked up. "Do you really think you can overpower me?"

"I promise I will never underestimate you."

"That's almost a compliment."

She drew closer, threads from the ragged hem of the shirt fluttering around her thighs. The next moment she stood close enough that her toes brushed his, the contact oddly intimate. She smelled like Clary's shampoo and the soft musk of Clary's skin. Memories of Vivian tangled with the present, weaving lust and anger and a fierce protectiveness into emotions he couldn't understand.

He bent his head so their faces almost touched. "Are you really going to kill me?"

Her lids lowered, the sweep of her lashes anything but demure. "I told you I play with my food."

The worst thing was, he understood the impulse. There was a part of her that was very like a buried part of him, and that intrigued and appalled him at the same time. They were both black-hearted. The only redeeming quality he had was that he understood why that was wrong.

He kissed her forehead lightly. "Stop this, Vivian. Go home."

She tilted her face up to him, catching his lips with hers. "And miss humbling you? I don't think so. I paid a high price to be here. Higher than you will ever know."

He wondered what that price was, but then her fingers slipped beneath his shirt to caress his bare back. Wondering took a backseat to more basic sensations. His breath sucked in and she chuckled low in her throat.

"How much humbling is enough?" he asked, his thumb stroking the clean line of her jaw. He'd almost gathered enough power. Almost.

"I'll let you know."

His hand closed, for the briefest instant, around the fragile architecture of her throat. He drew it away at once, too aware of what he might be tempted to do. Instead, he kissed her back, finding the hem of her shirt and the soft skin beneath. He stroked her then, firm and gentle as he slid his fingers lower to explore the sensitive places he knew brought the best results.

She nearly came right then, but he pulled back. She cursed softly, the look in her eyes frustrated and demanding. She stretched, rising on her toes to lock her lips to his, taking him without quarter.

It was then he unleashed his spell, releasing all the power he'd gathered and knocking Vivian back into oblivion. Maybe turnabout wasn't fair play, but Clary needed a fighting chance. Her body sagged in his arms, suddenly limp. She sighed softly, the bloom of sensual pleasure turning her cheeks rosy. He gathered her up, carrying her back to the bedroom and settling her beneath the comforter. She breathed gently, kiss-swollen lips parted as if she'd fallen into a natural doze.

He prayed it would be Clary who woke up, but at the very least this gave him a moment to think.

He slipped out of the bedroom, closing the door softly behind him, and retreated to the guest bedroom. The smudged outline of the chalk circle remained on the floor. He stepped over it, the scene between Laren and Clary replaying in his mind as he entered the en suite bathroom and turned on the shower to warm up. If Vivian was the perfect demon seductress, Clary embodied everything he valued among the mortals—liveliness and humor, loyal affection and a kindness that lit the world wherever it could be found. She made him believe in fabled beasts that housed the humbled soul of a prince.

That he, someday, might be worth redemption.

Merlin shed his clothes and stared into the mirror over the tiny bathroom sink. He and Vivian were too well matched to survive an actual fight, and he couldn't risk hurting the very woman he meant to save. The only positive was that Vivian, vain and self-protective, would be equally careful as long as she intended to stick around and make his life a misery. The situation might have been amusing, like something out of a broad, tasteless comedy, except it was unimaginably dangerous. Between them, they could break the world. They could break Clary.

He needed ideas, and a shower, even a fast one, always helped him think. He stepped under the stream of steaming water, grateful to ease the tension from his muscles. It wasn't just frustration knotting his shoulders—that potion had left toxins behind. Since waking, he'd felt like a bundle of aches. The shower was deliciously hot until a blast of cold announced someone else was using up the heated water. Merlin yelped, the spray pounding in his face as he fumbled with the controls. He slammed off the water, dripping and bad-tempered. "Vivian!" he roared, because only a demon would leave a man in a freezing shower. Grabbing a towel for modesty, he stormed toward the master bathroom.

But when he flung open the door, it was Clary who emerged from the cloud of steam, wrapped tight in a white cotton robe. Her irritated expression left no doubt who was ascendant. She stabbed him in the chest with a forefinger. "What was that?"

"What?" he asked defensively.

"I like a romp as much as the next girl," she bit out, a blush flaming up her cheekbones, "but that was uninvited."

Yes, this was Clary.

"The potion wasn't my idea." He gripped his towel tighter. To be fair, they needed to talk, but he wanted to dry off first.

"That was revenge sex. I *hate* revenge sex."

"What was I supposed to do?" He flipped wet hair out of his eyes and grabbed the robe he'd left on the back of the master bathroom door. He rarely used it, but today seemed like an excellent time to start. "Vivian would cheerfully kill us both if the mood struck her."

"I don't know about that."

The uncertainty in her voice sent a cold finger down his spine. He finished knotting the tie of his robe and turned to face her. "Of course she would. You don't know her like I do."

"Maybe, maybe not." Clary's eyes were dark with anger. "Now that I've been stuffed in the basement of my own skull, I know what it feels like. Don't do it again."

Merlin felt his jaw drop. "So what—"

She cut him off with a slice of her hand. "You two need to work things out like grown-up wizards. I refuse to be in the middle anymore."

Clary pushed past him and stalked into the bedroom, slamming the door behind her.

Clary sank onto the edge of the bed, then sprang up almost at once and began rummaging through her clothes. She rarely dressed with modesty in mind, but this time she chose plain black slacks and a white blouse that buttoned at the neck and cuffs. She wanted to look the opposite of Vivian.

When she bent to slip on low-heeled boots, she could feel aches in unfamiliar places. Vivian's possession had blurred the details, but she knew what had happened. She straightened, brushing the creases from her pant legs, and studied herself in the mirror. She looked composed and businesslike, the way she would going to a job interview.

Her calm features hid a storm of turmoil inside. The sexual encounter she'd just had was bone-shattering, extreme, simply *more* than she'd had with any other man. Vivian's complete lack of inhibition was part of it. Merlin himself was—she searched for the right term and came up empty. Highly experienced. Enthusiastic. A textbook of hormonal fantasy. But she categorically refused to participate in bedtime gymnastics from the backseat of her own brain. She wasn't Vivian's plaything.

No, Clary Greene would not be used or drugged or knocked out again. She wasn't a meal for the fae or a convenient container for stray demons. If sheer annoyance could lock hellspawn in the deepest, darkest recesses of her mind, Clary had it covered. Vivian was toast—and so was Merlin if he tried stabbing her with any more concoctions that messed with her magic. If that was getting rescued, it was too hazardous by half.

She was looking after herself from now on, thank you very much. Of course, that made no sense because she was still infested by a crazed hellspawn, but she'd deal with that once her blood pressure came back to planet earth.

She was combing her damp hair when a phone pinged. She looked around to see Merlin's smartphone sitting on top of his dresser. It pinged twice more in short order. Whoever was texting him was insistent, and in her current mood the piercing sound tempted her to smash the phone to splinters. She crossed the room in two strides and snatched it up.

The texts were from K. Art. As the social media coordinator at Medievaland, she knew that was King Arthur. There were three messages, and they were short, probably because Arthur couldn't type to save his life.

Do not update.

Malediction ware beware. Tisthelan.

Going darke.

Darke? Tisthelan? Clary squinted at the phone, momentarily distracted by the strange spelling. Once in a while olde tyme English slipped into whatever the knights wrote, which made the actual content hard to figure out. Malediction ware? Did he mean malware? It was hard to tell with medieval people. She was pretty sure Perceval still believed there was a teeny tiny angel inside the motherboard. Of course, after you've met a talking dragon, everything was relative.

With the phone in hand, Clary went in search of Merlin and interpretation. He was brooding over a mug of tea and looked up at her with an expression reminiscent of a sad golden retriever. He was as confused and hurt as she was, but she wasn't ready to talk about demon sex quite yet. If ever. That would have to fester until she was good and ready to rip that bandage off. Significantly, she noted there was no wheatgrass in sight.

She held up the phone so he could read the screen. "Does this make any sense to you?"

"No." He took the phone and set it on the counter, saying nothing about the fact she was snooping on his phone. "Should it?"

When she didn't answer, he poured her a mug of tea and slid it along the countertop. His wary look said he expected another round of their previous argument.

"Going dark sounds serious," she said. "With or without the *e*. It's like he's been hacked or something."

"You're the computer expert."

"You're the Arthur expert. Could he be in trouble?"

By way of reply, Merlin crossed to the table, set down his tea and opened his laptop. It came to life with a faint beep.

"Wait," Clary said. "Does your software automatically update?"

"Of course. It's more secure that way."

His face fell as he connected the dots to Arthur's first message. He dove for the keyboard, but not quickly enough. A low, malevolent chuckle sounded from the laptop's tinny speakers. A spark flew from the power connector, singeing Merlin's fingers as he reached for it. Clary's breath caught as she sensed Vivian stirring to life, but rather than triumph, the demon seemed to be as puzzled as she was.

"My computer's possessed," Merlin said in affront.

Clary had heard that before, but never so convincingly. With a swipe of her boot heel, she kicked the cord out of the wall socket. It wouldn't help immediately, but the battery had to run down sometime. "Have you tried hitting Escape?"

Merlin shot her a withering look just before a cloud of green fog rolled out of the screen. Merlin jumped back, staying well clear as the cloud hovered over the table. It shimmered a moment, sparkling and bobbing like a bad special effect.

"What by all the coven's pointy hats?" she muttered, circling the table.

The cloud seemed to dissipate, though the laughter kept going. At first, she thought the manifestation had been harmless, but then saw the green goop eating its way through Merlin's books and papers. With an oath, he grabbed a jar of powder from his spell cupboard and began sprinkling it over the mess. The green goop bubbled and hissed, which was bad enough, but then it seemed to coalesce into something with clumsy tentacles. It tried to lift itself by crawling up the neck of the study lamp.

Merlin slammed it with a fireball, scorching the table, but the goo sizzled until it was no more than smoke. Clary slid the balcony door open to get rid of the stink of rotting fish.

"That's malware all right," she said under her breath.

"It was trying to manifest," Merlin replied.

But whatever that was didn't belong in the mortal realms. "Was that a demon?"

Not quite, Vivian replied. *Nevertheless, they are test-*

ing your electronic highways to see if they are safe for us to travel. We are made of energy, after all.

Did you know about this? Clary demanded, deeply unhappy that her visitor was awake.

The modern age offers some interesting opportunities. Vivian's tone sounded oddly detached. *That is what Tenebrius told me. This is Gorm's plan to bring us from the Abyss.*

Before she could reply, the screen of the laptop bulged, a green and glowing hand stretching toward Merlin with grasping fingers. The enchanter looked down his nose at the apparition. "Seriously?"

The laughter was suddenly drowned out by a cacophony of voices, crackling static, scraps of music and what sounded like tearing sheets of metal. It grew and grew as the TV switched on to a football game at full volume, then a radio and then a stereo playing jazz. The hand was conducting like a demented maestro. Sparks fountained from the overhead fixture, and a car alarm sounded from the street below. It was only a matter of time before something caught on fire.

"Did I mention how much I hate demons?" Merlin grumbled with disgust.

Clary stalked toward the laptop, approaching it from behind as Merlin stayed just out of reach of the grasping hand. Though it had no eyes, it seemed to be able to track his every movement. Clary clenched her teeth, fighting the panic welling inside her. When she was just within reach, she jabbed at the laptop, hoping to slam it closed.

But the hand snaked around, faster than she could follow. It closed on her wrist with a grip like ice, startling a cry from her lips.

The grip was so cold that Clary's muscles jumped in protest. She staggered back, pulling away with all her weight, but the fingers squeezed tighter. For a glowing green hand made of static, its strength was terrifying. She was aware of Merlin reacting, grabbing the lamp and swinging it at the laptop, but he seemed far away. Her senses were filled with the demon's chill touch and a mounting agony that rose like spears of ice through her gut. She doubled over, her captured wrist twisting painfully.

"Clary!" Merlin snapped, worry sharpening her name into a command. When she didn't respond, he dropped the lamp and clasped her face in his hands and tipped her face up to his, but her vision blurred. Somewhere in the back of her mind, it occurred to her that his attempt to smash the screen must have failed.

"Clary?"

Chapter 14

Clary's consciousness slipped as if the present was a slick surface. Gravity—or the demon's power—pulled her into an inky pool to drown.

Wherever it was, whatever state she fell into, there was no air. Her lungs began to burn as her throat spasmed, every scrap of her flesh suddenly on fire. She caught a glimpse of a cave—no, it was a room made of stone. A marble bowl on a long pillar stood in the middle like a great big birdbath, and it was filled with green fire. Merlin was staring back at her, but it wasn't the Merlin she knew. He was younger, his expression filled with determination and eagerness. This wasn't the master enchanter at work—he was still a student.

Student-Merlin reached out toward the fire with one hand, the other holding up a gem. He began to chant, and as he did the green fire leaped from the bowl to the gem in a perfect arc of light. His expression grew triumphant, his eyes almost wild with the vision of possibility. Clearly, this was a breakthrough, though Clary had no idea what it meant.

She was seeing the past through Vivian's eyes, but even as that thought took hold, the vision began to melt away. It wasn't a simple fade to black, but a wholesale destruction that began at one edge and ate across, like a photograph held in a flame. If this was Vivian's memory—her life flashing before Clary's eyes—the demonic force from the computer was destroying them both.

Vivian shrieked in rage. *No, no, you shall not take my existence from me!*

Then the only thing that mattered was survival. Clary choked, unable to take a breath. Her lungs ached, seeming to fold themselves inside out as they struggled for air. Merlin's power flared, heating the air as his spell sizzled around the laptop in a corona of electricity, but it had no effect. Clary fell to her knees, dangling from the apparition's clutch. She was starved for air. Consciousness ebbed as black fuzzed the edges of her vision. Vivian held on one second longer and unleashed every ounce of power she had. Lightning flared around Clary's hand, frying the demon's fingers.

Suddenly free, Clary dropped to the floor. Breath surged down her abused windpipe in a loud, sawing gasp, but she was on her feet in an instant. Her head spun but she grabbed the black plastic of the laptop's lid and slammed it closed. A moment later the laptop went silent, only a weak wisp of smoke leaking from the edges.

It was in sleep mode.

"Well," said Clary, her face numb with shock. "That happened. I hope you do regular backups."

She looked around to see the table was scorched, the books and papers fried or covered in demon goo. Merlin picked himself up off the floor, his expression an odd mix of wariness and relief. "Are you okay?"

"I think so." She examined her hand, which was pink and tender from the discharge of power. At least it wasn't blistering. Vivian had saved her life, and Clary was reluctant to tell Merlin she was back just so he could zap her again. Maybe that was stupid, or maybe she had to find a resolution that didn't put her in the middle of their war.

"That was an excellent fireball," he replied, pulling a leather satchel from the mess of belongings scattered around the room. He pushed the laptop into it and buckled the flap closed. "That thing would have destroyed us all given a chance."

"Didn't it just want a way into this world?" Clary sank into a chair. She wanted comfort—a hug, a pat on the back, something—but the air between them was still tense. Clearly, they weren't ready to touch each other yet.

"If the demons reach our world, Camelot will be their first target. We banished them, after all." He frowned. "I haven't seen that trick before. It was a clever one."

Clary imagined the choking sensation again, the sharp panic just before the lightning speared through her. She shuddered. Merlin set the satchel down and put his hands on her shoulders for a second before dropping them. The gesture was still awkward, but it was filled with concern. "You did well."

"Yeah?" It was Vivian who had done well.

His eyes were dark with worry, but there was humor, too. "Yeah."

Clary felt for the demon's presence, but she had retreated, leaving behind an impression of strong annoyance. Odd as it might seem, Vivian showed signs of jealousy. "That thing in the computer wasn't a normal hellspawn, was it?"

Merlin shrugged. "It was energy with only a primitive consciousness. Demon essence, as opposed to an individual demon. My guess is that was the advance guard, and it had two functions—to test the plan, and to kill as many knights as possible."

That was an image Clary didn't need in her dreams.

When she didn't reply, he took a step back. "I'm going to take the laptop to my workshop and destroy it there." It made sense. Destructive magic was messy, and hostile residue wasn't something a person wanted in their home. Nor was this the kind of job Merlin would trust to anyone else.

"Do you want me to come?" she asked.

"No. Stay here." He took another cautious step away, probably wondering if or when Vivian would make a return visit. "Can I trust you to sit quietly for an hour?"

"Yes." She tried not to sound offended.

Afraid of a little witchling? Vivian's voice was faint, but it had lost none of its bite.

Clary ignored her. A sudden thought had popped out of her subconscious. "Tisthelan."

Merlin gave her a blank look. "What?"

"In Arthur's message. *Tis the LAN.* All of Camelot's files are on a local area network."

Merlin didn't look any wiser.

"Look." Clary hitched forward on her seat. "If demons are energy and want to get onto the great electronic highway, where do they start? There's endless streams of data, networks, wireless transmissions, cables, you name it. If they wanted to target the knights in particular, finding Camelot's LAN would be the perfect point of entry. From there, they could jump to individual devices and the people using them."

Merlin glared at his laptop case. "The vile thing came for me. Did I mention how much I loathe demons?"

"We have to get the word out. No email, no blogging, no gaming. No one touches any devices or the internet."

He nodded. "I will. I'll find a landline to call from. Be sure to take your own advice."

He touched her chin lightly, brushing it with his thumb. It seemed an unconscious gesture, but an uncomfortable silence followed. A few days ago they'd been master and student, not lovers. And not engaged in—whatever this three-way relationship was. It was beyond awkward.

Merlin turned away, picking up the satchel and heading for the door. "Don't go out and don't let anyone in."

Clary followed him into the living room and folded her

arms. "Aren't you going to lock me in with unbreakable wards or something?"

Merlin opened the door to the outside corridor and then paused, looking back with one eyebrow arched. "Would you trust me again if I did?"

It was an excellent point. She'd hate him for it.

So would I. I would make him pay.

"And no cooking, okay?" he said. The door clicked shut like a punchline.

Clary flopped onto the couch, depression hitting her like a wall. *Did I mention how much I loathe demons?* Illogical as it might be, she found it hard not to take the statement personally when she had Vivian inside her.

Her hand still smarted as if she'd dunked it in too-hot water. Apparently, shooting lightning bolts had its price. So did everything else that had happened that day—or days. She wasn't even certain how long she'd been in Merlin's suite. A glance out the window said it was growing dark. Since it was nearly summer, that meant it was evening. She didn't feel tired. She was too jittery for that.

No cooking? Vivian asked, not so distant anymore. *He's joking about my potion? He's grown cocky.*

Clary pressed her face into her hands, wondering for the hundredth time how she ended up with a high-maintenance demon inside her head. Not only was that weird to begin with, it was also evolving in a strange way. She'd started out paralyzed with terror, and she was still terrified, but she was also exasperated. It was also like having a cranky roommate that wouldn't shut up.

Why aren't you grateful I've chosen you for my vessel?

"I don't know where to start with that one."

I saved your life. You owe me everything.

"You keep borrowing my body without asking, so shut up."

I made us have excellent sex.

"You had sex. I got to watch."

Just as well. Merlin is too much for a mere wisp of a mortal like you.

Clary gave a strangled cough. "Oh, yeah? What's the matter, scared he'll fall for me instead?"

The demoness gave a low, growling hiss. Vivian seemed to loathe Merlin, but that glimpse of memory Clary had seen told a different tale. Vivian had been proud of her student.

It tried to take my memory, Vivian said, changing the subject.

"Did it mean to?"

I don't know. The sullen admission seemed dragged from deep inside the demon. *This is not my plot. I was invited to participate, but I had other priorities.*

Something told Clary that was a problem. "How did the other demons take that?"

Vivian seemed to consider her answer. *Tenebrius said that he would be in touch. I did not think he would send a disembodied hand to do the touching on his behalf.*

"That seems ominous."

Agreed. I would not be surprised if I was the target just as much as Merlin.

So the bad-guy demons weren't just nuking Camelot's tech toys so that they could invade Earth, but they might just be gunning for the creature cohabiting her skull. "Y'know, I think I miss the days when I was just a no-talent witch with a hopeless crush on my instructor." Which would have been around forty-eight hours ago.

You must admit I keep boredom from the doorstep.

There was a light rapping at the door. Clary straightened, recalling Merlin's orders not to let anyone in. Then she went to see who it was, because no one told Clary what to do.

Queen Guinevere waited outside. Clary froze. "Gwen!"

They were good friends—had been ever since Clary helped the queen adjust after she'd awakened in the modern age. For all her rank and importance to Camelot's future, Gwen was very much her own person. Clary had recognized a kindred spirit on the spot.

The queen stepped forward, one hand on her baby bump. "His Highness needs me to sit down."

Clary sensed Vivian's instant interest in the baby. *New life.*

"Please, come in," Clary said a beat too late. Gwen was already in one of the easy chairs. "What brings you here?"

"I know you're supposed to be in quarantine or something," Gwen replied, opening her shoulder bag and pulling out an ebook reader, "but you're the computer genius. This won't switch on."

Clary all but snatched the device out of the queen's hand. "You don't need that right now."

"But I do," Gwen said earnestly. "All my books are on there and I've got nothing but time to read. I was in the middle of a really good mystery when the battery died and it won't charge back up."

Clary's mouth had gone dry, picturing Gwen fighting off a possessed device. "How did you get here?"

"In a car. I know how to drive."

Of course she did. Clary had died a thousand deaths coaching her for the road test.

"About my books," Gwen prompted her.

"Can't you get paperback copies for now?"

Gwen shrugged, rubbing her stomach. "When you can't move, it's hard to go hunting through bookstores. I want my fix as fast as technology can deliver it."

The life is strong, Vivian all but purred.

Alarm trickled through Clary's chest, kicking up her pulse. The demons hated Arthur, and Gwen carried his heir. Was Vivian's interest a threat? "Didn't Arthur tell you to stay away from computers?"

"Of course. He drove Excalibur through his monitor earlier this afternoon. Apparently it began talking to him. At first I thought he'd just triggered that talking assistant thing and panicked. It turns out it really was possessed."

"Um, yeah." Clary imagined the scene all too well.

"But that has nothing to do with my ebook reader. My books are already loaded." Gwen's brow furrowed. "Can you fix it?"

Reluctantly, Clary turned the device over to examine it. "It could be the battery died for good, or maybe a connection is broken."

A healthy baby means a strong future for the kings of Camelot and their people. LaFaye's invasion would destroy it.

Vivian's words were filled with emotion, but it was impossible to tell if it was happiness or anger. Clary's hands stopped in their exploration of the ports and buttons. Her fingers still ached from blasting scorch marks in the dining room table, and all she could think about was her friend and the innocent baby just a few feet away.

"I think this is beyond repair." It was a lie, but Clary wasn't sorry. "Just stop by a bookstore on the way home."

"You've barely looked at it," Gwen said reproachfully.

"Do you really want to risk your safety—the baby's safety—on the fact that the wireless switch is off?"

Gwen's blue eyes narrowed. "I would never risk my baby. I'm not an idiot, and I have a library card."

"Then why are you here?"

Gwen's chin tilted so that she looked up at Clary, her expression stern. "You're in trouble, I can tell. You don't sound like yourself."

Clary's chest squeezed, a sudden sharp ache of affection. "You mean the ebook reader was just an excuse to come?"

Gwen lifted a shoulder. "I really do want to finish that story." Her smile belied the words.

"Thank you." Clary couldn't help a smile, however weak. "Arthur will be furious with you for coming."

"Arthur's always furious. It's his default setting, right next to fussing over my health. I wish he'd take up golf." The words were fond, tinged with just a little exasperation. "I needed to make sure you were okay."

"What if I wasn't?"

"You would never harm me or this child. I know you too well."

She is foolish, Vivian said. *She does not know me. She did not see the green hand. She does not know how the others would use a baby.*

Clary squeezed Gwen's hand, loving her friend and wishing she had never come. "You need to go."

"Are you sure?" Gwen looked sad. "I'd hoped for some girl talk."

"I'll come by later with an armload of books." It was another lie. She was too aware of Vivian staring through her eyes at the fair-haired queen and her unborn young. It was like Vivian wanted to drink them in.

They are fresh life. I have not seen it through the eyes of mortality before.

Something in Vivian's tone confused Clary as if the words meant more than she understood. Gwen seemed to sense her tension, because she rose to go. "Please be all right, Clary. I need my friends."

Her eyes had lost none of their warmth, but they considered Clary as if seeing her for the first time. Normally, they hugged, but neither of them moved. Without a word, Gwen turned and left, abandoning her device on the coffee table. Vivian watched her every move.

In the stark silence that followed, Clary swore under her breath. Was Vivian a danger to Gwen? Were the demons chasing Vivian a threat to those around her?

You need to go.

Clary decided the words weren't just for the queen.

Chapter 15

Clary grabbed the bag of clothes Tamsin had brought her and repacked the few items she'd spread around the bedroom. She zipped it back up with a decisive rasp of metal and put her hands on her hips. Packing was easy. The next steps would be hard.

You don't trust me around the queen. The demon gave a restless sigh.

"Ya think?" Clary grumbled.

Demons do not have children in mortal fashion unless there is a mortal mother to give it life.

"That's reassuring. I'd hate to encounter a hellspawn in the terrible twos." Clary's sarcasm was automatic, and yet she'd heard the longing in Vivian's voice. Was it possible to have maternal instinct when your species couldn't reproduce? "So where do little demons come from?"

We come to awareness from within the collective force of demon energy. We call that force the essence. That is what powered the attack on the computer. It was a waste, using a finite resource for such a thing.

Clary heard Vivian's anger and was curious. "The essence is finite?"

The essence came to be when the world was young, but we do not know how or where. Some say there is a distant homeland for the demons. Others say that we were made of the fire at the core of the world. The only certainty is that the Abyss is not the place where the essence was born,

*and that is why we are a dying people. There is nothing
to replenish us.*

It was the longest speech the demoness had made, and
for the first time Clary heard the teacher in her. It would
have been intriguing if she'd had time for a history lesson. Unfortunately, Vivian was trying to kill Merlin and
using Clary's body to do it. And then there was the suspicion Vivian's pals weren't such good pals at the moment.

"I need to get out of here," Clary said.

Vivian didn't seem to mind the sudden change in topic.
*I wouldn't recommend it, little fool. These are danger-
ous times.*

"Says the malign entity taking over my brain."

You make it sound as if there was effort involved.

"Not making me feel warm and fuzzy about your presence here."

And what do you plan to do about that, witchling?

That was the question. Ever since first meeting the
knights of Camelot, Clary had wanted to help in their battle against Morgan LaFaye. Now she was infected by the
enemy, a liability instead of an ally.

And whatever Vivian said, Clary had felt her interest
in Gwen's baby. Clary didn't understand demons, but Vivian definitely wanted to hold that child in her arms. The
only thing she could do to help Camelot and its queen—
and Clary's best friend—was to get Vivian out of there.
She could walk away, just as she'd decided to do back in
Tamsin's bathroom.

"Do I still have command over my own two feet?"

*Is it any wonder that you are a pathetic little witchling?
Do you really think you're going to save the world by asking that kind of question? If you're going to fly in the face
of all logic and common sense, seize the opportunity by
the throat. Don't ask permission.*

"Not helping, pussycat."

If you do manage to escape, what makes you think Merlin won't find you and drag you back home by the ear?

"Because your pride wouldn't allow it."

Vivian fell silent at that. Seizing the opportunity as instructed, Clary grabbed her bag and left.

Clary might not be an expert witch, but she'd had ample experience running away as a teenager. Renting a car or buying a bus ticket required showing ID that could be traced. Hitchhiking could be dangerous. Bicycles, however, could go long distances and were largely anonymous to most people. She was an avid recreational rider—who wouldn't be with so much gorgeous scenery around Carlyle?—and had a decent road bike at her apartment along with a stash of cash. She retrieved both, stuffing her backpack with necessities, and was out of town within the hour.

But the day had taken its toll. Determination got her as far as a cash-only motel two towns away, where she slept despite the dirty room and dubious lock on the door. It was the end of the next day before she reached the outskirts of Seattle, every muscle in her body begging for rest.

Vivian sniffed. *You contain an entity possessed of staggering power, and yet you sink to this primitive mode of transport. I'm unsure whether to be amused or embarrassed.*

"I'm sure you could sprout bat wings and fly, but I think someone would notice."

Isn't shock and awe the point of power?

"Only if you equate power with being blown to smithereens by paranoid security forces."

Modern mortals are no fun.

"They have their own problems." And if Camelot had its way, the supernatural world would not be added to the mix. Merlin had told her about the accords. Species who couldn't compete with the humans—the sasquatches and

merfolk in the Pacific Northwest were a good example—
strongly believed that their survival depended on invis-
ibility.

*We all have our own problems. No one asks about the
demons' side of events.*

Clary knew conversational bait when it was waved in
front of her and was tempted to ignore it. She wasn't sure
why the demoness felt the need to explain herself. Still,
there was nothing better to do while she slipped back into
the stream of traffic that flowed into the city's suburbs.

"Okay," she said, giving in. "Let's hear it."

When the end of the war came, Merlin's final battle
spell tasted like ash to the demons, and it smelled as foul
as the defeat it was. They all knew the moment presaged
living death.

The spell had been stolen from Vivian's own library and
crafted into a weapon against them. The thief—Merlin—
had slipped from her bed to copy it and then escaped back
to his king while Vivian slept. This, after she'd taught him
so much and opened his eyes to the truth of his enormous
power.

Such betrayal was the last insult in a war that had pitted
every species against Vivian's people. The army Arthur of
Camelot had cobbled together was an alliance of fleas, but
those fleas were legion, and they had won. They strutted
and crowed and claimed they were in the right.

True, the demons had fought for conquest and glory.
They'd fought for the mastery they believed they deserved.
Right and wrong didn't enter into it. Demons didn't bother
hiding their lust for power. They were dangerous, but they
were—unlike Merlin—honest about it.

Vivian had stood on the ravaged field of battle, among
the dead fae and humans and witches. Some of the demons
had killed with glee and others, like her, with a grim de-

termination to survive. Her people would succeed, or they would fall. Falling meant banishment to someplace worse than the blood-soaked dirt.

There had been death for demons, too, for immortality didn't mean that they were indestructible. Her kind was made from energy and magic and a rare concentration of power could blast them to nothing. Tenebrius had said noble words about their losses, but they'd been brief. After all, it was the living who were in trouble now.

Vivian had not felt mortality's shadow yet and wasn't afraid of death. Yet she had feared Merlin's spell, because she knew it meant the Abyss.

There were many names for it: Hades, Hell, the Underworld. Wherever demons had come from, they had passed through this desolate place to reach the mortal realms. The operative phrase was *pass through*. No one actually wanted to stay there, given the open pits of flame, rocky deserts and pools of toxic sludge that passed for lakes. Magic could make the odd oasis, but that was a far cry from a truly habitable world. Could anyone really blame them for wanting to stay away?

And yet Merlin was using her own spell to push them off the green earth, with its fresh water and birdsong, into the lifeless pit the petty King of Camelot thought they deserved.

The spell's release was a hot slice across her skin. It was a ring of force radiating from Camelot's highest tower, not quite seen except for a bend in space and time where the ripple passed over the surrounding land and sky. Clouds scudded away like foam in a ship's wake. Trees bowed and broke, the most flexible all but flattening before the force of Merlin's magic. And there was not just one wave of power, but pulse after pulse in concentric rings of crushing force.

The mortal realms would recover, but the demons would

not. The spell hit them like a war hammer, the force hurling them across the veil between worlds and sealing their path against return. Vivian flew end over end, losing all sense of her physical being as the magic smashed her to pieces and plunged her into the Abyss, a drop in a torrential waterfall of demonkind.

Down, down into the dark they crashed, into the sunless pit of arid rock. Here no birds sang, no trees stretched tall, no children laughed. Their freedom was gone, as surely as if chains bound their limbs. Here was their punishment on the command of Arthur, King of Mortals—but it was Merlin who had done it.

Vivian raged, yet she might have accepted her fate if it had come another way. But it had come like a knife in the back. She had loved Merlin, and this was the result.

For the first time ever, Vivian had felt the hot kiss of a tear.

Clary pulled her bike to the curb and pulled off her helmet to cool her head a few degrees. Vivian's memory left her solemn, unsure whether to offer her regrets. It wasn't like she sided with the demons, but banishment seemed harsh.

I'm not asking for sympathy, Vivian remarked in her usual dry tone. *Just that you understand we have our own story. There was a rational reason we wanted the mortal realms for ourselves. I, at least, am not a mindless evil who devours infant children on toast.*

"You say that like you're the exception."

Some questions shouldn't be asked. Where are we?

Clary didn't know Seattle well, but could tell this had to be one of the newer suburbs. It still had that semipermanent feel that came from half-finished construction and lawns just sprouting new grass. The afternoon light made all the fresh, colorful paint pop.

Very shiny, Vivian commented without enthusiasm. *There is something here I do not like.*

"In-ground sprinklers?"

Something is watching us.

"I thought you were keeping Merlin off our back."

For now. I am curious to see a little of the modern mortal realm and you have been showing it to me at an alarmingly grounds-eye view. I have been content to ride along.

Clary considered that. Since Merlin had knocked Vivian senseless in the post-potion aftermath, the demoness hadn't interfered with Clary's physical movements. Nor had she talked quite so much about vengeance. Something had changed.

But now wasn't the time to ponder that. "If it's not Merlin, then who's watching?"

Vivian uttered something Clary assumed was a demon curse word. *Fae, and they are carrying blades hewn from the black rock mined from the roots of the Crystal Mountains. Once blessed by the High Druids of ancient days, such knives can wound a demon. I thought they were all destroyed in the war.*

"Then how did the fae get them?" It seemed a stupid thing to worry about in the moment, but at the same time...

Clary sensed a rush of rage from the demon. It was pure, white-hot and fueled by the instinct to survive. It was also tinged by fear.

Tenebrius has betrayed me. He must have discovered that I lied when I agreed to spy for LaFaye. This is my punishment.

Clary froze. She was still straddling her bike, one foot on the curb and her helmet dangling loose in her hand. Her backpack was strapped with bungee cords to the rack she'd put on the bike for the occasion. The neighborhood had that post-apocalyptic quiet that bedroom communities get when everyone has left for the day. The only noise was a lawn sprinkler making a rhythmic *whoosh-whoosh* from the house to her left.

Her spine prickled in warning. Slowly, casually, she put the helmet back on and buckled the chin strap. "Where are they?" she asked softly.

Behind you. Go now.

Clary crouched over her low handlebars and started pedaling, rising from her seat a little to pump harder. Pain screamed up her exhausted thigh muscles, but Vivian's fright kept her moving. Now she could hear movement above the hiss of her tires on the pavement. It wasn't so much footfalls—fae were light on their feet—but the jingle of metal. She risked a glance over her shoulder to see two fae, long, white braids streaming as they ran, almost pacing her speeding bike. Despite the heat, they wore battle leathers, weapons belts strapped around their waists. It was the belts making all the noise.

Each fae carried a foot-long blade. They were black and gleaming, curved and tapered like a small saber. *Demon-killers*, Vivian hissed. There was no doubt they'd slice a human just as effectively.

Clary looked back to the road, struggling with the image of neat family homes paired with the deadly fae. Between the houses she could see a main road ahead, although she wasn't sure how to get to it. Like so many new developments, the streets were a maze designed to keep traffic slow and safe.

She'd just decided to forget the road and ride overland when something bumped the back wheel. Her narrow tire erupted into a sickening *thwap-thwap-thwap*. Clary skidded, just managing to control her fall as the bike went over. Pavement slammed her shoulder as she rolled free. She caught a glimpse of the fallen bike, a throwing star sticking from the mangled back tire. Well, that was one downside of the fashion for no fenders.

A split second later, an ear-splitting crack told her the helmet had saved her skull from the edge of the curb, but pain still flashed white behind her eyes. Hands snatched her upright. The fae was breathing hard, the thrill of the hunt plain in his dark pupils.

"Don't think I'm going to pause to drink your tainted soul, demon child." The fae's voice was low, almost a growl.

Clary was too stunned by her fall to speak. She could only react, and Gawain's fighting drills kicked in. She slammed the heel of her hand into the fae's elegant nose. The crunch of bone and flesh twisted her stomach.

The fae howled in surprise, reflexively clutching his face. Clary snatched at his blade, risking her fingers as she grabbed it free. It all happened so quickly, she barely had time to spin on her heel before his partner reacted.

Run!

Clary sped for the closest yard, but her legs were slow and heavy and the biking shoes that were so good at sticking to the pedals sucked for running. She dodged between houses, nearly tripping over the small, useless hedge separating one empty driveway from the next. The fae was gaining on her with ease.

"If you can do anything," she urged Vivian, "now would be the moment."

As soon as she spoke, she sensed the demon gathering power. It rose like an electric storm, crawling down her arms and raising the fine hairs despite the sweat soaking her skin. Then all at once, Clary was no longer Clary but a being of enormous power. She skidded—no, swaggered—to a halt in a backyard. There were no children there, but a swing set creaked in the silent breeze. She spun to face the fae, who came to a juddering halt and fell back at the look on her face.

Clary fell to one knee, clasped her hands in a double fist around the knife hilt and smote the ground. The world vanished into blackness.

Chapter 16

Vibrating with a mix of anger and worry, Merlin opened his dresser drawer and rummaged inside until his fingers found the amulet. It hung on a chain that had been sliced through by Lancelot as he'd torn it from the throat of Morgan LaFaye's pet assassin. The gem had the power to track magic. It also shielded the wearer from magical attack. Merlin had come by the gem almost honestly—Nimueh, the famed Lady of the Lake, had traded it in return for a favor. Merlin had accepted the deal mostly because he liked Nim and she'd been in trouble. For practical purposes, he was loath to use any tool that might draw the attention of the Queen of Faery. And yet now that his agate scrying stone was broken, he needed the gem's ability to track.

He pulled the amulet out from under a pile of socks. It was silver, star-shaped and set with a large ruby in its center. Merlin picked a piece of fluff from the chain, feeling the power of the stone awaken in his hand. It was a light trickle, but he didn't let the subtlety fool him. After all, he'd charged the stone himself once upon a time, when he was Vivian's student. He knew exactly how it worked.

If only he understood women half as well. Sure, he'd been gone longer than expected. He'd not only had to destroy the infected laptop, but also open a portal for Arthur to conduct negotiations with the goblin king in preparation for the coming war. In that window of time, Clary had fled. Why? He'd trusted her with that one thing—to stay put for a couple of hours. Clary was contrary, but she wasn't foolish. What was more, Clary on the loose meant Vivian on the loose, and that didn't bear thinking about.

But right now the *why* wasn't as important as how to get her back—even if that meant his troubles weren't over. There were enchanters who swore off sex, claiming it damaged the mental faculties, and at the moment he was inclined to agree. If he'd ever needed an argument for abstinence, this insane demon-infested situation was it.

Merlin raised the amulet, letting the star-shaped object spin on the broken chain. The ruby winked with every turn, beautiful and hypnotic. If it tracked magical signatures, surely Vivian would stand out in the crowd.

Vivian, who had suddenly begun to ask awkward questions about their relationship. What would make a demon do that? Then again, she'd always been curious. Experimental. Challenging. He was the one more likely to stick to old ideas. Her unpredictability had been good for him.

With a sigh, he dropped the gem into his palm.

His gaze fell on the stack of tattered paperback books on top of the dresser. Tamsin had put them in Clary's suitcase, but Clary had forgotten to pack them when she left. It didn't surprise him that Tamsin had sent the books, since she knew her sister so well. Clary called them her comfort reads, those favorite stories she read time and again because they were like visiting old friends. Through the course of her training she had apparently needed plenty of comfort because they had appeared again and again during her lunch breaks.

They were tales of adventure and romance, like any minstrel would tell, filled with exotic places and handsome lovers. The one on top—and the one he'd seen most often—featured a tent in a desert oasis, a camel and a harem girl swooning in a studly bandit's arms. That was Clary—smart, modern, independent to the point of madness and willing to embrace whatever she enjoyed, even if it was floridly improbable. She'd pointed out—in response to his acid commentary—that the fact that it *was* fantasy was completely the point.

The memory made his chest ache with an angry sense of loss. He sat on the bed, his senses all too aware that this was where they'd made love. He closed his eyes, unwillingly pulled under by memory for a moment. Her soft skin, the feel of her breath on his cheek, the feeling that once, just once, he was completely welcomed by another person. That was the one thing Vivian had given him that he had never been able to replace. Since Clary had become his student, he'd harbored a secret and unlikely dream that maybe, just maybe… He snapped his eyes open, pushing the emotion away. He couldn't afford to lose himself that way, certainly not now and perhaps not ever. Not with his track record for attracting doom.

The blankets were still tumbled, the light scent of Clary's perfume still lingering in the air. As hard as that was on his concentration, it would help focus the magical connection between them. Merlin straightened the coverlet and set the amulet down, staring into its ruby depths. With a few deep breaths, he slipped into a light trance.

The first impression was of blurred colors and rushing movement, like a film on fast-forward. Then he was seeing the world from—the back of a bicycle? Was there any more inefficient way imaginable to run away? Except, of course, his painstaking and time-consuming search of all the usual transportation routes had turned up nothing. Clary knew what she was doing.

So did Vivian. He sensed her watching for his approach and he faded back before her magical alarms detected his presence. His view adjusted to take in the surroundings. Suburbia. Houses, lawns, newly planted trees that would look good in about a decade. And fae with demon-killing knives. A crushing panic slammed his chest with the force of a train. Merlin jumped to his feet, all too aware that he might be too late.

Clary's gasp echoed in the surrounding blackness. She still clutched the demon-killing knife, but the only way she knew that was by touch. It was utterly dark.

Her memories of the past few minutes were fragmented, as they had been the last time Vivian took charge. She remembered the startled fae, the gathering magic and a thunderclap as she'd skewered the lawn. A portal of some kind had yawned and she'd jumped through. The fae hadn't been able to follow. Apparently, this was a demon-only escape hatch.

So where had the portal gone? Clary prodded the mental space where Vivian should have been, but all was quiet. Had using all that power exhausted her? A lick of panic said that, as little as she liked Vivian, she'd come to rely on her company.

Clary got to her feet, her muscles stiff as cardboard. Her shoulder hurt from falling off her bike and her wrist ached from hitting the fae, and she was trying not to be scared. After a deep breath, she summoned a witch light, the tiny ball of illumination bobbing above her palm until she willed it overhead.

Clary almost wished she hadn't. She was in a tunnel with rounded sides of hard-packed earth. It wasn't much taller than she was but it went on far past the witch light's glow. Behind her, the tunnel ended in a blank wall of dirt. Presumably, that end led back to the yard with the homicidal fae—and her ruined bike, her backpack and the real world. She unstrapped her helmet and set it aside, running her fingers through her flattened hair. After that fall, the helmet would have to be replaced. At least she still had her

ID and wallet—although she wasn't sure what good that would do her in the mystical demon sewer.

She wished Merlin were there. Besides his magical skill, few men could appear so calm while cracking an unruly imp over the head—and look so hot while they did it. Not that Clary particularly wanted to remember that incident. She hadn't actually meant to summon a rowdy, seven-foot creature with bright blue skin and a taste for smashing furniture.

Yes, if Merlin was here he would know what to do and, more important, she could tell him about the fae with demon-killer blades. Cautiously, she stood, picking up the knife. "Any idea what to do next?" she asked, hoping Vivian would answer.

Silence was her only reply. With no other options, she began walking, doing her best to watch in every direction despite the small space. It smelled musty, like a long-neglected basement. There had to be spiders, she thought with a shiver.

She considered what Vivian had said about Tenebrius working with Morgan LaFaye. It raised some interesting points. From what Clary had heard in the past, the demon Tenebrius and LaFaye hated each other. They had openly bickered at a tourney that had been held just before the queen had been imprisoned. Tenebrius had been the judge and awarded Arthur a prize of his choosing—one which Arthur had yet to claim—but the demon had been happy Camelot had beaten the Faery Queen's side. So why would Tenebrius ally himself with the notorious LaFaye now? And hadn't Vivian said she was the demon's friend?

Not in the human sense of the word. Plus, LaFaye is a superior ally. If she regains power, she can offer him freedom.

Clary released a breath, reluctantly pleased to hear Vivian's voice. "Then they deserve each other."

I agree.

Clary took another hesitant step. She'd become aware of a sound she didn't like—a sliding noise barely perceptible over the echoes of her own footfalls. "By the way, are you okay? You went quiet there for a moment."

I am tolerable. The word was curt. *Keep going. This pathway will lead to one of your great cities.*

"Which one?"

Does it matter? I didn't have much time to choose. This path was available, so I took it.

Since Clary couldn't argue with that, she didn't try. The only thing to do was to keep walking through the endless, featureless tunnel.

She had paused to rest for only a moment when the serpent darted forward. It was nearly the same black as the dirt floor and as long as a broomstick, moving with a strange sideways crawl. Clary would have missed it but for the sheen of the witch light on its iridescent skin. She shrieked, leaping backward to avoid the creature.

Kill it!

Without hesitation, Clary slashed with the knife, muscles taking over while her wits froze in panic. The blade bit into sinew, a flare of green light igniting where stone touched flesh. The snake writhed, the head curling back to bite at its pain. It was then Clary saw the fangs unfold like tiny twin scythes. They glistened with a milky yellow poison. She stomped on its neck, holding it still as she lopped off the head. Dark fluid drained from the stump, smoking as it hit the earthen floor and eating a hole inches deep wherever it touched. The blade was unaffected, but Clary backed away before the stuff could touch her shoes. She didn't want to think about what the snake's venom might have done. "What was that?"

A creature that dwells in demon passageways, Vivian said unhelpfully. *They are the realm's response to the wound caused by our magic.*

Like antibodies, Clary thought. Which meant the demons were an infection. Did that make her part of the disease? She stared at the scorched earth and neatly severed head. "Sorry, bud," she said to the thing. "It was you or me."

Vivian's chuckle was faint, but it was there. *You're beginning to sound like me.*

That was disturbing. "Are there more of those around?" *They never come alone.*

Clary moved on, picking up her pace to a jog, and then a run when she heard the whisper of skin on stone. She was out of breath by the time she reached a stone wall that abruptly ended the passageway. Vivian opened it with a flash of power, and she stepped through.

Clary stood for a long moment, trying to place the familiar scene. She'd been here before, but without context it took several long glances from left to right to remember the shops and restaurants that placed her on Portland's riverside walk. Clary zipped the long knife inside her jacket, careful not to do herself permanent damage. By then, she was already formulating a plan.

It was late afternoon, the water silvery and the sky filtered through a light haze. Tourists were everywhere, as were the tempting scents of the many restaurants along the route. She hadn't eaten since she'd gulped down a breakfast burrito on the road. She half-walked, half-ran to the nearest coffee shop, stocked up on caffeine and empty calories, and got advice from a pair of teenage boys working on high-end laptops in the corner booth. By the end of the conversation, she was fairly certain they would either own Silicon Valley or end up in prison before they were twenty. Either way, they'd given her the information she needed.

She took a bus, getting off near Powell's Books, and

found the store the boys had recommended. An hour and a half later she checked into a modest hotel with a small bag of new clothes and a large bag of tech toys. She'd kept the clerk at the computer store well past closing, but she'd bought enough to make it well worth her while. Besides, when two geek girls started talking, time flew in the nicest way.

The hotel room was old, with a queen bed, a desk and not much else. Still, it made up in space what it lacked in decor. Once she settled in, showered and ordered pizza, it was time to get to work. Neither the boys in the café nor the store clerk had heard of any unusual malware, which meant the demons hadn't surfed the electronic highway beyond Camelot. After all, these were the folks who would definitely notice glowing hands popping out of the screen and immediately try to figure out the code. Arthur's command to go dark had confined the problem, at least for the moment.

Sadly, it was a pretty sure bet that happy state wouldn't last, probably because Perceval would start texting some pretty girl.

And you have a plan beyond soldering Perceval shut in his own armor?

Vivian had gone quiet—and deathly bored—once Clary started talking computers. Clary was unapologetic. "You have your superpowers, kitty cat, and I have mine. Before I came to work at Medievaland, I was a programmer. My job used to involve shutting down computer viruses."

Clary opened another box, dumped the packaging on the floor and plugged in yet another device. She'd paid cash for it all, using up most of the emergency fund she kept in her apartment.

Not that I'm an expert on computer emergencies, but wouldn't a demon infestation be unique?

Clary answered without pausing in her assembly. "Yes

and no. With luck they can be isolated and erased. They're just electricity, right?" She opened the laptop and powered it up. It whirred to life with a cheerful beep. Clary's pulse jumped, loving the sound and smell of brand-new equipment.

Erased? Vivian's tone was icy.

Clary's stomach jumped at the sound. There was anger in the word, but also fear. Clary paused to check her thinking. She could understand why the demons wanted to leave the Abyss, but she'd seen a glimpse of the blood-soaked battlefield through Vivian's memory. She'd seen the manifestation that had crawled from Merlin's laptop. Even the snake in the tunnel argued that demons didn't belong in the mortal realms.

They sure didn't belong in her head. Clary's fingers ceased their flight across the laptop's keys. "I'm sorry I have to do this. I wish there was another way, but I can't let this pass. I have to try to stop it."

There was a long pause, and Clary sensed the demoness was considering her options.

I approve, Vivian finally said, her voice subdued but resolute. *Tenebrius does not trust me to guard his interests while he pursues his own, and he has betrayed me. He will not be defeated easily, especially if he is in league with LaFaye. Doubt won't help you survive.*

The demon had barely finished speaking when the door crashed inward, spewing pieces of wood across the floor.

Chapter 17

Clary bounded from her chair, every nerve on alert. The two fae who'd chased her before pushed through the door without a word. She recognized the one she'd hit because of his swollen nose and black eyes. This time, though, he had an automatic rifle slung over his shoulder. Apparently, they thought her worthy of bigger firepower. Clary felt a crazy twinge of satisfaction, but it was short-lived. The moment the fae were in the room, two more crowded in behind them, forming a deadly wall between her and the door. The last fae to enter closed what was left of the door and locked it.

The stone knife sat next to the laptop. She'd been using it to open boxes, but now she snatched it up. It wouldn't stop bullets, but it was all she had.

There was an instant of perfect quiet in the room. She was dimly aware of a chorus of voices in the hallway outside—evidence that the smashed door and parade of fae had attracted attention. The supernatural world was supposed to stay out of the public eye, but clearly that didn't matter to this bunch.

"What do you want?" she demanded.

By way of reply, the bruised fae raised his rifle. Clary's face went numb with panic, the rest of her body prickling as if she'd touched a live wire. She wasn't sure how much was adrenaline and how much was Vivian's rising magic.

He squeezed the trigger. Clary jerked aside, the bullet a hot kiss beside her ear. Her breath deserted her. A witch's reflexes were fast, but Vivian's were faster, and suddenly she was moving too quickly to think. She shrieked in pain as a fireball left her hand. There would surely be blisters if she lived long enough to burn.

The fae scattered as her attack slammed into the wall, leaving a scorch mark on the bland wallpaper. It gave Clary seconds to slash at a fae, but he ducked, sweeping low with one foot and knocking her down. Clary's knife spun out of reach under the queen-size bed. His second blow hit her hard enough that the room reeled.

In a second he was on her, one hand at her throat while he fumbled for the rifle. She was at a bad angle to fight back, her only defense to claw at his face with her already burned left hand. The fae's head jerked back, keeping just out of reach, but Clary grabbed the front of his coat, pulling him down. He pulled away, but not before she grabbed his jaw. The moment her fingers touched his face, Vivian released another blast of power. Clary swore with pain as the fae flew backward. He hit the ground, but didn't move again.

The other fae rushed in as she dived behind the desk. A rush of mad, protective anger flooded her at the thought of all her beautiful new equipment being shot to smithereens. She grabbed the folding luggage rack and hurled it. The gesture forced her to stand, which was a mistake. Three rifles discharged. She dropped to her knees behind the heavy desk, but not fast enough. A bullet clipped her shoulder, the fiery bite giving way to throbbing agony. Nausea swelled as Clary went icy cold, then burning hot with the shock and pain.

Then the wall behind the bed vanished in a blast of icy blue flame. Everyone turned, even the fae who was towering over the desk to shoot Clary like a fish in a barrel.

That's my boy. It's about time these fools learned who they've annoyed. Vivian's voice was nearly a purr.

Not nearly so confident, Clary inched just high enough to see over the edge of the desk. She was sweating, her breathing shallow, but the wound in her shoulder was bearable now, hot pain instead of a howl filling every corner of her mind.

A dark pinprick appeared in the center of the blue light, swirling like a child's top. It grew and grew, flaring outward until the darkness was as tall as a man, then taller, then reaching the high, plastered ceiling. Merlin stepped out, his face set into hard lines of fury. Clary cringed when she saw he held one of the black snakes just behind its head.

He hurled it into the knot of fae. It flew like a knotted rope, unfurling just in time to sink fangs into one of the enemies. A blast of gunfire sprayed the ceiling, shattering the overhead light and raining down plaster dust. Another fae swiped with a demon-killing blade, hacking the snake in two. It was too late. The fae who had been bitten was corroding, pieces of his body collapsing inward as the venom ate everything inside the fragile structure of his skin. A stink like rotten fish sauce choked the room. The only mercy was that he never made a sound.

By that time Merlin had stepped from the portal onto the bed and then jumped lightly to the floor. He had no gun, just a ruby pendant on a broken chain that he stuffed into his jeans pocket. The remaining two fae swiveled to face him, muscles coiled and rifles at the ready. Clary was sure they would have fired, except for the two well-armed fae who emerged from the tunnel and stood to flank Merlin.

With a flash of pleasure, she recognized Laren. The other, named Angmar, she'd met only once before but knew he was a friend of Gawain's and a leader among the rebel fae.

"You!" spit one of Clary's attackers. "Merlin the Devil!"

His rifle twitched, but Angmar shot him dead. In the same instant, Merlin lunged, knocking the weapon out of the remaining fae's hands and throwing him into the dresser. The fae slid to the ground, dragging the lamp and telephone with him. Outside, the howl of sirens split the evening air. Clary rose from behind the desk. Blood ran, hot and sticky, down one arm, but she couldn't stifle a grin.

"Hi," she said. "Thanks for dropping by."

"You're shot," he snapped as if she'd done it on purpose.

"I think I'll be okay," Clary said, answering the question he hadn't asked.

Merlin's expression was slightly wild, as if he didn't know whether to laugh hysterically or burn the scene to the ground. His amber gaze flicked over her, the computer equipment and the wreckage of the room. Finally, it came to rest on the last living bad guy, who was staring defiantly into the barrel of Angmar's gun.

He lightly placed two fingers on the captive fae's forehead. "It's time to tell us what you know."

Merlin was certain his nerves blackened and shriveled to ash when he saw Clary grinning at him, blood soaking her shirt and dead fae all over the floor. She was chaos packaged in a small, perky blond bundle, but he couldn't keep his stomach from dropping in pure relief. Even though the amulet had tracked her to the hotel, he hadn't breathed easy until that moment.

Merlin's interrogation of the remaining fae took less than a minute. When he was done, Laren and Angmar dragged the prisoner through the portal back to the rebel compound. Merlin had saved some of the demon essence from the laptop, and the rebel fae were eager to see if it could be used for a cure. As a one-time special bonus, they had a handy subject to test.

Which left Clary and her makeshift computer lab.

Laren had helped her shove it back into its shopping bags and send it through the portal. They'd gathered every last weapon, too, including the demon-killing knife and every cartridge they could find. With the aid of magic, Merlin had scoured the room of evidence. The police had been breaking down the door when he'd hustled Clary through the portal, which he redirected to the safety of his living room.

Once they were there, he rounded on her. "Did you use a credit card anywhere?"

She shifted uneasily. The room was lit only by a floor lamp in the corner. The soft light touched one side of her face, highlighting the gentle curves of brow and cheekbone. It struck him, as it had so often, how she never seemed to notice her own beauty.

"I paid cash as I went," she returned defiantly. "And I registered the room under the name Kitty Salem. It wasn't the kind of place that asked a lot of questions."

Kitty for Vivian, Salem for witches everywhere. Cute, but he wasn't in the mood to be amused. "Good, because the cops are going to be very curious. I'm pretty sure someone got a good look at you and probably the fae. There will be witnesses."

"Or not. People don't go to a no-tell hotel to be good citizens."

She had a point, but Merlin's chest was a knot of anxiety. It wasn't just the fae with demon knives, or the police, or the possibility that LaFaye would know her amulet had been in use and by whom. It was that he might have lost Clary.

"Why, by the blasted Abyss, did you run?" he roared.

Her chin came up. "Can I get a bandage before we dive into the details? I got shot."

"That's not an answer!" he snarled, but he marched her to the bathroom, a hand on her good elbow.

When they got there, he sat her on the edge of the tub and crouched to examine the wound. After rummaging in a drawer for blunt-tipped scissors, he gently began cutting away her sleeve.

"I was afraid, okay?" she finally offered. "On top of everything else, the demons know Vivian's last known whereabouts was inside my head. They sent fae assassins to punish her for sitting out this fight."

The prisoner he'd questioned had said as much, but Clary's frightened words made it personal. Merlin glanced up from his work. Her face was pale, but that was no surprise given the bullet wound, not to mention the day they'd had. What worried him more was the hollow look in her eyes. It went beyond shock and fatigue to a much darker place.

"What do demons do with human babies?" she asked suddenly. "What about Vivian?"

"Vivian?" he asked, trying to figure out where this was coming from. "I think she likes them."

"But she's a demon."

"Humans like baby animals. We don't need to be a cat to like kittens."

"That's weird," she said, then hissed through her teeth as he peeled away the soaked fabric of her jacket and shirt. "We're like pets to them."

"*Weird* is a sliding scale where you and I are concerned." He peered at the wound. "Vivian is as dangerous as a box of vipers, but she's selectively vicious, unlike some of her kin."

"Speaking of vipers," Clary said quietly, "where did you get the snake?"

"The same tunnel you passed through. The amulet was very thorough about tracing your journey. Once I knew where you were, I called for backup." He washed around the wound, relieved to see it looked much better once the excess blood was gone. "Congratulations. The bullet passed through."

"If she is so dangerous and you hate demons so much, why did you study with them for so long?"

The question stripped away centuries, returning him to the hillside where Vivian had first taken his hand. There was bitterness between them now, but it could not erase that golden sun-soaked day when she had come from nowhere and turned him from a disappointed youth into a man who understood his own worth. Her lessons hadn't just been about magic.

"She had something I needed." It was the truth, but it wasn't the whole answer. "There are times I wish I had never met her, especially when I understood the destruction and depravity that come so naturally to her kind."

Clary said nothing. He finished dressing the wound, certain he'd done an adequate job but planning to call Tamsin anyway to be certain Clary had the finest care. He rose, setting his tools aside and offering a hand to help her to her feet.

"Is that all you think of them now?" she asked. "That they're horrible and disgusting?"

Her movement was lithe and filled with energy despite the bandage and ruined clothes. Yes, this was Clary, always full of fire. That was a comfort, even if all her talk about demons was not. "What else is there to think? They did their best to conquer our world. They try to justify it by saying it is their nature to rule. They have no means to return to whatever homeland they came from so they'll rule ours instead. They're cruel and violent and make no apologies for it."

Clary looked down at where his hand held hers. "And yet you were lovers."

Merlin had been about to work the conversation back

to the subject of running away, but this stopped him cold. "It's complicated."

Her fingers tightened around his. "Explain it to me. I know it's none of my business but I'm really confused."

He didn't want to have this conversation, but after what had happened with Vivian and her potion, he had to say something. "A relationship like ours was—it's like a puzzle made of a hundred parts. I suppose all are, in a way. One shared experience, then another, then a joke you both laugh at. Before you know it, all those separate impulses become a single bond."

"So it wasn't all bad?"

"No. When I met Vivian, I was lonely and isolated and she was like a breathtaking bonfire."

"But it didn't last?"

"How could it? You know what she is. You saw what she did to me. To you."

And that was completely true. And yet a corner of his heart, one not crushed by regret for his betrayal, had missed her. She wasn't good or kind like Clary, but she had a quick wit and a stunning depth of knowledge.

No, there was no relationship more complex than his feelings for the demon. After an acquaintance of over a thousand years, how could it be otherwise? Awe, lust, admiration, terror, guilt and gratitude were all there. So was resentment. He didn't want to face the fact that he'd pretended to return to her side only to steal that spell. It had been the act of a coward, and it had been the act of a man doing his best to save Camelot from destruction.

And now? It was history, where she should have stayed for both their sakes. He was holding the hand of the woman he wanted now.

A frown pleated Clary's brow. "Do you hate her?"

"I don't trust her, and I hate what she's done to you." He studied Clary's anxious expression. She hadn't moved an inch, still holding his hand as if he might vanish if the contact was broken. "The only reason she isn't working with Tenebrius is because she's here to kill me."

"How can you be absolutely sure of that?"

"She doesn't forgive."

Not like Clary, who had helped bring Laren home to himself even after he'd tried to take her soul. And that was, perhaps, the moment Merlin understood just how much he wanted—needed—Clary in his life. It hadn't hit him all at once, but filled him as gradually as an incoming tide since the moment Clary had taken the fae in her arms. He wanted that kind of redemption. Not that he deserved it.

And he'd talked enough about the past. It was the present-day Vivian he had to worry about now. "Is she awake?" he asked Clary.

She pulled her hand away from his. "No. She hasn't stirred since you knocked her out. As far as I can tell, she's entirely gone."

Chapter 18

The lie all but burned Clary's lips.

Why did you say that? Vivian asked.

The answer was simple and very practical. Vivian was inside her and Clary was beginning to suspect she couldn't leave. Whatever Vivian had said about seeing the sights, there was no reason for her to have gone along on her cycling adventure, or to sit there listening to Merlin call her a box of vipers. No, she was stuck until something or somebody removed her. Therefore, in a sideways fashion, what Merlin thought of Vivian applied to her, as well. Unless, of course, he had reason to think the demon was gone.

That's terrible logic, little witchling. Vivian almost sounded sympathetic.

Maybe, but it was all she had. She didn't want him to think her a demon, or even a demon's walking hotel room.

Merlin's gaze swept over her. "Are you sure Vivian is dormant?"

"Yes," Clary said firmly.

Silence became a tangible thing as if the feeling between them was resonating off the bathroom's tiled walls. Suddenly suffocating, Clary turned and walked out, leading them back to the living room. She clenched her fists to hide the sudden trembling in her limbs. How had this happened? How had she ended up lying to the one man she wanted most to think well of her?

"Ordinarily, I don't think what I did to Vivian should

have quieted her for more than a day or two," he said. "Demons are strong. Immortal."

"But not invincible."

"No, and I keep returning to the fact Tenebrius has declared her an enemy. I see LaFaye's hand in that, but I also see Tenebrius's forethought."

Vivian came to attention. *What does he mean?*

"If she has gone quiet, something unexpected occurred. I think that was Tenebrius. It would be easy to sever the energetic bond between realms while she is vulnerable. That would be like pinching an umbilical cord or an intravenous line."

Clary sensed Vivian's startled reaction. *He said that was an accident!*

"What happens then?"

"Loss of strength," he said. "Hibernation."

Clary sat down, trying to digest the information. Was that why Vivian couldn't leave?

It's not untrue, Vivian said in a way that said it wasn't the whole story, either.

"But what about the fae with knives?" Clary asked.

"An instant solution," said Merlin. "Instant death is better than hibernation if you're shutting down a loose end who knows more than they should."

"That's horrible!"

"That's demon politics," Merlin replied, his expression grim. "I wouldn't wish this on anyone, not even her."

"Especially not her?" Clary asked gently.

"She wants to kill me."

"She didn't."

"I hesitate to take that as a sign of affection."

"I'm just trying to be fair."

"Stopping LaFaye and Tenebrius will help Vivian." He looked away. "Right now things can go back to normal for you."

"Normal?" She gave a faint smile. "I'm not sure what that is anymore."

Merlin knelt at her feet, smiling slightly as he brushed the hair from her eyes. "You'll be fine."

Except Vivian was still there. This would be the moment to confess she'd lied, but then he kissed her, nibbling along the angle of her jaw. "What are you doing?" she asked, a rush of pleasure making her voice husky.

"I'm punishing you for running away." His fingers ran lightly down her arms, carefully avoiding her injury. "It may involve some extended interrogation." Then he kissed her forehead, a soft, lingering gesture that said she was precious to him.

"This is an odd form of punishment." Their discussion had been so serious, she wasn't quite ready for his lightened mood. She hadn't wanted to hear about how much he both admired and loathed his ex-lover, even though it made perfect sense. Take away the supernatural parts—and maybe the killing parts—and it didn't actually sound all that different from anyone talking about their exes. At bottom, even the most powerful witches and wizards and kings and queens were still people.

"I'm happy you're all right," he said, rising and pulling her to her feet.

"I'm glad you're happy." She should say something, tell him she was far from demon-free, but then he'd get that look on his face. The one that meant he hated demons, and that contempt would be for her.

"We should get you cleaned up and in bed," he said. "You look ready to fall over."

The words were solicitous, but they somehow let her know that if she wanted to fall over in his bed, he'd definitely be there to catch her.

It was everything she'd ever wanted from him, but now it made her breath quicken in apprehension as much as desire. She was playing with fireballs, and she should know by now that she'd get burned.

He kissed her, his hot mouth sending her pulse into triple time. Images from the potion aftermath crowded her head, and her knees grew weak. It was too much.

She pushed away, her stomach in knots. "I need to sleep." She ducked her head, desperate to hide the lie that must be branded on her features.

He stroked her hair, his touch gentle with a sympathy that made her squirm. "Of course. I'll use the guest bedroom. Get all the rest you need."

Clary was certain she wouldn't sleep a wink.

"You realize if this works I've earned my right to fight with the rest of Camelot's forces," Clary said to Merlin the next day. Her voice was bright and cheerful, even if the rest of her was exhausted.

Merlin grunted in typical male fashion—that way of implying volumes they thought other people understood.

They'd both been busy that morning. Clary guessed it was as much to cover the frustrated desire between them as the need to fight their enemies. At least on Clary's side, work was a safe way to avoid the thorny question of Vivian's presence. Maybe in time she'd grow used to the idea of having her lover's ex in her head, but she wasn't there yet.

She'd reassembled her equipment on the dining room table, doing her best to ignore the scorch mark they'd left the last time they'd battled demonic malware. Currently, she was typing code, adjusting a program she'd written before in hopes that it would dissolve a demonic entity. Well, energy was energy, electrons were electrons. She'd give it something that would scramble its zeroes and ones. Meanwhile, she was waiting for Merlin to follow his grunt with something she could respond to.

"Use your words," Clary replied. "Or don't. I just don't want to guess what you're thinking."

He narrowed his amber eyes, reminding her of a disgruntled tomcat. "You used to be an obedient student."

"No, I wasn't." Though she did recall being marginally more respectful. In awe, actually. "Okay, fine, but I had your ex in my brain for a while. It colors things."

Merlin left the room.

Clary sighed but her fingers didn't stop moving. Merlin was avoiding any further conversation about Vivian. Apparently, he'd said all that he meant to on the topic.

Clary wasn't sure what would happen if a choice came along that pitted her interests against Vivian's or if the demon would ever resume her revenge against Merlin. For the moment she had all but vanished from Clary's mind, which seemed to be her way of resting.

The timing was good because Clary needed to concentrate. With this computer emergency, she finally had an opportunity to show what she could do instead of repeatedly screwing things up.

She'd blocked off every one of her workstation's connections to the internet until she had her strategy in place. Now she was typing furiously, all too aware she had no time to waste. In her opinion, the entity would eventually give up on invading Camelot's tech and move on to easier prey, which was pretty much the rest of the world. So far, they'd managed to keep everyone from touching their devices, but it wouldn't last.

And Clary's foe was bound to be unpredictable. Sure, LaFaye hated Arthur because he had Camelot's crown and she believed it should have been hers. Sure, the demons hated Camelot for sending them to the Abyss like bad dogs. It made sense they'd designed an attack specifically to invade the tech toys of Arthur's crew. But Clary understood things that got into the computer ecosystem developed a mind of their own. Infections infected. Trojan horses found things to invade. Someone would slip up and check their social media account. She had to confine the entity and destroy it, stat.

Clary sat back, rereading her last few lines and poking a key when she found an error. Her shoulder hurt, but it was better than before and she could live with the badass scar the bullet would leave behind. Moving on automatic, she drank a mouthful of coffee, not minding that it was cold. A quiver of excitement hovered in her stomach—not random butterflies, but quiet fireworks of pride. She was at the top of her game.

To give credit where it was due, Vivian had made some suggestions about the physics of the demonic collective. Any programmer except a witch would have despaired at translating her supernatural physics lesson into code, but Clary felt good about what she'd done. Very good. This was her personal superpower.

The front door slammed and she recognized Arthur's deep voice. The king, it seemed, had to come to Merlin if he wanted a front-row seat for this particular show.

A shadow fell across the table. She looked up to see the two men blocking the light. As always, Arthur wore his sword, Excalibur. The king's reddish hair looked slightly wild as if he'd been trying to tear it out. Given the circumstances, she supposed it was possible.

"Hello, boys," she said, forgetting for a moment that she was talking to a king and his enchanter. Vivian really was a bad influence.

However, Arthur simply nodded. "How does your work progress?"

"I'm ready." The words left her with confidence. She put one hand on the crystal sphere sitting beside the laptop. It wasn't the precious object Merlin's red stone had been, but a workaday crystal ball. Every witch coven had one. So did the rebel fae. If they couldn't trust digital communications, magic would have to do. "Everyone's on standby."

"Tell me what will happen," said Arthur.

Clary had to hand it to him. For a medieval guy, he made a good attempt at grasping the modern world. All the same, she put it in layman's terms. "If I poke the entity with a big stick, it's going to run. So I've given a bunch of friends their own sticks to keep it from getting away."

She held up a flash drive. "These are the sticks in question. Camelot spent a fortune in overnight courier fees. Mine is the biggest stick and coordinates all the others, which is why I had to write a bunch more code."

Arthur's eyes lit up. "I see. This is like a boar hunt. You will deliver the killing blow, but it will take other spearmen to keep the boar at bay."

"Yeah, okay," she said. "This isn't how one typically eradicates a bit of nasty on the web, but this isn't a usual computer bug."

Arthur gave a small smile. "I understand. Please proceed."

Clary proceeded. She gave the crystal ball a tap and it flashed red, the signal to all her fellow geeks to unleash the code. Then she popped online just long enough to type in a string of characters, hit Return and disconnect again. A heartbeat passed, then another.

"That's all?" Arthur demanded.

"Wait for it," she said. Her screen began to scroll, listing the zillions of places her code was coursing in search of its quarry.

Merlin moved to stand behind her, putting one hand on her shoulder. It was a simple gesture, one a teacher or a friend might make just as easily as a lover. Despite her best efforts, her thoughts chased down what was becoming a well-worn path. They had begun to move toward a relationship, but she was still confused by her—and his—

connection to Vivian. In some unconscious way, was he Clary's lover, or Vivian's? Where did they overlap? Would everything end once Vivian was gone, or if he found out the demoness was still around?

She should have been content that, for now, he was behind her and supporting her contribution to Camelot's defense. It wasn't enough. For the first time, Clary wasn't asking why he'd want to be with her. She was certain she deserved Merlin for herself.

Clary's moment of distraction ended with a frantic flutter of orange light from the crystal ball. Laren's face appeared in its center. Lines of tension bracketed his mouth.

"There is something amiss. Our equipment is overheating and there is something wrong with our monitor. The screen is..." He trailed off with a look of disgust, then seemed to gather himself again. "It is not conducting itself as a screen ought to behave."

He'd barely finished before other voices began crowding in. The image in the ball flashed between one face and the next. Clary recognized some of the witches, and others were strangers. All had agreed to help her, but now their panicked exclamations melted into a confused babble.

She smacked the top of the ball, taking control of the conversation. "Hang on, all of you. You're doing great. Help is on the way."

"My CPU's too hot!" someone cried. "The computer is trying to shut down."

Clary tapped the ball again. "You're magical. You fix it."

She began typing like a madwoman. She'd anticipated something like this might happen, and had countermeasures ready to go. She re-established a link and launched one file, then another, before shutting down again.

"What's happening?" asked Merlin.

She jumped at the sound of his voice. She'd been concentrating so hard, she'd nearly forgotten she was in a physical space with real people around her. "Our green gooey friend is looking for a way out of the trap. I've just set bait to draw it back this way."

"What kind of bait?" he asked.

"Something that looks like an escape route." She smiled up at him. "It isn't."

Admiration flashed through Merlin's eyes. He'd watched her struggle so hard with her studies that she knew he'd appreciate her confidence now. She flushed with pleasure, but turned back to the screen, all too aware of Arthur's assessing gaze. Her flustered mood was short-lived. What she saw on the monitor snapped her to attention.

It had turned a putrid shade of lavender that, here and there, shaded to a greenish-blue. That was bad enough, but it was bubbling and lumpy, like carbonated cottage cheese. The smell made Arthur step back.

He waved a hand. "This stinks of a battlefield two days in the sun."

Clary's mouth watered dangerously, but she launched her final assault. The bubbling became more frantic, and Arthur drew Excalibur, holding it in both hands, in case the laptop mounted a savage attack—an image that would have been funny if it hadn't been all too possible. Clary scooted her chair back just in case.

The cottage cheese bubbled into a cauliflower, then began to change pixel by pixel into something else. The change came randomly so that it was impossible to guess what image it might be, but it held its shape, still protruding from the screen. Clary rose from the chair, backing up until she felt Merlin's solid form behind her. One of his hands touched her waist as if to steady her. She heard Merlin's indrawn breath when the picture resolved into a face. Excalibur twitched as if it took all Arthur's willpower not to strike.

The heart-shaped face had large gray eyes and an elegant bone structure that hinted at mixed blood—fae and human or fae and witch, or perhaps some of all three. The hair was black and lustrous, the skin pale as the moon.

LaFaye, Vivian hissed from deep in Clary's mind.

Chapter 19

Clary stared. She'd heard a lot about the Queen of Faery, but she'd never seen the woman before now. "Well, I guess there's no question about a fae-demon alliance now."

The eyes turned Clary's way, and she shrank back just a little. She hadn't expected the image to respond, and there was nothing friendly in the fae queen's glare. "Do not become too confident, witch. This was a scouting party, nothing more."

The voice made them all tense. It came from the laptop's speakers, the tone tinny and crackling with static. If the image noticed the poor audio, it didn't seem to care. The gaze rested on Merlin for a long moment, sparking with hatred, before moving on to Arthur. "I bid you come to the Midsummer Festival in the Forest Sauvage. My emissaries would hold parley with you."

Arthur raised Excalibur until the tip was inches from LaFaye's coldly beautiful face. The apparition's expression twisted with anger. The sword was the one thing she feared, for it cut through every enchantment, even hers.

"I have allowed you the luxury of imprisonment," said the king. "Are you certain you want me to seek you out?"

From what Clary knew, the Lady of the Lake's prison was the best Camelot could manage, and LaFaye's current stunt was proof that the jail was growing weak. Arthur's brave words were equal parts threat and wishful thinking. Even so, there was no mistaking the fear in her eyes as Excalibur's point drew near. She gave a reptilian hiss.

"Come, Arthur," said the Queen of Faery. "Come and face your destiny if you dare."

With that, her image dissolved into a fluttering mass of random black shapes that were immediately pixelated and erased by Clary's code. The laptop's screen flattened back to its normal shape, but Clary's heart continued to pound.

"Is she truly gone?" Arthur asked quietly, lowering the sword but not sheathing it.

"She was never truly here," Merlin replied. "That was a projection, nothing more."

Still, Clary scooted her chair back to the desk and initiated a scan. They were silent as the image of a tiny witch on a broom sailed back and forth across the screen. Eventually, it burst into a shower of stars. "It's clean," Clary announced, voice shaking with relief. "The internet is officially demon-free."

"This is your victory," said Merlin. "You should be proud."

To Clary's utter surprise, the king pulled her from her chair and planted a kiss on her cheek. He gave an infectious laugh. "Praise all the saints. Now Gwen can download her stories and stop threatening to order my knights to the bookstore three times a day."

Clary raised her chin. Morgan might have called the internet invasion a mere scouting party, but Clary knew better. They'd slammed a door in the face of their enemies. That had to be a victory worth cheering about, even if it was just the first of many battles.

Merlin threw open a window, admitting a welcome gust of fresh air. "So who's up for a picnic in the Forest Sauvage?"

Humiliation was a nuanced experience, and Morgan LaFaye had plumbed every depth. She was a skilled enchantress, educated by the finest witch and fae practitioners and possessed of a natural talent unseen in a thousand years. She was a monarch and a warrior in her own right. And yet…

The queen paced her quarters, trying not to notice the threadbare path she'd worn in the carpet. The objects around her blurred with the speed of her steps, but that didn't matter. They were so familiar, she barely saw them anymore.

Fear raged like a storm battering her from the inside out. As good as she was, she had been trapped in this prison. Now she'd suffered the shame of another defeat. Morgan wore that embarrassment like a leaden mantle, not just for herself, but for the whole of her family. They had cleared the path for her to inherit Camelot's throne with cunning and violence, and she had failed to seize that gift and wield it like a queen. Did she even deserve it?

Of course she did. As always, Merlin had interfered. Merlin, who had saved the infant Arthur. Merlin, who had brought him to kinghood. Merlin, whose strumpet Vivian had refused to join with the others and assist La-Faye in her hour of need. Well, Tenebrius would punish that dereliction.

And now Merlin's protégée had shut down Gorm's escape route. There would be no sudden attack on Camelot, no escape for the demons and no freedom for Morgan.

She flung herself into a chair, kicking aside the footstool so hard it flipped over. Why had she trusted her future to a spell she didn't understand? Like most who had spent even a brief time in the modern world of the humans, she was acquainted with smartphones and video streaming, but that was a distant cry from knowing how to write that into a spell. Computers were a crude magic of their own, and one she'd never bothered to learn.

And demon magic? Her power had refused to blend with theirs, unbalancing the incantation. No wonder it had failed. Her magic was too pure to blend with the demon dregs.

LaFaye jumped to her feet. "Gorm!"

The summoning circle flashed, and the tiny demon appeared in a cloud of theatrical smoke. She all but leaped across the room and snatched the creature up by the scruff. It dangled, the expression in its yellow eyes vacillating between being mournful and brimming with reproach.

"You failed me," she said in a low, bitter voice.

"I told you the spell was a prototype," Gorm wheezed. "I learned much. Next time it will work much better."

"Is that an excuse?" she raged.

"It could have worked with some practice. Your magic is a little different than ours, like AC and DC currents."

She didn't want to hear it. "My magic is pure. Yours failed."

The creature waved its hands, begging her to let him go. They were ugly, wrinkled little paws. Rage howled inside Morgan and trembled through her limbs. She hated the monster. She hated that he'd tricked her, exposed her inadequacies. Most of all, she hated that he'd raised her hopes and then failed. As the seconds ticked past, she grew light-headed, the world dimming to grays and blacks around her.

"There won't be a next time," she said, her words quiet now. "I don't permit failure."

She wrapped her hands around his throat, summoning every scrap of her anger and feeding it through her ferocious power. Gorm kicked and squeaked, eyes bulging as she squeezed.

He was just a little demon. When Morgan was finished, there was barely any stain at all.

"The Midsummer Festival is where every species in every realm agrees to a truce and comes out to play." Tamsin grabbed Clary's arm and dragged her forward. Clary followed obediently, still feeling slightly woozy from the portal that had brought them there. The Forest Sauvage was a no-man's land between all the realms. It was wild and dangerous, full of strange monsters and even stranger magic, but it was also home to many wonderful things.

The fair was held in a large meadow, or series of meadows, separated by stands of trees. The vendors' pavilions ringed the main field, each one decorated in a different pattern. There were stripes of green and white, blue with stars and red silk ringed with prancing lions. Each sold something different—wine or gold work or instruments inlaid with mother-of-pearl. At one end of the meadow was a stage and there a band of dwarves played a raucous reel on fiddles and wheezing small pipes. Children of all species romped together on the grass in a bounding, wing-fluttering chaos of delight. The sight made Clary laugh out loud.

"Aren't we supposed to be, y'know, organizing an army or something," Clary wondered out loud. "This feels too much like a vacation paradise after the past few days."

Tamsin's expression turned serious. "Enjoy the peace while it lasts. The crazy is never far off in these parts."

"What are we supposed to be doing?"

"Arthur is meeting with the goblin king, Zorath. Gawain is with him."

Clary nodded. Merlin had been mysterious about his immediate plans, but that was normal for him. "Then I suppose we're free to explore."

The two sisters wandered the booths, and slowly their mood lightened. It was impossible not to be tempted by the bright, fluttering scarves and baskets overflowing with every kind of bead or broach or ring. Clary was a natural magpie, and any fairground could part her from the last dollar in her purse. This was no different; only her wonder was more intense. Each item was exquisite, from the polished statues of tiny dragonets to the huge clay drums that sounded like captive thunder. Best of all were the hideous goblins who had brought their sparkling hoard of gold and gems to market. She'd heard about Gwen's adventures with the goblin king, when she and Arthur had slain a troll and saved the goblins' precious mines. The feat had cemented Arthur's alliance with King Zorath, and the shared peril of the quest had gone a long way to healing the relationship between Camelot's king and queen.

However, as beautiful as the treasures were, it was the happiness of the fair that stole Clary's heart. Everyone greeted her like an old friend, even if they'd never met.

I have not seen this place for many, many years, said Vivian wistfully. *It is as delightful as I remember it.*

"I thought demons still came here once in a while," Clary said in a low voice, not wanting to alert bystanders that she was chatting with her personal hellspawn. While she could talk to Vivian within her own mind, it somehow made it harder to discern which thoughts were her own.

Only Tenebrius comes now. He is strongest and able to leave the Abyss for periods of time. He keeps a castle in these parts.

Clary remembered Tamsin's story about that castle, and fervently hoped to avoid it. "Do you know where LaFaye is imprisoned?"

The Lady of the Lake's white tower. You can see it through the trees.

Clary searched the horizon. "I thought there was a glamour that hid it from view." She finally found a smudge of white against a dark backdrop of green.

The magic is growing thin. Lady Nimueh is a mighty sorceress, but LaFaye is formidable.

To Clary's eyes, the distant tower looked like a broken fang waiting to strike. After the image in the laptop, she never wanted LaFaye's gaze on her again. But then, the evil queen would be hunting larger game than Merlin's student witch.

That is exactly why we shall succeed, said Vivian with bloodthirsty satisfaction. *No one will see us coming, and I will have my vengeance on Tenebrius and his dark queen for what they've done to me.*

"I really don't like the sound of that."

The demon didn't reply, because Merlin appeared at Clary's elbow. "I have set perimeter wards throughout the fair. If Tenebrius or his fae friends arrive, I will know it."

"So, what next?" Clary asked.

"We wait." Merlin gave a careless wave toward an enormous tent that filled a nearby clearing. "Arthur is enjoying the hospitality of King Zorath. Goblins always dine before serious negotiations, and ambassadors from a dozen of the mortal races are there."

"What's there to negotiate? Surely everyone wants La-Faye gone."

He shrugged. "There will be battle plans, plans for dividing up booty and decisions about which champion leads the charge. None of it means much once swords are drawn, but the pride of monarchs is tricky business."

"I bet Arthur misses Gwen for this part." The queen was a masterful negotiator, but she was too close to her time to travel.

"Probably," Merlin agreed. "But he has Gawain, who can be diplomatic when he chooses. Have you had a chance to look around the fair?"

Tamsin, who had obviously been eavesdropping, looked up from examining a tray of earrings. "You should definitely show Clary around."

She shot Tamsin a scowl, but it was mostly out of old habit. Tamsin had set her up on far too many awful dates during their teenage years. Merlin looked between them, suspicion plain on his face. All the same, he gave Clary a slight nod. "Do you want to see the sights?"

Clary shrugged but she smiled, too. "Okay."

Merlin offered an arm and they set off down the row of pavilions, walking slowly but with purpose. "Don't bother with this part of the grounds. It's just a better version of Medievaland. The really interesting things are outside the main field."

"What do you consider interesting?" she wanted to know.

He gave a slow smile that was actually charming. "Have you ever tasted the desserts that the naiads make?"

"The what?"

"Naiads are water spirits. There are not many left in the human world, but they still live here where the waters are pure." He led her into what was clearly the refreshment area. It smelled of wood smoke and cooking aromas, some redolent of spice and one a savory, mouthwatering blend of mushrooms and sage. She veered that way until Merlin pulled her back. "Don't eat anything made by the spriggans. You can never tell where it's been."

He took her instead to a corner of the meadow where a stream ran close by. After the smoke, the air seemed crisp, an earthy tang replacing the heavier smells of meat and spice. The space was crowded with all manner of folk, some with wings and antennae, others in full chain mail. Clary waved to Beaumains, who was standing in line and chatting with a pretty girl who was green from head to toe. Whatever the naiads sold, it appeared to be a universal favorite.

When they got to the head of the line, Clary saw the naiad serving dishes of what looked like crushed ice. Every time a customer paid—sometimes with gold, but sometimes with a shell or a flower—the naiad knelt and took another dish from the cool stream. Clary was entranced by the creature's grace, and also by the fact she was entirely translucent. It was hard to see where she was until she moved, and the light seemed to bend and curve to show her presence.

Merlin paid in a type of coin Clary didn't recognize. The naiad accepted it—she was definitely corporeal enough to deal with solid objects—and lifted their desserts from the shallow water.

"Thank you," Clary said, shocked a little by the freezing temperature of the dessert. It was only then that she discovered the entire dish—including the bowl and spoon—was made of ice.

"Enjoy," the naiad replied in a lilting voice and then turned to the next customer.

Clary walked away, Merlin at her side. "The trick," he said, "is to eat the whole thing before it melts."

Obediently, she dug the spoon into the ice. The first mouthful made her stop in her tracks. The sun was hot on her shoulders, but her mouth was filled with a refreshing explosion. She couldn't name all the flavors, but she recognized many. There was that earthy tang, but there was something floral, too. There was honey and the rich ripeness of berries, the snow of the mountains and the spice of herbs. It was a mouthful of everything good about the summer forest.

"Oh!" The exclamation was hardly profound, but it came from her heart.

Merlin grinned, and there was something boyish in it. "I have this at least once every summer." And he stuffed a spoonful into his mouth.

Clary couldn't remember him ever sharing an ordinary personal detail. She'd seen his home, even his bedroom, but this was different. Surely someone who had lived for centuries had thousands of likes and dislikes—or maybe the need to define one's tastes changed as time blurred memories together. Or, and this made more sense to her, his heart was here, in this land caught between worlds. Maybe this felt more like home.

She paused between spoonfuls, even though cold water was beginning to drip through her fingers. She was getting an ice-cream headache. "What was it like, being the king's sorcerer in the old Camelot?"

The sadness in the look he gave her broke her heart.

Chapter 20

"What do you think?" Merlin said. "It was the time before everything happened."

Before he had destroyed the world he knew and half the creatures in it. Clary could see him retreating, the relaxed mood they'd shared dissolving like the icy dessert. He looked away as if wishing to be anywhere but next to her. "I mean," she said, stammering a little, "was it like this, with pixies and naiads and goblins? Did the supernatural walk freely, or did they hide from humans like the witches do now?"

He seemed to relent, giving her a sidelong glance. "They were in the open back then."

She took a final spoonful of dessert and set the bowl on a stump to melt in the sun. "It must have been beautiful."

He didn't reply, but walked slowly toward the trees. Not sure what else to do, Clary followed. She sensed he was deep in thought, maybe lost in memories older than the oaks around them.

When they came to another clearing, he directed her to sit on a fallen log. Clary obeyed and watched as he picked up a fallen branch, breaking off leaves and twigs until he was left with a makeshift wand as long as his forearm. He walked the circumference of the clearing, drawing a line in the grass. A human would not have seen it, but her witch's sight made out the faint yellow glow he inscribed. When the circle was closed, he turned to her.

He'd regained his composure, even offering a faint

smile. "It is far easier to show you than to describe it."
And then he raised his hands and spoke words of power,
showing what Camelot's enchanter could really do.

Clary blinked and gasped as mist rose from the glowing circle like a cylinder that reached the sky. Then it
shimmered into focus, turning to pale stone with arched
windows overlooking rolling hills and a pristine sky. The
view said they were high up, so high that birds flew below
and the horsemen on the green seemed tiny as a child's
toy. But the enchantment did not stop there. The illusion
rolled toward her like an unfurling carpet, showing a stone
floor with brightly woven rugs, shelves of scrolls and ornately bound tomes, a worktable with flasks and jars and
a crooked inkwell complete with feather pen. Clary discovered she was sitting on a low bed strewn with furs.

"This is where I worked," he said.

The illusion was remarkable. Clary stroked the furs,
even lifting one to see what was underneath. The mattress was far thinner than anything on a modern bed, but
it seemed perfectly comfortable. "How did you do this?"

I taught him well, Vivian purred from some distant
place inside her.

"It is real," he said. "For a brief time, at least. We are
invisible to passersby."

Clary rose and walked to the window. The wide embrasure was cool, the stone gritty beneath her hand. Outside,
a breeze snapped the rows of multicolored pennons that
decorated the rooftops below. There were a dozen smaller
buildings inside a crenelated wall. A drawbridge stretched
across a moat guarded by pinnacled towers. Everywhere
there were people in medieval clothes—ladies on dainty
horses, soldiers and many, many workers. A knight rode
across the courtyard, his destrier's feathered hooves clopping on the cobblestones. "This was Camelot," she said,
her breath barely above a whisper.

"It was," he said. "It was a time that only remains here, in the kingdom of magic and memory."

"But Camelot still exists," she said, turning to look him in the eye. "Arthur and Gwen have built something new. It doesn't look the same, but it's just as real. It serves the same purpose."

"Of course," he said, the words subdued. "It is not in Arthur's nature to give up."

And neither had he. She could see it in the yearning look he gave the scene outside his window. The light limned the clean lines of his nose and jaw, showing off his austere good looks. She imagined him in the costume he'd worn at Medievaland, with the robe of stars and his wizard's staff. He was indeed her rebel prince of magic, filled with storm and daring. He was everything she'd dreamed of in her future mate.

"This was before the spell that destroyed the fae and damaged the witches," he said, "before the demons were banished and Camelot collapsed. Before I sent the knights of the Round Table into the stone sleep. Yes. This is what I crushed beyond recognition with a single act, and if faced with the same circumstances, I'm not certain I could change anything. Camelot had all but lost the war."

In anyone else, the words would have seemed like self-pity. Merlin was stating plain fact. The only thing that softened his statement was the knowledge that he was still trying to fix his mistake. No one could say he hadn't taken responsibility for what had happened.

He leaned on the side of the window, looking out at the hills. His broad shoulders filled the loose T-shirt he wore, the short sleeves baring his tanned and well-muscled arms. One hand rested on the sill, the fingers curled into a loose fist. Clary put hers over it.

"I will take comfort when I've healed the damage I've done," he said.

"That doesn't mean you can't have company." She leaned forward, leaving a light kiss on his cheek.

His hand turned, catching hers, and squeezed it. "My history should frighten you away."

"I know," she said. "You're the greatest enchanter of all time, and the one who fell the furthest from grace. All the little witches are told to eat their peas so they don't end up like Merlin."

His eyebrows arched. "Now you're mocking me."

But she'd made him smile—almost. "We've figured out a cure for the fae. This story of Camelot isn't over yet."

His gaze melted as if her words had far more power than she knew. This time it was he who kissed her, tugging at the tender flesh beyond her lips. He teased her with his tongue, begging permission to explore. She caught his tongue, sucking it deeper into her mouth, sharing the summer-forest taste of their icy dessert.

All the misgivings she'd felt the night before receded in the face of his grief and the need to show him he was not alone. She had to make him believe there was a future without the pain of loss she felt in his desperate kiss. She cradled his face with her hands, holding him as if he was something precious.

He backed her to the bed, pushing her down to the feather mattress. Clary let herself fall, the soft furs tickling the bare skin of her arms and face. She stretched, luxuriating in the unexpected comfort. But then she saw the heat in his amber eyes and suddenly became self-conscious. The hunger was impossible to mistake.

He bent over, resting his hands on either side of her hips, and bent to kiss the bare strip of skin between her top and the waistband of her jeans. The faint prickle of whiskers made her shiver, and then he kissed her again, just above the first spot. His tongue dipped hot and wet into her navel. She curled forward, her fingers in his thick, dark hair, and then he was on the bed with her, straddling her body as he kissed and licked his way upward. She pulled off her top, abandoning it among the furs. She'd wanted this moment, not as Vivian's host, but for herself. She tugged at Merlin's T-shirt until he stripped it off, revealing the sculpted muscles of his chest and stomach. She ran her hands down his torso with gleeful greed.

He stroked her, the pressure of his fingers deft even through the fabric of her jeans. She squirmed, arching into it, wanting him with a need that went back to the first time she'd heard his name. Then, he'd been a legend, a mystery to unfold. Now she knew him as a real man. She'd found more grief and less fantasy, but she'd turned her dream into something with value. She found his lips again and drank him in, heart pounding as if she would fly to pieces.

With Vivian and the potion, he'd held himself on a short chain, disciplining an almost violent need. This was equally intense, but tempered with a tenderness she had barely suspected. He was offering her the man he kept hidden behind his chill wall of reserve.

They shed the rest of their clothes, one item at a time. Clary was never sure how much of that was Merlin's magic, spurred on by impatience. He slipped his fingers through her intimate folds, drawing a moan of pleasure from her throat. There was something to be said for a man with a thousand years or more of practice.

And then his fingers slid out and he kissed her there, doing everything she had ever imagined, and then a dozen things more. Pressure built and churned, the eye of the storm low in her belly. Desire spiked in short, sharp bursts, each one tearing a piece of her self-control away. She held on as long as she could, refusing to let the moment end, but that was impossible. Eventually, Clary was forced to surrender, pleasure erupting as magic crackled over her skin. The power was neither his nor hers, but a twining web spun of their combined arousal. She cried out, a sound between jubilation and a sob.

And then he was beside her, pulling her close with an urgency that mirrored her own. He slid inside her, the sensation so intense she came a second time. He began to move, a languid rocking that soothed and made her restless at the same time. Until now, he had barely touched her breasts. Perhaps he had been saving that path to fresh sensation because now he set to work with a will, kneading and sucking and rolling the tips with his tongue. Tension corkscrewed inside her again, driving her to push his gentle rocking to deeper strokes. He met her need and doubled it, going deeper and faster. The magic around them became a snapping corona, flaring as he made his final thrust. He roared, a wordless shout of triumph as he came. Clary crested a moment later, shuddering beneath him a final time.

They fell back, exhausted. Clary curled into his side, their limbs tangling. The air was warm and comfortable, the bed soft as a cloud. She should have fallen asleep, lulled by the soft rhythm of Merlin's breath. His hand stroked her hair, twining the strands through his fingers.

Except her mind would not be still. She'd wanted this, no question. It had been a gift between them, the door opened by his unexpected willingness to share his memories of the Camelot he'd lost. Except…

Her thoughts trailed off, hating her conclusion. Merlin didn't know she still held one of the demons he'd sacrificed everything to destroy.

Don't, Vivian said, her voice profoundly sad. *Nothing but unhappiness lies that way.*

Merlin made a sleepy sound and kissed her ear. She rolled toward him and buried her face in his neck.

Then Vivian did something unexpected. At first, it felt like being dissolved in champagne, a million bubbles popping along every nerve. All at once, Clary was wide-awake, filled with unstoppable energy. Vivian wasn't lurking inside her, like a guest sharing the same house. Not anymore. She'd spread herself through Clary like the liquor in a cocktail, an indivisible part of the mix.

Merlin must have sensed something, because he rose on one elbow. Clary glanced down his long, lean form and wanted to purr. It was a strange kind of sharing, and yet it was perfect. They both got the full benefit of the view—and whatever else was on offer. She drew herself up, pushing him down on the bed and imagining a lengthy menu of treats. Merlin's eyes were half-lidded, almost speculative, but his slow smile was that of a very happy man.

Then the ground shook, and not in a good way.

Merlin leaped from the bed, aware the world he'd left beyond the walls of his remembered tower had changed for the worse. How long had they been there? He couldn't be certain, but it could not have been much more than an hour. He began snatching up clothes, tossing some to Clary and pulling on others. It was only when he did not hear her moving that he turned to look at her.

Her green eyes were panic-stricken. "Come on," he said, touching her cheek and forcing her to meet his eyes. "Remember you are the student of Merlin and a powerful enchantress in your own right."

He'd seen her in her element, using her skills to trap and defeat the thing in the computer. He'd seen her fight the fae and struggle to measure up to her own dreams. Courage like hers was uncommon.

She blinked, as if coming awake, and met his gaze. Her eyes had a luminous quality that was hers alone, and they regarded him with a sweetness that almost made him shy away. He was not used to such affection, especially in this place with all its reminders of disaster. He did not deserve it, and yet he would shed his last blood to keep her from changing her mind about him.

There was every chance that might come to pass. For all the terrible things she knew of him, there was more. And yet he couldn't face that now—he wouldn't. Not so soon after the beauty of their lovemaking. He leaned forward, kissing Clary's velvet mouth once more, drawing out their peaceful interlude for another second. She kissed him back, sipping at his lips as if it were the last time they would ever touch.

Then the ground shook again.

"What is that?" she whispered. Then she seemed to snap out of her daze and hastily began pulling on her clothes.

"It sounds as if they started the apocalypse without us."

He waited until her sneakers were tied and then commanded his replica of the tower to vanish. The bed and other furniture went first with a faint explosion of mist that wafted away on the breeze. The carpet receded to the walls, leaving only the grass behind, and then the walls themselves turned to a thick, gray fog, blotting out the view of Old Camelot. With a final wave of his hand, Merlin cleared the air, and they saw the cause of the disturbance. Far in the distance, a huge stone sailed through the air toward the Lady of the Lake's white tower. When it struck, stone sprayed into the air and the ground shook beneath their feet.

"They're using a catapult," he said, answering the question forming on her face. "I believe it's a trebuchet, to be precise, with just enough magic to break through every ward Lady Nimueh has set around her tower."

"Who is *they*?" Clary asked, her voice rising with panic. She grabbed Merlin's hand, and he squeezed hers in reply.

"The fae armies have arrived." He gave her a thin smile. "Shall we go save the world?"

Chapter 21

They did not run. Merlin had seen too many battles, with enemies waiting in ambush and arrows flying where he least expected them. He held Clary's hand and proceeded with healthy caution toward the goblin tent where he hoped Arthur would be. Their path took them first through the clearing where the food vendors had been. It was empty of people, but fires licked at the wounds in the grass where the tents had been. Food, dishes and even articles of clothing were strewn on the lawn. A dead pixie lay facedown, wings torn like a broken kite. He kept Clary moving, hoping she did not see it.

An ax rested beside the path, meant for chopping wood rather than battle, but he took it anyway. Sometimes a weapon was more efficient than any spell, and he guessed he would need all his magical strength before the day was done. As they reached the main clearing he stopped, Clary's soft form bumping into him.

"What's up?" she asked.

The coast was clear, so he pulled her forward without replying. The stage was empty of musicians now. The tents where the merchants had sold their wares were abandoned. A few had collapsed, the colorful silk deflated over the silhouette of the tables beneath. Others had obviously been looted. The goblin's display of treasures was empty, the ground a trampled mess of mud.

He could see figures running in the distance. He was certain by their swaying gait that the figures were dryads, the tree-people who lived deep in the woods of the Forest Sauvage. They were normally peaceful, but like the Charmed Beasts who spoke the human tongue, they had sided with Camelot and its king after Arthur had saved them from enslavement by the fae.

The white peak of King Zorath's pavilion lay ahead. At least it was still standing. Merlin slowed his steps, pulling Clary close to his side. Guards blocked their approach, but he recognized the two knights at once. Owen of the Beasts stood to the left of the pavilion's entrance, and Beaumains stood to the right, one arm still wrapped in a bandage.

"The king was asking for you," Owen said, the soft Welsh lilt of his voice at odds with his stern expression. "There has been trouble."

"What happened?"

"The king will tell you. He said to send you in immediately when you arrived."

Clary released Merlin's hand. "I should find Tamsin."

"She is with the wounded behind the tent," Owen said.

Merlin caught Clary's arm before she could get away. "If there is the slightest whiff of trouble, come find me."

Her eyes widened, the expression pleased and a little rebellious. "What's to say I'm not the cause of it?"

And then she was gone. The remark had been pure Clary, carelessly flippant, but there was enough truth in it to make Merlin wince a little. There were times when the woman could be marketed as a kind of bipedal land mine.

He shook himself and went in search of Arthur. It didn't take long—he was deep in conversation with Zorath, the goblin king.

Goblins were warty, lumpy, peculiar-smelling creatures and the king had all those qualities in spades. They also came in a variety of hues, including green, blue and a scarlet red. Zorath was red, as wide as he was tall, entirely bald and wore a cloak of ermine and a diamond-studded crown.

Merlin bowed low to Zorath as well as Arthur, knowing goblins appreciated a show of respect.

"I'm glad to see you," Arthur said to Merlin in a "where were you?" tone.

"I was on the far side of the grounds," Merlin replied. "What's happened?"

"It was a flock of birds," said Zorath, who looked mightily offended.

"I beg your pardon, Majesty," said Gawain, who approached from Arthur's right. "They were not birds as we know them, but like the creatures who attacked on the tourney ground at Medievaland. I have seen such apparitions in the Forest Sauvage. They were the creatures of the demon Tenebrius, whose stronghold lies not five miles away."

"Great," Merlin muttered under his breath.

"The attack is everything we feared," said Arthur. "The fae and demons are working together to free LaFaye from her prison."

"We're outnumbered three to one, and they're better trained and better armed," Zorath complained. "Could it get any worse?"

"Undoubtedly," said Merlin. "And it probably will, but we don't have any other option. We have to fight."

Merlin had said something similar to Uther Pendragon, Arthur's father, just before a battle. There had been war back then, too—the tangled web of royal families were forever squabbling about who got to wear the crown. The witch-born family of Morgan LaFaye wanted it for their darling little sociopath, and Uther wanted it for his unborn human heir. The king had made Merlin promise to look after the interests of his child. Merlin had believed himself more than capable of looking after a single babe.

Then came the day when he visited Uther's castle, expecting a grand victory celebration. The king had defeated the witches in open battle, and his crown was safe. It should have been the start of a new peace.

But suspicion stiffened Merlin's spine as he galloped through the castle gates. The stable yard was deserted. So was the great hall, the bakery and armory. When Merlin flung open the doors of the feast hall, he found the figures of men slumped around the high table. Even from across the room, he could tell they were knights and lords by their dress. Food sat on great platters of gold, but it crawled with flies. Merlin's stomach churned at the sight, but as he drew closer he saw drifts of dead insects littering the table. Warning sounded deep in his gut.

He touched the first man he came to. Stiffness had obviously left the body, because he rolled easily to one side. Merlin sprang back, pulse jumping as he saw the man's face. It was swollen and blue-black, the skin cracked and crusted with fetid fluids. The few drops of liquid left in his cup might have seemed innocent once, but now was black and sluggish and smelled of something foul.

Merlin's mouth turned dry. Poison. A coward's weapon.

He circled the table slowly, looking at each hideous face and trying to put a name to it. When he got to the red-haired man at the head of the table, the one with the jeweled goblet and wolf's-fur cloak, he recognized Uther. Merlin had failed to protect his friend.

He backed away from the horrible scene, barely able to understand what he saw. He knew what poisons a witch could brew and was certain this was the handiwork of Uther's enemies. With a desperate roar, he bolted up the stairs to the chambers of the queen. Bodies lay in his path—servants, page boys and knights. The poison had reached them all, which made Merlin suspect the castle's central well.

The scene in the queen's chamber was a repetition of all

he had seen so far. A pitcher and silver cups sat on a tray, though a few of the cups were scattered as if dropped by a suddenly limp hand. Sunlight slanted in through the high windows, shining mercilessly on the fallen ladies of the chamber. Only the queen's visage had been untouched. She was dead and pale as parchment, but her loveliness was unchanged. She had not drunk the poison, but the blood-soaked sheets told another story. She had died giving birth. Merlin spun around, wondering where the child had gone.

And there it was, a boy, in a basket by the hearth. The ashes of the fire were long cold. Merlin bent over the basket, dreading what he would find. The babe's skin was chilled, his breathing uncertain, but the prince alone lived out of all the castle's occupants. A careless oversight on the assassin's part, and one that would be rectified if word of the heir's survival got out.

Merlin gathered the child up, holding him close to share the heat of his body. Anger bit inside his gut, his chest, the back of his throat. Who did this to their fellow beings? To a mere baby? Merlin's own infancy had been filled with everything a child needed—safety, plenty and love. He'd had much while this child had lost everything. Worse yet, the princeling had lost it because Merlin had underestimated their enemies. If he'd been more suspicious, Uther might still be alive.

There was nothing in the place that was safe to eat or drink, so Merlin rode away at once. He knew a knight, Sir Hector, who lived far from this castle and had a family of his own. It would be safe to hide the prince with him until the boy came of age. Then Merlin would help him reclaim Uther's throne.

Perhaps Merlin wasn't meant to save Britain himself, as his druidess mother had believed, but through a great king. He could teach this Pendragon child, show him the way of statesmen and shape his character. This boy would be wiser than Uther, craftier than his enemies and far, far wiser than Merlin.

He decided to name the boy Arthur.

That boy stood before him now, a grown man with ice-blue eyes and his father's reddish hair. Arthur was every inch a king, but he was still Merlin's friend and, in a way neither man often acknowledged, the orphaned child he'd held in his arms.

"What do you need me to do?" Merlin asked, knowing he'd lay down his life to spare that boy's—or his king's.

"We take the battle to the tower," said Arthur.

Horses were brought for the knights, but the goblins went on foot. A contingent remained behind—including Tamsin and Beaumains—to guard the wounded. Merlin wished Clary would stay behind, as well, until he saw Gawain and Tamsin's farewell. Judging by their heartfelt kiss, he wasn't sure if it was worse to leave the woman he cared for behind or to have her with him as they rode into danger. His one comfort was the improved strength and reflexes the connection with Vivian granted her. Still, he insisted Clary wear light leather body armor and strap a long knife to her hip. He did the same, adding his favorite sword in a back sheath.

Their progress eastward through the forest was quick, as if the path itself opened up to speed their way. Merlin rode at Arthur's side, with Gawain in front and Clary in the relatively safe position behind him. Owen of the Beasts rode beside her, ready to be of assistance since she was not a strong rider. No one spoke, leaving only the clop of hooves and the jingle of harnesses. The woods themselves were quiet, as if every living thing was on alert. That made Gawain's shout to halt easy to hear.

Merlin reined in, straining to see what was the matter. It was only when Gawain edged his horse aside that he saw the fox bowing low in the middle of the path. It was a little larger than an ordinary fox, but it looked otherwise the same, with black stockings and a white underbelly. The only extraordinary marking was the splash of green at the tip of its tail, which marked it as one of the Charmed Beasts of the Forest Sauvage.

Owen made a sound of pleasure, for the fox was his particular companion. No one would call it a pet, however. Charmed Beasts were their own masters, though they had allied with Camelot in return for the protection of the Pendragon kings.

"Greetings, Senec," said Arthur to the fox. "What news do you bring?"

"Your Majesty," replied Senec in a melodious tenor. "The Lady of the Lake sends word to hurry. The defenses of the tower will not last."

"How many fae have come to fetch their queen?"

The fox hesitated. The beasts made excellent spies, but their ability to count was limited. "They brought many soldiers. Enough to fly three different banners."

Three different armies of fae translated to thousands. Arthur held a quick consultation with Zorath, and a large contingent of goblins split off, moving at a quick march to approach the tower from the south. Once that order was given, the king spoke to the fox again. "My thanks to you, Master Senec. I have one more task to ask of you."

"What is your command, Your Majesty?"

"There are eagles among the Charmed Beasts. Do you know their location?"

"Of course, Your Majesty."

"Find them and tell them it is time to summon every creature that will fight with me. It is time to make our stand against the Faery Queen and her demon allies, once and for all."

With a final bow, Senec turned and was gone. The company rode on, sunlight flashing through the leaves and dancing on the knights' armor. The ground rose as they went, passing fast-moving streams fed by mountain snows. Eventually, their path opened onto a broad platform of rock that formed one side of a valley. The white tower stood on the other side and some distance to the south. It was a good vantage point—close enough to see the enemy, but well out of bowshot. It was an excellent point from which to mount a charge.

The white tower rose like a delicate spear of crystal, the thick mountain pines forming a dramatic backdrop. At last Merlin spied the gleam of the enchanted lake that stretched near Lady Nimueh's castle. Unfortunately, it was surrounded by what looked like a living carpet of heavily armed fae. They were packed so thickly and in such number the mountainside below the tower could not be seen.

And crouched in the middle of the throng was the trebuchet, a great wooden machine on wheels at least five times as high as a man. Its base was triangular, the long throwing arm balanced on the point. As Merlin watched, the arm swung forward, its enormous slingshot whipping up and over to cast a huge boulder skyward. The stone cracked against the white tower and the ground shook, making the horses sidle.

Merlin had assumed there was a touch of magic that allowed the assault to pierce the enchantments that defended the castle. Now he could see there was far more to it than he'd assumed. There were fae in blood-red robes standing near the machine, scribing symbols into the boulders they hurled. Demonic symbols. It made sense, but now the magnitude of the magic in play became clear. This was the kind of magic that could turn the Forest Sauvage into a desert, or simply erase it altogether.

Cold, prickling fear ran up Merlin's shoulders and perched at the back of his neck. Arthur turned to him, the glittering chill of his eyes confirming that he knew exactly what was at stake.

"Give the signal," said the king. "We engage now."

Chapter 22

Clary heard Arthur's words and the finality in his voice. It was rare that she, who had grown up without kings, truly understood what his crown meant, but she did then. She felt the burden of it in her gut. His order would cost lives, but not giving it would cost more.

With only a slight hesitation, as if he was thinking the exact same thing, Merlin raised his hand and a bolt of bright green light exploded into the air. The signal. There was an instant of quiet, like an indrawn breath. Her insides went tight, holding a gibbering panic at bay. It felt as if every fae head had just turned their way. They'd passed some point of no return.

Then a storm of goblin arrows flew in perfect unison, buzzing as the fletching caught the air. The first volley had barely risen when a second came from the south, showing the fae were trapped in the bowl of the valley. Fae shields flew up, deflecting many of the arrows, but a respectable number found their mark.

"Loose!" The goblin king's voice echoed off the valley walls, and another flurry of arrows sailed from the goblins' recurved bows. Zorath had shed his regalia in favor of a studded leather cap that had seen much use. This wasn't his first battle.

Gawain, Owen and Perceval gathered protectively around their king, and it struck Clary how few knights there were. She'd heard the original Round Table had numbered one hundred and fifty, but only a fraction had been found and awakened in the modern age. Two were injured, thanks to Vivian's stunt at Medievaland, old Sir Hector had retired from the battlefield and Lancelot was off guarding the white tower with the Lady of the Lake.

And yet, when the goblins finally charged, so did they. It happened suddenly, with a cry and a churn of hooves and a horrible drop in Clary's heart.

"No, wait!" she cried, half rising from her saddle until Merlin caught her arm.

"Be still," he said, squeezing hard until she met his eyes. "The fae aren't going to leave just because we ask nicely."

"But there is only a handful—"

"We cannot ask allies to fight unless we draw our own swords."

But all she could think about was that Arthur was Gwen's husband and Gawain was her sister's husband-to-be. She didn't want to live in a world without Perceval's impudent laughter or knowing that there was no Owen to nurse stray animals back to health. These weren't the shining knights from the movies—these were people she loved. But then, couldn't that be said of all soldiers?

She sank back to her saddle, trembling with fright and anger. None of this should be happening. The urge to smack LaFaye's perfect face rose like a silent scream. "What do we do?" They were the only ones left behind.

Merlin's expression spoke of banked fury. "What we always do, stand on the balcony while the knights battle below. Except this time our magic is aimed at the enemy."

So the shows at Medievaland had been rehearsals. That gave her a point of reference, at least. "How do we destroy their army without hurting our own?"

Merlin dismounted and then helped Clary down before securing the horses. "First, we take care of the trebuchet. The assault on the tower weakens the spell that keeps Morgan imprisoned."

She looked down the valley at the machine, careful not to let her eyes rest on the chaos of men and weapons. If she saw a friend in trouble, she'd lose her focus. As she watched, the fae released the next shot, and the huge beam swung the catapult. A boulder flew into the air, and this time she could see the corona of dark magic sizzling around it. It crashed into the top of the tower, knocking a layer of stone away. The top of the tower crumbled, leaving only a shard like a broken tooth. Clary's chest hurt at the sight, but her curiosity was stirred. "How come the Faery Queen won't be killed when the tower comes down?"

"The spell that jails her will break before the tower falls altogether. I do not doubt that LaFaye already has an escape plan in place."

The knot of tension in Clary's chest made another twist. "Let's make sure those plans don't do her any good."

Unexpectedly, he kissed her, his mouth hot and urgent. When he pulled away, he rested his forehead against hers for a moment, his eyes squeezed shut. "Thank you for being here."

Where else could she be, when everyone she cared about was in peril? "I'd say no problem, but it probably will be."

He huffed, a kind of half laugh, and turned to the scene below. Clary stood at his shoulder, folding her arms and frowning down at the blasted machine. Then she pointed. "What's going on there, by the wheels?"

Merlin narrowed his eyes. "Dryads."

They seemed to erupt from nowhere, sinking their long fingers into the wood and tearing it to shreds. As they watched, the fae turned as one toward them, dealing swift death to one of the graceful creatures as the others slipped away, only to reappear and attack a different corner of the machine. Their courage shook Clary to the core.

And yet the trebuchet swung again, sending another missile toward the tower. With a jab of his fingers, Merlin shattered the rock to powder. A roar went up from the battlefield, some voices defiant, others enraged. The strike left him panting.

"Don't stand in the open," he said, pulling her behind a screen of trees. "They know we're here now. And watch for anyone attempting to reach us."

Clary nodded. It was her turn next, and she already had a plan. She could feel Vivian stirring, but the demoness remained inconspicuous, merely nudging Clary's spell where it lacked finesse. With her help, Clary launched a very realistic swarm of hornets upon the fae working the trebuchet. All productivity stopped as the otherwise perfect fae launched into a manic dance of slapping and shaking their cloaks and hair. Meanwhile, the dryads finished their destructive work.

"Good one," Merlin shouted, and launched a fireball at a mounted fae general. It struck him squarely on the breastplate and sent him toppling backward from his horse.

Their run of luck didn't last. The next moment fae rained from the trees, trapping Merlin and Clary in a circle. She recalled Merlin's warning that they'd exposed themselves, but she hadn't heard anyone approach. But then again, all fae moved like shadows.

Merlin's sword left its sheath with a hiss, the motion continuing in a downward slash that killed one attacker before the leaping fae touched the ground. Clary shrieked in pure surprise, but had the wits to draw her knife and fall into a crouch. By then, Merlin had run the second fae through, freeing his sword again by kicking the carcass to the ground. Like all the most experienced knights, his sword work was more efficient than pretty.

Clary counted three fae left. One made a grab for her, but she dodged, sensing Vivian's subtle assistance as she weaved and slid a spell onto the blade. When she slashed, it hit its mark, leaving a red stripe down his arm.

"Go away," she snapped, furious that she'd been forced to cut him. He didn't seem to care, because he lunged with his own blade. She twisted away, slamming her heel into the side of his leg. She heard a horrible, wet crack as he slid off the lip of the valley and went tumbling down the path where Arthur had ridden into the fray. She'd probably dislocated his knee.

When she turned back, the other two fae were dead. Merlin leaned on the point of his sword, sucking in deep breaths. His face and arms shone with sweat, and she could see fresh gashes on his armor. The sword ran with blood, but none of it seemed to be his.

"I've never seen you fight," she said, her voice colorless with the shock of what had just happened. "I thought you just trained for the exercise."

His mouth twisted. "I wish."

Clary's chest squeezed at his tone. Knowing there was nothing useful to say, she watched as he wiped down his sword on a rag torn from the tunic of a dead fae. Unwilling to touch the dead, Clary wiped her knife on the grass and put it away. Her hands began to shake as adrenaline left her system. Now that the crisis was over, her mood was sinking fast.

Merlin spun toward the trees, sword raised. Clary jumped in fright, but this time she could hear someone approaching—not fae, then. As the bushes parted, a tall man came into sight, carrying an unconscious female form. Though she'd met them only once, Clary knew they were Sir Lancelot du Lac and Nimueh, the Lady of the Lake. The powerful enchantress was one of the fae who still had a soul, and one moment in her luminous presence had told Clary everything about what the fae people had lost.

The woman was dressed all in white, but the gown was tattered and muddy, her feet bare and covered in cuts. Her tangled hair was unbound, its silvery length almost reaching the ground. Dulac, as he was known among the knights, was in battered armor, and it was plain that he'd been fighting. Clary nearly dropped to her knees. If Dulac and Nimueh were here now, like this, everything had gone pear-shaped.

Merlin sheathed his sword and sprang forward to help the knight lay his burden on the grass. "Nimueh!" he said, urging the woman to wake. When she didn't respond, he looked up at the knight. "How long has she been like this?"

"Not long, but she's exhausted." The knight's face was pale as he knelt beside his lady. "She fought hard as any warrior, but she cannot hold out any longer."

Clary stepped forward. It was on the tip of her tongue to argue that they simply *had* to keep fighting, but she strangled her fear. It was plain the two had done all they could. "Get your lady to Tamsin. Take my horse. There's a hospital set up at the fairgrounds."

Dulac's steady brown gaze met hers. "Thank you."

Merlin nodded. "Let Nim rest now. We'll need her fire-works later."

As Dulac gathered the unconscious woman in his arms again, an enormous crack resounded over the valley. Clary spun to see a diagonal split crawl across the white stone of the tower. The top half slid off, crashing to the earth in a cloud of dust. The lower portion exploded, fountaining rock into the sky. Flames followed in a rush that reached almost as high as the original spire. They died almost at once, but the point was made. The enchantments that guarded the prison were gone and Morgan LaFaye had escaped. Although she was safely on the other side of the valley, Clary began to tremble.

Dulac galloped away with his lady, barely sparing another word. The Queen of Faery would take revenge on her jailers if they were caught. Clary watched them go, so brave and so weary, and wondered if everything was lost.

Merlin touched Clary's shoulder, making her jump and then sag against him. Her throat ached with unshed tears.

A long, piercing note rang over the valley. "That's Gawain's horn," said Merlin. "Arthur has sounded a retreat."

And then he threw a spell into the seething mass of warriors. Like a long bullwhip, it seemed to crack and then ripple outward in a blur of violet light. A demon spell, Clary realized as Vivian fed her the knowledge. One that Merlin had learned from her. It seemed to only touch the fae, and not for long, for as they fell to their knees as if struck, they picked themselves up again almost at once, angrier than ever.

That spell takes a great deal of strength, Vivian explained, *and mastery to ensure it does not hurt your friends. No one could perform it twice in one battle.*

But it gave the retreating army a moment, and that was what they needed. Swords swung and spears stabbed, and Clary could see clearly now how badly outnumbered Camelot's allies were. The goblins had borne the brunt of the fight, and far too many lay dead on the valley floor. The remainder took the opportunity to escape.

Arthur and his men reached Clary and Merlin just minutes later, along with the goblin king. A sob of relief escaped Clary. Perceval had an impressive gash over his eye, but they were all alive. The two kings listened grimly as Merlin, leaning with exhaustion against a tree, told them about the Lady of the Lake's flight.

"We must regroup," said Arthur.

"And do what?" Zorath demanded, his voice rough with grief.

Arthur said nothing, his face like stone. Clary bit her tongue, wanting to butt in, but she had nothing useful to say. They couldn't give up, and everybody knew it, but what hope did they have to win?

Merlin broke into the uncomfortable silence. "We have

to move before the fae pursue us. There is nothing to be gained if our retreat becomes a rout."

Clary was about to point out that she'd given her horse away when she saw something in the sky. "Look!"

Everyone turned to see the eagles soaring into the late-afternoon sky. She saw a pair, and then two more, and then there seemed to be dozens splitting off in a dozen directions. "Master Senec has delivered my message," said Arthur. "The eagles of the Charmed Beasts are summoning our distant allies."

But seconds later something else was in the air. Scraps of black floated upward from the treeline, seeming to tumble and waver more than fly. They were fast, though, matching the eagles for speed. When a handful caught up to one of the majestic birds, they swarmed it, and moments later the eagle plummeted to earth.

"No!" Clary exclaimed under her breath, not just for the eagle but for the hope it had represented.

"Hellspawn," Gawain snarled. "That is the work of the demon Tenebrius."

Arthur shifted in his saddle, seeming to come to a decision. He turned away from the sky and looked them each in the eyes before turning to his enchanter. "You asked me what I need you to do," he said to Merlin. "I need you to cure the fae, however impossible that may seem. The only way to win this war is to turn them against their own queen."

Chapter 23

The enormity of Arthur's demand left Merlin hollow, but he had promised Uther Pendragon that he would safeguard his child. He had promised his mother to safeguard their people. And there was an inevitability to the task. Merlin's errant spell had damaged the fae, and he had sworn long ago to heal that wound. Perhaps the unlucky stars that cursed his existence had finally aligned. Maybe this was his moment to make things right.

"I agree," he replied. "This is not a war we will win in open battle. This was our only chance for that, and we lost."

"Do you have a plan?" Arthur asked. "Is there anything you need to carry it out?"

"My student—" he nodded to Clary "—and another horse. She rather generously gave hers away to Dulac."

There were no spare mounts, so Perceval offered his. Minutes later Merlin was cantering to the west, Clary just managing to keep up. When they finally reined in, she was breathing hard. "Where are we going?" she asked. "What is this plan of yours?"

The sky had turned to the dusky blue of early evening, that rich color that came the hour before sunset. The sunlight had turned Clary's skin to a pale honey shade. He watched as she self-consciously combed her fingers through her wild mop of hair. Somewhere in her past there must have been people who told her that if she only dressed like a lady or tamed that spiky tangle of locks, she might have been beautiful. That would be like telling a wood violet to climb into a window box, or a robin to sit quietly in a cage. It made no sense. She was flawed and unruly, and that was part of her perfection.

He realized she was waiting for an answer. Reluctantly, he turned his thoughts back to the coming disaster. "It's more of a guess than a plan."

Her look was dubious.

"It's a good guess," he said, just a little defensively. "Do you remember the fae Laren and Angmar dragged away?"

"Yes. I doubt I'll forget them trashing my hotel room anytime soon."

He supposed not. "Angmar called me just before we left for the Forest Sauvage. I'd given them a sample of the demonic essence that corrupted my laptop. It restored the soul of the fae who attacked you, just as a taste of your soul cured Laren."

Clary's eyes widened, showing off their green depths. "Really? I guess it kind of makes sense. The demon essence, or whatever they call it, must have demon DNA. Do demons have DNA? And why does demon DNA restore fae souls?"

Merlin shrugged. "Because it was a demon spell that stole them." He really hoped it was that simple. There was a lot of guessing going on in the conversation, but that was the problem when it came to demons. Nothing about them played by ordinary rules.

"However," he continued, "an enormous number of soulless fae requires an enormous amount of demon essence for a cure. Happily, the material Tenebrius used to infect the computer was extremely dense. A modest amount will go a very long way."

A silence fell as she digested that. An evening breeze was rising, bringing the smell of earth that had baked in the sun.

"And so you think if we got our hands on more of that goop, we could use it to dose the fae?" she asked.

"Yup. And on a battlefield a whole lot of fae will be in one convenient place."

"I couldn't figure out a good disbursement model," she said. "I couldn't figure out the math."

"Container." Merlin made a shape with his hands. "Spell." He mimicked an explosion, with particles raining on the earth below.

"Oh." She nodded her understanding, but didn't look enormously happy about it. The light was fading, blurring and softening her features. A distant bird trilled its evening song. "And so where are we going to get the goop?"

"Tenebrius had it, or at least I assume he was the one who did, to carry out the attack on Camelot's tech. Only a top-level demon ever has access to their essence. I'm hoping he has more stored there." He pointed at a distant roofline that appeared past a broad apple orchard. "That's his castle."

"Are you crazy?" Her words were quick and low. "When Gawain and Tamsin went there, they barely got out alive."

"Do you have any other ideas where to get what we need?" He nudged his horse forward, picking up the broad trail that led through the abandoned orchard. "I don't think demon goop is available online, though I've never checked the dark web."

Clary made an exasperated noise, but followed. "What do you want me to do?"

"I can send you back home, if you prefer."

"And sit around biting my nails? No, thanks."

"Good, because someone has to tell Arthur if my plan doesn't work."

It was almost too bad that Vivian had gone dormant. He could have used her firepower. But if it was only magical talent he needed, he would rather have taken Nim.

Gawain would be a far better guard, or Master Senec a better spy. But Clary alone understood the whole problem, from Laren to the laptop to Tenebrius's betrayal of Vivian. She'd proven herself a fighter and could think on the fly. All things considered, Merlin couldn't wish for a better partner.

They rode in silence through the rows of trees, the horses' hooves muffled on the soft ground. Green apples were just forming on the trees, filling the air with a hint of their tartness. The beauty of the place was broken once, when they found the corpse of an eagle. It was one of the Charmed Beasts they'd seen attacked, and its feathers were all but torn away.

"This means Tenebrius left LaFaye and came this way," he said. "Another reason to remain alert."

Clary nodded, tears standing in her eyes as she gazed at the fallen bird. They stopped just long enough to bury it in the loamy soil and then resumed their ride.

The moated grandeur of the demon's castle loomed ahead. Twin towers guarded an archway that framed a portcullis and drawbridge. No guardsmen were visible, but that didn't fool Merlin for a moment. The place would be watched.

When they reached the edge of the orchard, they stopped again. The first stars were showing against an indigo sky as he dismounted. "I could tell you to stay here with the horses, but I doubt anywhere in this area is safe."

She dismounted stiffly. He was sore, so she had to be in minor agony. "If it's all the same to you, I'd rather stay close."

He nodded, scanning the drawbridge and towers. Using magic would act like a beacon. If he was going to get in quietly, he would need to use old-fashioned burglary skills. "Can you swim?" he asked, eyeing the moat. At least there was nothing nasty about the water itself or the stream that fed it.

"Sure. I was a lifeguard in college."

"Good. If anything touches you in the water, kill it. It might just be a fish, but I wouldn't take any chances."

They removed their armor, shoes and weapons, keeping only their knives. Barefoot, they crept to the water's edge. Merlin slid into the moat without making a noise and dove, the chill darkness swallowing him whole. He kicked forward, sensing the movement of water that meant Clary was behind him. The distance to the castle's outer wall wasn't far for a strong swimmer. He came up for breath when he touched stone, but still barely raised his head above the waterline. He knew from Gawain's adventures in this place that there was a watergate that led to the castle yard. Clary bobbed up beside him, spitting out water. Merlin pointed to his left, and they began their search for the gate.

It didn't take long, but they were wet and cold once they were back on land. Lights shone inside the main keep and guided them across the yard.

"How do we get inside?" Clary whispered.

Merlin craned his neck to see a window above. It was just an opening in the stone, without glass or shutters, but it was large enough to climb through if they could reach it.

Clary followed his gaze. "Give me a boost."

He did, feeling the distracting blend of muscle and softness as he hoisted her upward. Then, like a shadow, she was through the window. Merlin dug his fingers into the stone and, using main strength and bruising his toes, followed her upward. When he pulled his chin over the broad sill, he saw the window opened into an empty passageway. With another heave, he swung himself up and in.

Clary was crouched against the wall, all but invisible in the shadows. Her tense posture told him she felt the heavy atmosphere of the keep the same way he did. Dark magic filled the place, thick and cloying, as if the air was filled with heavy smoke. There was no smell, and yet a sense of alarm filled him, primal as a fear of flames. It was the scent of a predator, and they were the prey.

He crouched beside Clary, putting an arm around her to stop her shivering. "Gawain said there was a library in this tower," he said, keeping the words barely audible. "We should start our search there."

They rose as one, thinking they were safe for that moment. They had been quiet, so quiet, and yet not silent enough. Merlin looked toward the staircase, but the shadows thickened into a solid shape that turned and tilted its head to fix them with a black, glittering eye. It wore a hooded robe that hid most of its face, but he knew what was beneath the folds of cloth. It had no name, but he'd seen it long ago. It was Tenebrius's watchman and a kind of horrific pet. It had the face of a crow, the body of a man and the appetite of a ghoul.

He gave Clary a shove in the opposite direction, and she ran. The crow sprang forward, the hood falling back to show its razor beak. Merlin had no weapon but his knife, which seemed tiny against the slashing talons of the creature's hands and feet. He snapped a kick to its chest, grabbed the beak and twisted, smashing it headfirst into the wall. Then he ran for all he was worth. Clary was far down the hall, and he had to sprint to catch up. He could hear the birdman stirring and knew the smart thing would be to get out of sight.

There was a door ahead, with a round arch and a plain iron knob. Clary looked over her shoulder, a question in her eyes. Merlin nodded, and they ducked through the entrance. Merlin fished his key chain from his pocket, and lit the tiny flashlight he kept there. It was cheap and the beam was small, but it worked well enough when magic wasn't a good option. The light revealed an earthen tunnel that existed, for no apparent reason, twenty feet above the ground.

"Demon tunnel," Clary said softly. "How come we got in?" She was pressed against him, shivering slightly in her wet clothes. He pulled her closer.

"This might not lead anywhere," he said, choosing not to answer. "Sometimes they were built for storing things the demons wished to conceal."

"Like the goop we're looking for?"

"Exactly."

They walked on a few steps. The space was honeycombed with chambers, though most appeared empty. Merlin swept the beam around, then up, and then in the corners just in case of snakes.

"You know about these places," Clary said, keeping no more than two steps away. "Vivian must have taught you about them."

It was a statement, but he knew there was a question inside it. "Yes, as her student I lived in her household for some time before the demons were exiled to the Abyss."

She was watching him closely, and he wondered how much Vivian had told her about those days before she'd gone dormant. Some things were best left alone. Vivian, of all people, would know that. It was with some relief that he found a chamber with shelves to the ceiling, each one overloaded with objects. "Here," he said, leading her forward.

The room had a moldy smell as if some of the contents were ancient. On the first shelf alone there were earthenware jars that looked vaguely Egyptian, wooden apple boxes filled with old uniforms and an ice-cream maker still in its original box. Demons were natural pack rats. The next held magical paraphernalia, most of it old and rickety. The third shelf held only one object, and Merlin knew it was what he was looking for. It was oblong and papery, like a giant egg or cocoon, and about the size of a football. But it wasn't the appearance that told him that this object alone held demonic essence. It was the aura that radiated from it, the same suffocating dread he'd sensed in the hallway above.

Yes, he'd lived with demons. At first, he'd thought them all-powerful, and then he had seen them as simply *other*— a species that didn't quite belong. Like a foreign plant that escapes the garden into the wild, they overran the other species around them. What they wanted, they took—livestock, houses, children, wives. It was easy to believe they'd come from some other world where there might be natural predators to keep them in check.

Merlin had understood it all the day Tenebrius had found a tiny Hebridean village that sat on an island the demon desired for himself. He'd drawn a claw across the throat of every inhabitant and tossed their corpses into the sea. Then he had done the same to the neighboring islands and burned any house that spoiled his view.

After that, Merlin fled from the demons, ashamed of his association with them. Ashamed that he had studied at their feet. Revolted by what they were, and what his time with them said about him. It was only when Arthur had begged him to rid the mortal world of the demon scourge that he had returned to Vivian one last time. He'd gone back to betray her by stealing her battle spell, and then that had horribly backfired. He should have known that nothing good ever came from a demon.

The thought made him wonder what terrible blunder he was making now. Yet now, as before, he couldn't see another way forward. The object on the shelf before him was the fae's best hope, Camelot's hope, and maybe even redemption for himself.

"What are you thinking?" Clary asked, worry puckering her brow.

"Nothing good."

He reached out, grasping the container, and lifted it from the shelf. It was solid, but not terribly heavy. Still, it took all his willpower not to drop it and back away in disgust. It hummed with energy, the thousand upon thousand potential individuals swimming in an unformed state. This was the primordial ooze of demons, and Tenebrius had tried to weaponize it. Merlin tucked the egg under his arm, hating the papery feel of the cover. It felt like dead skin.

He glanced at Clary, using the sight of her as an antidote to his mood. They'd found what they needed and they could leave this place. The egg might give them a cure. There was still a chance to turn everything into a win.

Clary gasped, her face turning to a mask of horror. "Snakes!"

Chapter 24

The strip of winding shadow struck, arching into the air. Speed blurred all detail, but Merlin saw the flash of deadly fangs aiming for his leg. His power flared, but he throttled it at the last moment, remembering the danger of using magic here in Tenebrius's private domain. Saving himself would expose Clary.

But she moved fast, driving her knife through its skull. Merlin jumped back to see her blade quivering in the stone floor, the serpent pinned like a specimen in a display case. Its tail twitched once, and was still. She backed away slowly, disgust twisting her features.

"How did I do that?" she asked hoarsely.

Merlin let out a shaking breath. Lucky for him that even if Vivian was dormant, she'd left some of her reflexes behind. But there was no time to talk about that now. Another rope of darkness skittered across the floor in a strange, sidewinding motion. Clary squeaked as it twisted toward her.

Without thinking, Merlin scorched it with a handful of flame. For an instant, the serpent glowed bright white edged in orange, its body stretching and drooping like molten glass, and then it collapsed to ash. Clary grabbed his arm, fear and gratitude plain in her tight grip. As the light faded from the ash, the room grew dark, and that was even worse. Merlin knew there would be more snakes hiding in the inky shadows. There always were.

"We need to leave," he said softly. "I've used magic,

and now Tenebrius will know we're here." He'd managed to stifle his power when it came to himself, but he hadn't been able to hold back when she was at risk.

Clary swore under her breath, then freed her knife from the stone floor. "How do we get away without running into more wildlife?"

Merlin considered. Even if they survived the snakes on their way back to the main castle, the creature with the crow's head was outside the door to these hidden rooms. Plus, they'd already tripped whatever magical alarm system the demon employed. A speedy getaway would be more valuable than a stealthy one.

With one hand, he drew an archway in the air. A thin line of luminous white followed his fingers as if he was sketching with light. The white thickened and seemed to crack apart, like the seal around a door. Brilliant blue rays escaped the gap like windblown banners, flaring wide. With a swipe of his hand, Merlin cleared the doorway, settling it back to black. Soon the dark orchard shimmered into view. The branches of the trees swayed in a silent wind he could not feel. It was just an image, the reality far away—and yet close enough to reach in two strides. With the egg of demonic essence under his arm and Clary's hand in his, he stepped through the portal.

The horses whickered as they stepped out of nowhere, but stood obediently as Merlin stashed his prize in the saddlebags. Merlin and Clary donned the clothing and equipment they'd shed to enter the moat and within a minute, they'd mounted and set off at a brisk pace.

They rode in silence as if holding their breath. It was possible that Tenebrius wouldn't notice the egg was missing for some time, the same way no one noticed a missing golf club until it was time to use it. All the same, Merlin expected spies, or magical trip wires or a perimeter alarm to sound as they left the orchard for the road. Nothing came.

"That was too easy," Clary finally muttered.

He wanted to tell her not to jinx their good fortune. Instead, he tried for a reasonable explanation. "Perhaps the demon goop masks our presence."

"What, like disguising our scent?"

"Perhaps."

But he might have spoken too soon. He reined in, hearing a sound like the wind in a ship's sails. It was moving across the sky toward them like low, rhythmic thunder. His chest tightened so hard it felt as if his heart had been forced to beat sideways. Without hesitation, he nudged his horse into the cover of the trees, grateful when Clary's mount automatically followed. They hid just in time. The creature in the sky flew low, the skirts of its tail rustling against the tips of the trees. A smell like rotting carrion swamped them, making the horses stamp and quiver. Merlin's own stomach did an uneasy roll.

"Tenebrius, in his hunting form," Merlin whispered.

They said nothing more, watching the dark shape pass over them. He reached forward, patting his horse's neck and whispering comfort into its flattened ears. The spell was small and simple, yet it was enough to keep their mounts from panic until the demon was gone. Even in the dark, they could see the great carrion bird had savage claws and a beak hooked like a scythe. But it moved on without pausing or so much as looking their way. It was searching for something or someone else.

He waited a few minutes, then a quarter hour, listening to the wingbeats pounding the air. They seemed to go north, then east. Once they faded, Merlin continued to listen, his ears almost physically straining to catch a last clue to the demon's destination. If he hadn't been on another mission, curiosity would have made him follow.

They waited a long time to ensure the coast was clear before they moved. Then Merlin turned his horse's head toward the fairgrounds and set off at a gallop with Clary at his heels.

As with most trips, the road back seemed shorter. Even so, the sky was turning from the black of midnight to the indigo of earliest dawn when they crested the ridge that marked the halfway point of their journey. From there, the path they followed descended to a wider road that ran the length of the forest. Merlin almost relaxed, but then he saw a flash as steel caught the silvery gleam of starlight. Alarmed, he reined in, signaling Clary to do the same.

"What is it?" she asked in a barely audible voice.

"Fae." Now that he knew they were there, he could see past the glamour that hid the army. Thousands of soldiers marched along the road below, their column stretching as far as he could see in either direction. Their armor did not match, but nonetheless it gleamed with careful polishing. White hair hung in long braids, and slender hands held bows that curved like wicked smiles. They moved silently, as only the fae could. Merlin sat straighter in his saddle, the awareness of danger awakening his own urge to fight. LaFaye must have ordered the hills of Faery emptied to gather this army.

Clary reached out to touch Merlin's arm, and then she silently pointed. Merlin followed her gaze to a small figure on a gray mare. Merlin's stomach burned with sudden hate. He knew that dark-haired woman from a hundred nightmares. It was Morgan LaFaye herself, freed from Nimueh's prison. Beside her horse's head was Tenebrius, striding in step with the others. He was dressed as usual in beautiful silken robes and seemed utterly relaxed as if he hadn't just flown there in haste to greet them.

The queen turned to say something to the demon, and Merlin caught a glimpse of her face. The pale oval was indistinct at that distance, and yet he knew it was the same as they'd seen in the laptop, exotic and beautiful as a poisonous bloom. Merlin clenched his fists on his horse's reins, making the beast toss its head.

"Where are they going?" Clary asked.

"I don't know," Merlin replied, wishing again he had the leisure to spy on Tenebrius and the queen. "But if I don't get to safety with this egg, it won't matter."

It would have been so easy to draw another portal, or send a message through a spell, but Merlin knew LaFaye would sense another enchanter's magic this close. He'd take that risk for himself, but Clary was no match for the Queen of Faery or for Tenebrius. He would have to rely on other skills. Merlin turned his horse's head and retraced his steps, leading them away from the marching fae at a brisk pace. As if there weren't enough reasons to hurry, soon dawn would deprive them of the cover of darkness.

He glanced at Clary's worried face. "Change of plan," he said. "We can't get back to Arthur. This army blocks our path."

"I guessed that much," she said, and he saw how tired she looked. "Where can we go?"

There was only one place he knew of in the forest with strong walls, decent beds and no monsters. "The castle at Camelot."

Her look was pure confusion. "Camelot?"

"You were expecting a five-star hotel?"

"Wasn't Camelot in England?"

"The castle is here, too." It was not the same place where the Knights of the Round Table had lived so long ago, but an almost-identical twin created by the magical realm for reasons deeper than anyone knew. It was solid enough, every detail preserved without decay down to the raisins in the larder and the oats in the barn. The main difference was that none of people who had lived and worked in the real place dwelled in this twin. To Merlin, the joyless silence made going there like visiting a grave. Tonight, however, that grave was their refuge.

The path he took led them through the deepest part of the forest, where the track disappeared in places and in others led them to bogs, or bramble patches or streams too treacherous to ford. Merlin, however, knew the land and found a route despite its tricks. All the same, dawn was breaking by the time the castle came into view. It stood on a rise overlooking the surrounding land, the round, pointed towers and crenelated walls gleaming in the rosy light. He heard Clary's indrawn breath and saw delight wash the fatigue from her face.

"It looks like something from a storybook. Which tower is yours?"

Her words struck dagger-sharp. "It's not here anymore. It hasn't been since Arthur banished me after the war." Arthur's wrath had been worse than any punishment, but Merlin had deserved it after what he had done to the fae.

She stared in disbelief. "But you're not banished anymore."

"It is true that I am welcome at Arthur's court again," Merlin agreed. "It seems the forest still has reservations." He spurred his horse forward, putting an end to the discussion.

They passed over the drawbridge and between the towers that guarded the entrance, the hooves of their mounts ringing off the walls. The sound crawled over Merlin's skin as if an invisible pen were writing out his sins in a tattoo. It was too quiet here, just like in Uther's castle of death.

They found the stables and tended the horses before anything else. Caring for one's mount was the first lesson any warrior learned, and they'd ridden the poor beasts hard. Besides, if magic failed they were the only means of escape. He had to be sure they were there for Clary.

She got as far as removing her animal's saddle before she sank onto an old three-legged stool and leaned against the side of the stall, her face white with fatigue. She watched Merlin work, her eyes slightly glazed. "I should be helping you," she said, voice thick with guilt.

Merlin had been watching her fade, and smiled at her words. "Rest and don't worry about it. I'll look after both horses."

She lifted her head, blinking owlishly. "You need to be doing stuff. Magical stuff. I should be doing this."

Clary was tired to the point of being useless, but she wouldn't thank him for pointing that out. "Physical work is good for thinking."

That much was true, and he liked the warmth and smell and gentle sounds the horses made. Merlin was reluctant to end the peaceful interlude, knowing it would be the last. Finally, though, he retrieved the egg from the saddlebags. "Let's go inside." He put an arm around Clary and led her toward the keep.

"To a nice, soft bed?"

He nodded. That was where she was going—to Guinevere's old chamber. It was hung with green silk and the bed was piled high with down pillows. Plus, Arthur had built his queen a bathing chamber lined with a mosaic of tiny marble tiles. Clary could sleep there safely and in as much luxury as the forest could provide. They entered the door of the keep, and Clary halted for a moment to stare openmouthed. The grand entrance was hung with colorful banners. Weapons and shields hung on the walls, evoking all the pomp and grandeur of Arthur's court. To one side was a sweeping stone staircase, the banister carved in the likeness of a sinuous dragon with its head as the newel post. He observed her wonderment with a twinge of pride. The old place hadn't lost its sparkle.

He helped her up the stairs to the chamber he sought.

"Rest," he said, giving her a gentle kiss as he sat her down on the bed.

Clary looked up at him, cracking an enormous yawn. "I can't just sleep. What's happening with Arthur? What's that army doing? Don't you have a big spell to prepare?"

All that was true, but she'd pushed herself to the point of exhaustion. He kissed her again, this time on the forehead. "A warrior sleeps while she can, because she doesn't know when the next opportunity will be."

"And what are you going to do?" she asked, stifling another yawn she obviously resented.

"Nothing much. I'll be back in a few minutes."

It was a lie, but she was already settling back onto the bed, too exhausted to notice. He left the room before she could argue, carrying the egg back to the main floor, and then down another staircase into the bowels of the earth. Few people knew that Camelot had a dungeon, much less how to reach it, but Merlin did. He'd put it there, after all.

This was where the battle would be won or lost, and he had a great deal of work to do before everything came to an end.

Chapter 25

Clary woke with a start, unaware that she had even fallen asleep. She pushed off a thick blanket that had been spread over her. She didn't remember it from when she'd first entered the room, so she guessed Merlin had checked on her at some point. The thought brought heat to her cheeks. For months all he'd done was scold or challenge her, or teach her in that strangely terse but patient way he had. Tenderness still wasn't something she was used to from him. As she sat up, she realized he'd also pulled off her shoes. The sight of them lined up neatly beside the bed made her stomach do an odd flip. They'd stripped when they'd made love, but caring for her as she slept seemed twice as intimate.

Light streamed through the open shutters of the window, telling her that the day was far advanced. There was a bathing room adjacent to the bedchamber with a round wooden tub that was filled with water scented with rose petals. A minor spell heated it enough that Clary was able to wash thoroughly and dry herself with the soft linen towels folded beside the tub. A change of clothes was laid out on a nearby trunk. Merlin again? Clary guessed the hip-length tunic and loose pants were made for a page or squire. They were far from flattering, but they sort of fit and they were clean.

She pulled on her shoes and went back downstairs, looking for Merlin and breakfast. She would have called his name, but the formality of Camelot's castle, with its intricate sconces and miles of embroidered tapestries, awed her. For all that she loved Medievaland, she was a hamburger and binge-TV kind of girl. Besides, she had no guarantee what might show up if she began shouting at the top of her lungs.

She wandered outside the huge front doors, vaguely remembering from history class that castle kitchens were in a separate building so that they couldn't burn everything down. She began a circuit of the yard, pausing to say hello to the horses and finding a smithy and a carpenter's workspace before finally locating the kitchen.

It was there she found Merlin sitting at a large trestle table and frowning into a cup of smelly herbal tea. The familiarity of the image struck her. The wood, brick and sparse furnishings were a lot like his apartment. His decorating choices, not to mention his fondness for weird beverages, weren't fashion forward, as she'd assumed. They were what he was used to.

When she sat on the bench across from him, he pushed a platter of cheese, fruit and nuts her way. "Sorry it's a bit primitive, but this is what was in the kitchen stores," he said. "Breakfast cereal hasn't been invented yet."

She fell on the food while Merlin poured her a cup of the tea, which turned out to taste better than she expected. In fact, everything did. It might have been a function of her hunger, but she didn't think so. This was food as it was meant to be, pure, raw and grown as nature intended. She had to force herself to chew slowly before she inhaled it and gave herself a stomachache.

Merlin watched her with something like amusement in his amber eyes. "I trust you slept well?"

"Like a rock," she said around a bite of the soft, creamy, white cheese. "What about you?"

He looked into his tea. "I caught a nap. I had things to do."

It must have been a short nap, judging by the circles

under his eyes. Grim lines framed his mouth. She reached out and put a hand to his cheek, feeling the brush of his stubble. "Talk to me." It was a demand, not a plea.

His glance was sharp, but she saw his defensiveness wane and she caught his gaze and held it. "I sent a message to Arthur, telling him where we were and what we'd seen," he said. "I expect he'll join us here. This castle is defensible."

"Won't we be sitting ducks? LaFaye will know exactly where we are."

Merlin's smile was sharp. "There are some advantages to that."

Like gathering all the fae in one place so that they could cure them. That led to another question. "Where's the egg?"

"I put it in a safe place and, to borrow your slang, warded the hell out of it."

"Do you know how we're going to use it when the time comes?"

"I have some ideas." He'd put a hand over hers where it touched his face. He pressed his lips into her palm, sending tingles up her arm and into her core. When he looked up, his eyes were hot with an emotion she couldn't quite read. "I don't know what will happen in the next twenty-four hours, but parts of it will be ugly."

Her breath stopped for a moment, but she deliberately calmed herself. "I know."

She felt Vivian stir. The demoness had been unusually quiet that morning, but now her presence reminded Clary of just how much she was hiding from Merlin. She had no illusions that they'd make it through an entire battle without Vivian showing up.

If you are going to destroy LaFaye and her demon allies, Vivian said in something close to a growl, *you will indeed need my help. I have knowledge only a demon can provide. Together we shall crush them to ash.*

Which was great for Camelot, but would probably kill her. Even if it didn't, there was the whole demon-ex-girlfriend-in-my-brain issue. Clary's relationship with Merlin would be toast.

Merlin was studying her expression. Whatever he saw there did nothing to lighten his mood.

"Come." He held out a hand. "There's something I want to show you while we have a little time."

"How much time?"

"Enough. The fae are still hours away, and I have prepared everything that I can."

She rose from the table and grasped his fingers. His skin was warm from the earthenware cup he'd been holding, and the sun caressed her shoulders as they stepped back into the courtyard.

All the same, his words sent a chill through her. Whatever was going to happen was not far off now. The happiness they had in that moment, in the sun and quiet of Camelot, was measured in scant hours.

She moved close to him, wanting to lean into him like an affectionate cat. On a primitive level, she recognized his physical strength and skill as a warrior. He was also the greatest enchanter in the mortal realms. It was natural that she would turn to him for protection, but there was more to her need than that. He understood her. He saw Clary Greene for herself.

The whole time she'd been his student, from the first lesson to their adventures in the demon's castle, he'd watched over her but never stifled her. He'd let her take her share of danger and learn from her mistakes. No one had ever shown that much confidence in her. No one had cared enough to give her that much space while still catching her every time she fell. For that reason, she was as prepared as she could be for whatever job she'd be asked to do in this war.

He was ever thus, Vivian said, startling Clary. *Some lovers try to grant one's every wish. He will teach you to grant your own wishes. Sadly, fools mistake that for lack of passion. They don't see the genuine care in his actions.*

For a demon, thought Clary, that was deep insight.

I've learned much from you, said Vivian. *One cannot be a teacher without having the curiosity of a student.*

Clary couldn't help wondering what on earth her demon visitor was finding in the chaos of her brain.

That mortal relationships are as complicated as a painting. So many colors. So many layers, one atop the other until it is the combined effect that we see. A demon's existence is far simpler in that regard, but I am grateful to understand another point of view.

With that, Clary sensed Vivian fading into the background once more, no doubt to dig up some new and juicy contradictions from her subconscious. Or plot some suicidal revenge fantasy against her demon buddies. Yup, there was nothing but good times ahead.

Merlin led her to a garden behind the keep, set out in neat squares like a checkerboard. Clary recognized many of the herbs from her studies. Some were for cooking, some for dyeing cloth and others for medicine. The combination of scents made an intoxicating aroma in the warm sun. Bees swarmed the plants, the low buzzing an instant invitation to a nap. Merlin drew her to an arbor festooned in a red and white climbing rose. Clary paused to sniff the striped petals.

"This variety of rose has disappeared from modern gardens," said Merlin, touching a cluster of blossoms with something like affection. "But that's not what I brought you here to see. Go through the archway."

Clary did, and stepped from day to night. She spun

around, looking up into a sky crowded with stars. Beneath her feet was an endless stretch of pale sand. "What is this?"

"It's from your book," he said with a lopsided smile. "An oasis in the wide desert, alone with the midnight stars."

She spun around to see the same unlikely purple tent as on the cover of her favorite romance. Gold fringe festooned the sides, and lamps of pierced metalwork hung from poles staked in the sand. The lamps threw elaborate patterns of light on the sides of the purple silk, tiny cousins to the stars above. A slight distance away, she saw the lumpy silhouette of a sleeping camel. Beyond the tent was a dark pool surrounded by palms that waved languidly in the breeze.

"Awesome," she whispered, unable to find her voice.

He came up behind her and his hands slid around her waist. "It is a fantasy, nothing more."

But it was *her* fantasy, her favorite one, and he'd remembered it. She closed her eyes and leaned back against his chest where the steady beat of his heart reassured her. "I always came here in my mind when I needed to escape. You made it real."

She understood why he'd done it. With demons and fae and war, anything could happen. They might never have another chance to be together. This might be farewell.

"Come inside the tent," he said, distracting Clary from her dark thoughts.

The tent flaps were already drawn up, showing a spacious interior. A scatter of Oriental carpets covered the floor, creating a thick, springy surface. An ornate couch— or bed, she couldn't tell which—occupied one end of the space. The other held a table covered in golden dishes. Clary looked closer, lifting a cover to release a cloud of spiced steam. Clary identified saffron rice, almonds and a medley of pears, squash and roast lamb in a peppery sauce.

"There are figs in honey," Merlin pointed out, "spiced wine, and shaved ice with quince and lemon."

Clary knew without asking that these were his weaknesses. A pang of uncertainty assailed her until she saw yogurt pretzels, pumpkin pie and a golden platter laden with neat rows of seafood tacos. Her weaknesses.

"You know what I like." She shouldn't have felt so astonished, but she was. "You know what we both like."

"There is fantasy enough for us all," he said softly and turned her in his arms. She slid against him, her body fitting perfectly in his embrace. "There is enough to please every part of you, which is what I want to do right now."

Merlin was seducing her. He'd built an entire world to do it. Clary tried to swallow, but her tongue was thick and unruly. "You don't need fantasy," she said. "You had me the moment you remembered the oasis. That was the real you, not any daydream."

He gave a slight shrug. "If you've got the magic…"

She kissed him then, taking his mouth with all the frank hunger that rose in her like a drug. He tasted of tea and of himself. She gripped his shoulders, rising on her toes to balance as she drank him in. When the kiss finally broke, she drew a deep breath. "You built this place for my dreams. Where are yours? What do you want?"

Merlin hesitated. "I want you to be happy." Every last, delicious inch of her.

The scene he'd created was born of the same skills the demons used to create their pockets of comfort in the wastelands of the Abyss. Once in a rare while, he appreciated the beauty their power could weave. Was it possible that their legacy was capable of good or ill, and the outcome dependent on the one who wielded it? Some people said that of guns. Others said guns were a temptation to do wrong.

Merlin wanted to believe he could make things come out right. He knew better than to think one woman's love could change him—he had to do the work himself—but she could make the journey so much better.

He slid his hands beneath the neckline of her tunic, finding the wing of her collarbone. He bent and kissed it, smooth skin scented by the rose petals in her bath. He groaned, kissing his way to the cool flesh of her shoulder. Clary was a delicacy more delicious than any food and more intoxicating than the rarest wine. "You're everything I need."

She pouted, and it was adorable. "Still, you must have more vices than naiad ice cream and spicy rice."

"My favorite flavor is Clary." He cupped her face in his hands. "We fight well side by side. Do you know how long it's been since I could say that?"

Her brow furrowed. "I don't think that's in any magazine quiz about finding the ideal life partner."

"I'm not ideal. I'm not even particularly good. If you knew me, I doubt you'd remain in the same room."

"That's not true," Clary said in a low voice.

But it was.

He finally found out the truth after living with Vivian for years. They had shared a long day of labor, conjuring a spell that strengthened the borders of demon territory against encroachment by trolls. Demons regarded the monstrous creatures the way gardeners viewed slugs—a nuisance, but one possible to contain.

That night Merlin lay on the furs at Vivian's feet, drowsing as she read to him from a tome of history. Books were how they spent their hours, reading or being read to, for not even Vivian ever stopped studying magic. As subjects went, it had a learning curve that stretched to infinity.

"This passage was written by Agoricus the Great," she said.

Merlin knew the name of that demon. It had taken all

the druids of his island homeland to destroy him. "Do I want to hear what he has to say?"

Drunk with relaxation, Merlin rolled to his back, staring up at Vivian's beautiful, feline figure. The firelight played with her form, kissing the curves and shadows of her face. Her violet eyes were intent, regarding him with speculation.

"You should. He was the mightiest of the demon princes of his time, and it is significant that he was slain by your mother and her friends."

"He was an arrogant fool?"

Vivian's smile had teeth. "Didn't you ever wonder why I took an interest in you?"

Something in her tone was different, and cold foreboding made Merlin sit up. "Tell me."

"Didn't you ever wonder why demon magic came to you far more easily than any other kind?"

But now Merlin was mute with apprehension. By this time, he had seen what Tenebrius had done in the Hebrides, and a thousand other cruelties. The only thing that kept him with the demons was the gratitude he felt for Vivian.

"Agoricus the Great was your father," Vivian said almost smugly.

"What?" He was on his feet.

"Your mother conjured the strongest warrior to sire her babe. She neglected to specify what species." Vivian shrugged. "When I learned that you existed, I wanted you for myself. Half-demon, half-druid witch. What a fascinating specimen you would be."

She leaned forward, caressing him with her gaze. "What a weapon to hide among the mortals."

Revulsion hit him, and not just because Vivian had withheld that truth. He was half a demon. His mother had slain his father in order to protect her tribes from the demon's devastation. Worse, Merlin had sworn to protect his people and yet here he was, fawning at the feet of his demon mistress. He disgusted himself.

He grabbed the book from Vivian and flung it into the fire, letting his father's words burn to ash. "How did you know?" he roared.

Vivian raised a single brow. "Agoricus bragged of bedding the great druidess, Brida, and of siring a son. He knew you would be a power in the world. When he fell at your mother's hands, I searched for you and coaxed your steps my way. When you arrived in that olive grove, you all but knocked on my front door."

Merlin sank to the floor, his head in his hands. Where did he belong? He was too much a mortal for the demons, seeing their cruelties for what they were. But if the humans discovered his father's name, they would do their best to kill him on sight.

He hated Vivian for plucking him from his penniless ignorance.

He hated himself for being her tool.

He hated himself for being stuck between worlds.

He had returned to the human kingdoms that night, and did not return again until he came back to steal her accursed spell. If Vivian had done her best to turn Merlin into a weapon to use against mortals, he would thwart her and be a weapon *for* the mortals. He'd banished her kind to the Abyss, freeing the world from demon evil.

And he'd broken Camelot, and the fae, the witches and, yes, the demons doing it. If he'd needed proof of his father's blood in his veins, it went far beyond his unusual amber eyes. He'd inherited a demonic talent for destruction.

Merlin deserved whatever doom befell him.

Chapter 26

Clary ran a hand over Merlin's forehead. Her touch was warm and firm as it smoothed his brow. "A penny for your thoughts. You disappeared somewhere inside your head for a moment."

"I wouldn't waste the money," he said, turning his face into her palm as she stroked his cheek. "They weren't good thoughts."

Clary smiled, but it was tinged with determination as if she flatly refused to be anything but delighted. In many ways she was an innocent who deserved all his protection. In others, she was every bit a fighter as the rest of Arthur's court. The contrast fascinated him.

"If they're bad thoughts," she said softly, "I'd like to hear them so I can chase them away."

He cupped her face with his hands. "If I asked you to return to Medievaland, would you go?"

"No," she said simply. "I came to fight. I have magic, too, you know."

"I know. I taught you."

"And you're a good teacher."

"I can take everything but watching you get hurt."

"Right back at you. But you're not leaving, so I'm not, either."

And they kissed, mouths teasing in tentative nips. He bit the tender flesh inside her lips, bidding her to open to him. Once their tongues tangled, he lost himself in the taste of her. It was the sweetest, most sensual reprieve from the darkness eating at his heart. Clary was the anti-dote to everything he was.

In one swift move, she pulled off her tunic, dropping it at their feet. He traced the edge of her bra with his tongue, exploring the rough lace and smooth skin beneath it. Tension built between them, rising until they could take no more.

It was impossible to say who moved first, but suddenly they were fumbling with their clothes, trying to undress without ending their embraces. He lifted her in his arms, her bare legs wrapping around his hips. The skin-to-skin contact, hot and frantic, almost broke his control. He carried her to the bed, but she stayed where she was, clinging to him, her lips locked with his.

Her bra was gone. Merlin's tongue found her nipple and began a teasing assault. A shiver rocked through her and she tilted her head back, inviting him to take more of her. He did, laving her in long, teasing strokes and rolling the tips of her breasts until they were flushed and erect. She writhed beneath him as he suckled one breast and then the other, blowing on her wet nipples until she shuddered with need.

Finally, she released her grip, sliding down his body with her own. The promise of her lithe, soft flesh ripped a moan from his throat. Her fingers were clumsy with haste as she unbuttoned his jeans and when she sank to her knees, his pulse pounded like war drums. She touched him, first with her palms, stroking his fullness until it throbbed with need. He buried his hands in the wild mop of her hair, the silk of it between his fingers a sensual delight.

His breath hitched as she stroked him and took a long, slow lick. If he knew her preferences, she knew his. In the spirit of wickedness, she nibbled at all the points that would unravel his self-control. He shifted uneasily as her teeth grazed him.

"Please," he moaned.

"Please stop?" she teased, giving another lick. "Or please keep on with what I'm doing?"

"More."

She gave him more, until he hovered on the edge of explosion.

"Enough." He pulled her up, all but tossing her to the silken covers of the bed. "Now I please you."

The thundering of his pulse countered the ragged syncopation of their breath as they tried to kiss and move and bite all at once. He kneaded her breasts, drawing a sigh from her lips as she arched into him like a cat begging for attention. He drew a nipple into his mouth, letting his teeth graze the point as he sucked it to a stiff peak. She writhed beneath him as he attended to the other, bucking against him in her quest for relief. He slid his fingers between her thighs, testing her readiness. She was hot and slick with need.

And yet, he went slowly, drawing it out with kisses that began at the clean angle of her jaw and worked slowly between her breasts. The scent of their desire made his head swim with lust. He wasn't just loving her, but claiming her for that moment in time, and he did it thoroughly. He devoured the sweet and salt of her skin, the softness of her thighs and the delicate architecture of her bones. He found the hidden points of pleasure and brought her gasping with surprise. He wasn't a wizard for nothing.

When he finally entered her, they were both ready for the intimacy, making it a slow communion of body and soul. They had made love before, but this time he gave more of himself to it, pleasuring her but also sharing everything that pleased him. Clary took the lesson to heart. Soon it was impossible to hold back, and his body took over. Clary gave a lusty, hiccuping cry and dissolved with pleasure, digging her nails deep into Merlin's flesh as he drove hard to the finish and filled her with heat and warmth.

She spasmed her release around him, squeezing tight in wave after wave. Then his mind broke apart, and there was nothing but delicious female flesh and the need to possess it. He dissolved in the ecstasy of her and cried out, a sobbing, triumphant shout.

He relaxed into the mattress, letting the silken softness cradle him as he held Clary in his arms. She buried her face against his chest, her breath like a featherlight kiss. She seemed so small, the fire in her quiescent with satisfaction. He ran a hand down her back, tracing the slope of waist and hip. She was perfection.

Merlin's thoughts rested there, refusing to acknowledge the darkness gathering around them. He'd created this moment for them both, one taste of bliss before the storm began. He refused to look ahead into the gale. It would do no good to break their hearts now, when they needed all the courage they could get.

She propped herself on one elbow, her gaze soft with their lovemaking. "Thank you. I never suspected you had such a romantic side."

Merlin wasn't sure he'd call that lost corner of his heart romantic, but it was intensely private. At least, it had been until now, when he'd shared it with her. He stroked Clary's cheekbone with his thumb. "I wanted to show you a side of me no one else ever sees. I want you to know how much you matter."

He said nothing more, because there was nothing more to say. Tears stood in her eyes, though a faint smile hovered on her lips.

Remember me this way, he thought. When he kissed her again, there was pain in his heart, for they would not get through this war without baring all their truths. He wasn't ready to face what she would see in him.

* * *

The Queen of Faery felt regal once more. She was bathed, her hair dressed by expert maids, her midnight blue riding habit was trimmed with sapphires and her mount was a black mare of the finest bloodlines. Best of all, she was freed of that blasted tower—literally blasted free—and able to roam where she willed. And best of all, she had flunkies to do her bidding. She had let it be known that her royal will was to expunge Merlin and his puppet prince, King Arthur of Camelot, from existence once and for all. Merlin first, then Arthur and then all the rest.

Her spirit would feel infinitely lighter with their corpses lined up for her inspection. She would walk from one to the other, admiring each in turn and knowing she had established the ultimate power over each one. Hers to hold, and hers to destroy. It would be like Christmas or an especially satisfying day of shopping. They would never threaten her happiness again.

It would not be without risk. Arthur possessed the sword Excalibur. She feared that enchanted weapon, for it was the one blade that could cut through her enchantments and end her life. For years, that had stalled her plans out of pure cowardice, but no more. If she'd learned nothing else from captivity, it was that being careful had gained her nothing. No more caution.

The endgame was well in motion now. She rode through the Forest Sauvage at the head of an army, the tall, silent trees standing sentry on either side of the road. They'd had archers poised to kill any of Arthur's spies, whether on foot or in flight, but she'd called them off now. It didn't matter what Arthur knew, because nothing could help him anymore. She spoke little, too agitated for ordinary conversation. Besides, the only words that mattered had been the order to march on Camelot, for that was where Arthur was sure to flee. By the time the sun set, his crown, his sword and his life would be hers.

And better yet, she'd have Merlin and his witchling. Why he had taken on a student after so many centuries, she'd never know. She supposed it didn't matter, because what could a beginner do in the face of the Queen of Faery's superior power? Morgan mentally pictured them roasting on a spit. After today, neither would have the chance to interfere again.

Tenebrius appeared at her left stirrup. The demon had joined them some miles back, but went on foot. It was doubtful any sane horse would carry such a creature. Morgan looked down, enjoying the sensation of rising above him.

"Do you have a plan for battle?" he asked.

"Of course." She flicked a fallen leaf from the skirts of her new riding habit. "I have discussed it at length with my generals."

There, that put him in his place. This was need to know, and he wasn't in the inner circle. Why would a demon expect more?

He bowed with a humility that had to be fake. "How would you like me to contribute my magic, my queen?"

She recalled the disastrous outcome of the computer attack. Filthy demon magic that had crippled her own. Resentment colored her tone. "Keep your spells to yourself until I give the order."

He laughed. The sound brought heat to her cheeks. "What is so amusing?"

"Nothing. Your advice is wise. It is difficult for any but the most accomplished practitioners to use demon power if they are not born to it. Some never do."

She raised her chin. "Few wish to. It is unclean. Besides, I am not using it, you are. We will each stick to our own spells."

He snorted, his yellow eyes narrowing to slits. "Have you seen Gorm, by the way?"

Alarm skated through her, though she did her best to hide it. "He is not my employee or my pet. I do not concern myself with his whereabouts unless he is summoned."

She spurred her mare forward, leaving the demon behind. In a dozen yards the forest road ended and a view of Camelot's castle opened up. Morgan reined in to stop and stare. The pale towers seem to float above rolling green hills, a prize that until this moment had been untouchable. "No more." The words were barely a breath, but they carried all her intention like a spell.

The moment was spoiled as Tenebrius came up to her once more. Morgan inwardly cursed at the demon for breaking into her daydream, but said nothing.

He fixed her with his strange yellow gaze. "You know that even I, who am stronger than any other of my kind, can only remain outside the Abyss for a limited period of time."

"You are confessing this weakness for what purpose?" she asked tartly.

"Now that you are free, what of my freedom? That was our bargain. We both get out of jail."

"I will attend to that when Camelot is mine." She was asking more than their original bargain, but what was he going to do?

He stood motionless, as if holding in a string of curses. "Would you like me to watch the skies as I did when your prison fell?"

She nodded. "Be on guard for a dragon of Merlin's acquaintance."

"A dragon. That's all?" His sarcasm was plain. "And what will you be doing while I tackle that detail?"

"There is but one thing left to do before the fall of Merlin Ambrosius and Arthur Pendragon begins." She turned to her sea of exquisite, heartless fae. A greedy glee assailed her at the sight. They were hers. *Hers.* She commanded them, and they would smash Camelot's court to pulp and hand her the glittering crown.

"I need a volunteer," she said to her shining host. "Who here would like to fetch my secret weapon against the king?"

Chapter 27

"It's time."

Clary heard Merlin's words. For a long moment she pretended to be deaf, but the inevitability of the moment dragged her to her feet and made her dress. They did not speak as he did the same. She dawdled, stretching out even these few minutes, and was still holding her shoes when they turned to face each other. He touched her cheek with the back of his fingers.

"Listen to me carefully," he said. "I'm going to need your help. Arthur is going to bring his men to Camelot and will need to get in the front gate. I don't know if he'll reach here before the fae. You need to help him get through the gate safely. Find a good vantage point and offer covering fire like we did at the tower."

It sounded simple enough, but she was paralyzed as she understood what he was actually saying. "You won't be with me?"

He shook his head. "I have to launch the spell that will cure the fae."

Her pulse kicked into a gallop. "Without me?"

"I have to work alone."

That meant they wouldn't be there for each other— but then, this was war. Things were getting real, and she couldn't rely on him for everything. "I'm afraid. I'll be all right, but I'm scared."

He kissed her brow. "You can do this, Clary. You're ready. This is everything you've trained for."

It is, said Vivian, surfacing from wherever she had gone. *This is the moment we fight.*

Tears burned the backs of her eyes as the razor's edge of panic cut through her. This was goodbye. "Be careful."

"I will," he said.

Even if they both survived, Vivian was inside her, itching to fight. Even if everything went perfectly, nothing was going to be the same. If she let Vivian fight—and why wouldn't she unleash a weapon like the demoness to save Camelot?—she would be obviously possessed, a hated demon. The alternative was to hide the truth, and that only served herself.

You do not hide from a just fight. Neither of us do. It is not in our nature.

That was the truth. Clary squeezed her eyes shut as Merlin kissed her lips one last time. Tears leaked from her lashes and she swiped them away before he could.

"Save the world, okay?" she said in a choked voice.

Clary ran, bursting from the tent and across the starlit sand. The camel gave a surprised snort, but the only other sound was the wind in the palm trees of the oasis. She stopped to pull on her shoes, not caring that she had sand on her feet. She looked back over her shoulder, but Merlin hadn't followed. She was glad and heartbroken at once.

The warm wind touched her cheek. She knew deserts were cold at night, but she'd always dreamed this one would be warm, suitable for gauzy harem wear and dancing naked under the moon. A pleasant, harmless untruth, like the rest of this desert scene. Merlin had made it just so that they could enjoy a moment of perfect joy.

She'd never be able to read that book again without thinking of this oasis. She couldn't help resenting that a little. Before today her daydreams had been easy, demanding nothing from her. Now Merlin had tangled her heart in them. But if he'd complicated Clary's hopes, he'd also given her tools. She wasn't the incompetent witch she'd been when she'd arrived at his doorstep.

"And I have a demon," she muttered. "I will not be afraid to use it."

Vivian sprang to life. *I thought you'd never ask.*

Clary finished knotting her shoelace and rose, trepidation seeping in. "Tell me."

The Queen of Faery ordered my death. I want her head on a spike. I have a plan.

Clary's brain froze at the audacity of the words. "Excalibur is the only thing that can cut through her magic. Not even the Lady of the Lake could beat her."

But I'm something she's never faced before.

The delighted anticipation in Vivian's voice sent chills down Clary's spine, but then her mind snagged on an important point. "What do you mean LaFaye ordered your death?"

I have been examining my state. Tenebrius told the truth when he said that I would die in your realm. Merlin assumed my trapped condition meant hibernation, but all connections to the source of my energy have been completely severed. I have limited time left.

There was fear in Vivian's voice, but also bloodthirsty exhilaration as if she was betting her last chips in a high-stakes game. Clary understood. Vivian had been mortally wounded, but she would go out in her own way and hold nothing back in one last, glorious fight.

Help me, Vivian said. *Help me with my revenge and you will be free of me and a clean, pure witch once more.*

"But you're dying!"

I will fight for the new life the queen carries, and for you and Merlin and your dreams. I will paint one of the many layers of your love before I am no more. I will be a chapter in your romance of camels and desert stars.

Clary's mind reeled. What would it be like to be mortally ill and alone, cut off from everything familiar, even your own body?

I will die fighting, as I must. Besides, I'm stuck with you. I couldn't be alone if I tried.

Clary swallowed back her tears, knowing Vivian wouldn't want them. "We'll fight together, then."

Clary would fight for a new Camelot, and Gwen and her baby, and the wedding Tamsin and Gawain would have if they ever stopped dithering about cake and decorations. Everyone Clary loved was on the line, and hadn't she trained with Merlin just so that she could fight when the time came? They always knew the fae would come. As Merlin said, it was time.

"Merlin should know what you face."

He will know when I choose to tell him. Now go back to Camelot.

Clary's hands were shaking, but she obediently crossed the sand and used her own magic to shove the portal door open, leaving her fantasy behind. She blinked as reality swam into view. It was still bright in the garden, though the sky had hazed over with a thin layer of cloud. As the portal closed behind her and vanished, Clary had the sense that only an hour or so had passed. And yet something had changed. The garden continued to release its heady aura of lavender and thyme, but the bees were gone. The birdsong, including the incessant cooing from the dovecote, had stopped. It was as if everything that could hide had fled to a safe retreat. "This isn't good."

LaFaye has moved the first piece on the board. Find out what that is.

Clary sprinted to the keep, mounting the winding stairs as fast as her feet would carry her until she reached the highest chamber. She was breathing hard as she took stock of her new surroundings. The room was empty except for some trunks, but it had windows on all four sides. She ran to each one in turn, seeing mostly sweeps of wood and meadow, but the west-facing view told her what she needed to know. There were fae as far as the eye could see and nothing between them and the castle.

They'd arrived much sooner than expected. Merlin had underestimated LaFaye's battle plans.

Merlin finished dressing himself, his movements so brisk they were jerky. It had taken all his resolve not to imprison Clary in some far distant realm where he knew she'd be protected from battle—but that was a coward's way to ease his heart. Trust was the greatest tool he could give her, and Clary had earned the right to do her part. He believed in her too much to put her in a cage, even to spare himself pain.

He left the desert, releasing the magic that had formed it the moment he had safely returned to the castle garden. He would have kept the oasis for Clary's future use, but he needed all his strength for the coming fight. She was nowhere in sight, which was a relief. The aching lump in his chest was a warning that his resolve wouldn't have survived another parting.

It was the same reason he hadn't told her that he loved her. If anything went wrong, an admission like that would have been a millstone around both their necks. He'd loved before, certainly. He had a heart and the world was filled with lovable people. But he hadn't loved like *this*, with a woman he wanted to be with forever. Ironic, given what they would face that day. Or perhaps it was fate's gift to him, a glimpse of who he might have been. There might have been a Merlin who was a good and loving man, content to at last find safe harbor and home.

His vision blurred, but he blinked his eyes clear. Nothing good came of being with him. His parents had created a monster capable of ripping the souls from an entire race.

His only possible redemption was to become the man who healed the world, regardless of the cost. He would use the cursed power he'd been born with for good. Then, only then, would he deserve mercy.

Merlin started for the dungeon, his long strides carrying him across the courtyard as they'd done so often before in better times. Back then he had the love of a king and every opportunity to indulge his curiosity. A word would send servants scurrying to bring him rare ingredients. There would always be an audience to gasp and clap at whatever magical wonder he desired to show off. He'd been an insufferable idiot who never realized how blessed he was until it all fell away.

He entered the keep and unlocked the secret door, passing through the layers of wards he had set last night. The stairs were narrow and dark even with the aid of the light he summoned. The dungeon was not a large space, but it had a table and a brazier and a tall pedestal that held the egg inside a cage of deadly magic. That was all he needed for now.

Merlin had broken the world, and now it was time to fix it. There was a very good chance the spell would kill him. The downside of giving Clary her fantasy of perfect happiness was that now it meant something to him, too.

He clenched his jaw against the agony of loss that splintered his heart.

Clary had found her way to the tower roof so she could see even better. More fae had arrived, circling the castle in a noose of steel. There had been losses at the white tower, but the troops she'd seen on the road last night had doubled the size of LaFaye's forces. More were coming from the forest and falling into place behind the others, rank after rank arriving as she watched. She had no idea how many

fae there actually were in their homeland, but she had a
sense every good fighter available was present.

And she could see another one of those freaking cata-
pults in the distance. The wheels of the trebuchet turned
slowly, bumping over the rolling grass while two long lines
of soldiers pulled on ropes as thick as their arms. Common
sense said that Clary would have to leave the tower once
it began its work, but she had some time yet. The army
was still gathering.

"Where is Arthur's army?" she wondered.

He is not far, but he hides himself.

Clary wondered how Vivian knew, but this wasn't the
time for idle questions. Instead, she continued to search the
enemies' lines and finally spotted LaFaye herself. Instinc-
tively, Clary ducked behind one of the huge merlons, the
square teeth of stone that made up the crenelations along
the tower's edge. A wild terror surged through her as if
she were a rabbit and the queen a hungry hawk.

Fear is smart, said Vivian in a voice that came close to
a purr. *Every good predator is careful and crafty.*

Clary's stomach rolled over, panic threatening her breakfast. But she peered around the slab of stone, taking a second look. She used a farseeing spell that Merlin had taught
her to bring the queen's face into focus. She looked the
same as when she had bulged out of the laptop—beautiful
except for her contemptuous expression. She rode a black
mare and her dark blue gown was spangled with gems. She
carried no weapons that Clary could see, but who needed
a sword when you were Morgan LaFaye?

Clary shivered when the first goblin arrows flew, their
song filling the sky with a deadly hum. As Vivian had said,
Arthur's forces were hidden and the fae wheeled around
in confusion, bringing their shields up a moment too late.
Dozens fell to the deadly shafts, even in the small slice of
the army Clary could see.

Yes! Vivian exclaimed.

Clary scanned the woods, finding no sign of the bowmen. Down below, LaFaye was doing the same, twisting in her saddle. She flung out a hand, and Clary sensed her power rippling outward. It peeled back the concealing magic that hid Camelot's troops.

Clary just had time to glimpse the goblins shooting from the trees when the knights charged. They came up the rise to her right like a silver spear of armor and horse, driving deep into the flank of the fae. It was all Arthur could do, she realized. The fae army was between the king and his castle. It belatedly occurred to her that she might have wanted to pull up the drawbridge, but that would cut off both friend and foe.

Leave it, said Vivian. *There are better ways to help.*

Clary leaned out to get a clear view of the knights, and understood what Vivian meant. They were driving toward the front gate, which would give them some cover, but their momentum had run out. With so many fae, they were mobbed. And yet, she couldn't help but wonder at the skill of Arthur's men. Lancelot lay about him with his battle-ax, hewing down fae with bloody efficiency. Excalibur flashed, and enemies fell as if a scythe had passed through them. It was lovely and terrible and everything she'd dreamed of when she'd read their stories as a girl.

Then a fae's spear struck Arthur's side, and he slumped forward. Clary's fireball struck before she'd so much as formed a thought. The fae went up in flames. And then she became a kind of witchy sniper, giving cover as the other knights circled around their king.

"By all the pointed hats in the coven, I'm doing this," she muttered. She was fighting like a pro.

Fae arrows skittered like claws against the stone of the tower as the enemy returned fire. She ducked, as safe as one could be in a battle, but aware that it would only take one shaft to end her warrior career. Perspiration ran into her eyes.

The goblin army clogged the area before the draw-bridge, preventing the fae from storming in, but there was still a sea of swords between the knights and safety. Progress forward was one step at a time, the battle so thick that Clary could sometimes barely find her friends inside the thickets of steel.

It seemed hopeless, the ranks of goblins thinning as La-Faye ordered attack after attack. The fae queen had not yet unleashed her magic, but Clary guessed she was holding back, saving her strength for a final, fatal blow. Numbers were enough for now.

Likewise, Clary kept Vivian in reserve and used her own smaller power to ease Arthur's way to the gate. Soon he wasn't the only one wounded. Perceval's shield arm drooped, leaving his side dangerously exposed. She covered him as best she could, but there was too much to watch at the same time.

And then a frenzied yell came from the left. A portal blazed to life in an explosion of light, and another army streamed through, some on horseback and others on foot. They were fae, but completely unlike the fae surrounding the queen. These were alight with passion, swords raised and eyes blazing, their long, white hair streaming with the speed of their attack. Clary recognized Angmar and Laren among them. These were the rebel fae, the ones with souls who had escaped from LaFaye.

The cavalry had come, but as the queen turned to face them, even Clary could see at once that the desperate rescue wouldn't last.

Chapter 28

Merlin knew the battle raged outside, but he could not afford distraction. The work he did was too delicate to let his mind wander. He'd cast the ritual circle first, building it strong enough to hold the magic he needed. Within it he scribed shapes, first in chalk and then in his own blood. That would direct the energy out of the dungeon and into the sky above the fae army he knew brawled outside the gates. Energy would be the first step of his ritual. The second and more dangerous stage would be igniting that energy with enough force to disperse it over the fae.

He removed the wards from the egg and placed it in the circle. It seemed so common—like something from an animal's burrow—and yet the power that surged from it crawled over his skin. Now that he'd taken away the wards, he was certain LaFaye could feel it, too, even at a distance. For an instant he remembered her as a skinny girl with serious gray eyes— smart, adventurous and stubborn. She might have been an ally if she'd grown up with a different family around her. But she hadn't, and something essential in her personality had been irreparably broken. After the harm she'd done, there was no turning back for her now. Pity stabbed him when he thought of that girl, but she was no more real now than the Merlin who might have been. They hadn't reached this point by accident. They'd both made choices. Now they would do their best to destroy one another.

He sat cross-legged on the floor and held the egg between his palms. The energy crawled over his hands like tiny claws, streaming between his fingers and over his wrists. It was thrumming as if aware, a slow, inhuman heartbeat that sent surges of power deep into his core. Merlin let his mind go blank, falling into the sensation. Images flickered by, but he didn't attempt to catch them. Riding a pony as a boy, his mother with her hair braided for war, the Mediterranean Sea, and Clary, her laughing eyes green as the first buds of spring.

He had promised himself to let her go. She had trained hard to take her place in this battle, and she had succeeded. Her triumph was his, as well. But he loved her, and that made everything hard. There were a thousand reasons he was here alone—for the fae, for Arthur, for all of Camelot and even for himself—but she was the most important. He had to win and if that demanded the sacrifice of his own life, so be it. It was the only way he could truly protect her.

There was a moment of regret, and the awareness of his own vulnerability. But Merlin Ambrosius didn't matter anymore.

He crushed the egg and let the demonic energy consume him.

The battle shifted as the queen's forces turned to rebuff the attack of the rebel fae. As much as LaFaye hated Merlin, the fae despised their rebel kin more, for they represented all that the fae had lost.

As the fae's attention swung away, Arthur's advance toward the gate picked up speed. Clary's fire knocked off the fae that remained behind to block his path.

In the distance more unexpected aid came as a stream changed course, flooding the path from the woods and turning it into a bog. The trebuchet was quickly mired, and all the fae heaving on the ropes couldn't prevent it from sinking deeper and deeper into the mud. Clary guessed the naiads were responsible, but caught no glimpse of the transparent beings. Then ropes of ivy snaked up the beams of the great machine, pulling it down into the muck. When the fae pulling the trebuchet drew their swords to hack the vines away, they were pulled down, too. It was a small victory, but it raised Clary's hopes.

She returned her attention to the knights. LaFaye had put her troops back in order, and Clary was hard-pressed to clear a path for Arthur's last rush to the gate. LaFaye hurled a spell at the towers guarding the drawbridge, shearing off the top three rows of stone blocks as neatly as if she held a hedge trimmer. The only thing that stopped her was the number of fae struck by falling stone. Clary didn't breathe until the last knight was safely inside and the remaining goblins manned the castle walls, raining arrows down on their attackers. The drawbridge creaked upward, leaving LaFaye's armies on the outside of the moat.

From where she stood, Clary couldn't see the knights once they were inside the castle walls, but she could hear orders shouted for water and bandages and for weapons from the armory. Instinct urged her to go help, but she had another job to do.

LaFaye was clearly up to something. The queen moved forward, a phalanx of guards around her. There was someone with her on a white horse, but Clary couldn't see who it was. The fighting around the queen stopped and the army parted. Those allies who weren't inside the castle had withdrawn for the moment, leaving their dead on the bloody banks of the moat.

"Arthur," called Morgan LaFaye. "Show yourself."

Silence followed, leaden and intense. Clary could hear the wind hum through the chinks in the castle's rock, as if the stone sang softly to itself. At last, a door opened below. Clary peered down to see four goblin archers emerge onto a stone balcony. Then Lancelot and Gawain followed, their shields held high. Finally, Arthur stepped out, moving carefully. His tunic was bloody, but he held his spine straight and his head high, and one hand rested on Excalibur's hilt. With his other hand, he moved Gawain's shield aside. It was clear that Arthur would allow his men to guard him, but he refused to hide.

"There is no victory for you here, Morgan," said Arthur, his voice carrying easily over the field. "It takes more than swords to rule the mortal realms."

"My army is insatiable for human souls. I command with an authority that you can only dream of."

Which was why, Clary knew, LaFaye had used her own sorcery to keep the fae from healing naturally. Merlin's spell had only begun the damage to her subjects. Time had healed the witches, but LaFaye had ensured her people never recovered. It was a hideous abuse of her power.

Arthur was clearly thinking along the same lines. "You command through treachery against your own. Gloating ill becomes you."

Clary's scalp prickled, distracting her from the exchange. She looked over her shoulder, but no one was there. The sensation was power cycling from below. The dungeon. Merlin. The spell that would return souls to the fae.

She had little idea how the spell would work, or how far along it was, but anything involving that much power was highly dangerous. A knot gathered in her gut and twisted hard when she thought of the risk to Merlin. She had intellectually understood that battle could bring death, but this was too real. This was something she couldn't face. She loved him. She loved him!

"How can I help him?" she said to Vivian. "I have to do something!"

Be patient. Everything depends on choosing the right moment.

Clary was about to make a scathing comeback when one

of the queen's guards dragged the white horse forward. All thoughts flew from Clary's head as an outraged cry rose from Camelot's men. Guinevere sat on the white horse, her face rigid with fright. Clary's heart dropped like a stone.

"I know your sorcerer is at work, Arthur," said LaFaye. "I can feel his spell like an itch along my skin."

Clary saw Arthur and his men stiffen. This was news to them. "Let my queen go, Morgan!" the king bellowed.

"And return your precious heir? I think not." Her reply was clipped and businesslike. "Not unless you hand Merlin over at once."

Arthur's fists clenched as he seemed to weave on his feet. Blood dripped from the hem of his tunic, showing his wound was still open.

"What do we do?" Clary demanded. "And don't tell me to be patient!"

Vivian didn't reply. She didn't need to.

A roar of amazement sounded from both armies as energy whooshed into the sky like Roman candles on the Fourth of July. The force of it hurled Clary backward, her nerves tingling as if she'd touched a live wire. She crawled to her hands and knees, teeth chattering. "M-Merlin," she breathed, gazing up in wonder.

Energy sparkled against the cloudy sky, white and gold and pink and blue, each fleck swooping up to crest and flutter down again like the spray of a fountain. It was beautiful, but the magic needed to command such power would tear anyone apart. Not even Merlin could survive it.

Agony yawned open inside her. "I should have told him that I loved him."

Vivian's sympathy was a light and unexpected touch. *He knew.*

A gasp escaped Clary as if she'd taken a wound. The

thought of Merlin, of that time in the garden, was more than she could bear. Hot tears washed down her face.

It is time, said Vivian, but Clary was turned to stone. *Now!*

Clary's attention snapped back to the field, blocking the wall of pain that threatened to unravel her. Gwen sat forgotten, the speed of events saving her from the spotlight, at least for the moment. LaFaye rose in her saddle, pointing toward the multicolored rush of energy. Her lips moved feverishly and a moment later a bolt of green lightning hurtled toward Merlin's spell.

Vivian sprang into action, her power ripping through Clary so fast it felt as if she would turn inside out. Perception scrambled, all sense of size and space dropping away as she fused with the coruscating light. The flow was powerful, but lacked the will and intelligence to defend itself. The green lightning struck, but Vivian batted it away, absorbing the impact with her own strength. The impact sent her spinning around, and she suddenly understood what she needed to do. Tenebrius had done his best to rip her power up by the roots, but she had conserved her magic for just such a moment. She had lain quiet, watching and waiting to pounce.

Merlin held a pillar of light, the stream of energy coursing between his hands and the sky. He jolted as Vivian's consciousness joined the stream. Relief and trepidation arrowed through him, making him drag in a noisy breath. He'd thought her gone, but she was definitely present now, the bright, lush hue of her personality adding its mark to the stream.

"Hello!" he said softly. Maybe he had betrayed her, and maybe she had struck back with her potion. Now, with the future balanced in his hands, those things seemed less important than her brilliant mind and incandescent spirit.

Hello, she replied. *You can't do this alone.*

He felt the juddering impact of the faery queen's attack and the force of Vivian's counterstrike. The gyrating twist the blow caused nearly knocked him from his feet. By the time he caught his balance, he knew what Vivian meant to do. He nearly staggered again.

"No," he said softly. "Let me. I owe you recompense for what I did."

Don't be a fool.

There was kindness in the voice that traveled through the steam of sparkling light, and that was worrying all on its own. Vivian had never been kind. Not in the way humans were.

You arrogant mouse. Did you think I was incapable of learning? Of choosing who I am?

"Why?"

Your Clary is quite a teacher herself. This time there was deep affection in her voice. For him. For Clary.

It humbled him. "I'm sorry. For everything."

I know. That's why you always frustrated me. You could never see how I cared for you.

He was too shocked to find the words to answer.

The plume of energy exploded into a fine mist, hurling Merlin into the stone of the dungeon wall.

Clary screamed and fell, the agony of the explosion seeming to tear holes in her mind. She curled into a ball, cradling her skull as the pain made her retch and twist. Only when the white-hot threads receded from behind her eyes did thought creep back to her. Something very, very bad had happened to Vivian. It felt as if the demoness had been torn away, with only a gaping hole left behind.

Shocked, Clary rolled to look upward at the shower of sparks in the air. *Dispersion*, she thought as the wind caught the colorful energy and floated it across the fae army. It was the second part of Merlin's spell, the dangerous process of showering the energy over the fae. Vivian had taken Clary's math problem and spreadsheets and solved the issue with the subtlety of a sledgehammer. And damaged herself irreparably in the process.

Clary closed her eyes, weeping. She'd wanted the demoness gone with all her soul, but still she felt her loss. What remained had been so drained by the explosion that it felt little more than a memory or a shadow. Vivian had been dying and she'd given everything to strike one decisive blow—one that would turn the fae on their evil queen.

Clary swallowed, praying this meant Merlin was safe, but knowing he'd been holding the energy stream when it had exploded. Sobbing, Clary scrambled to the edge of the tower. The demon essence fell everywhere like a fine snow. The fae stood transfixed, their eyes wide and faces upturned. The Queen of Faery waved her arms and screeched, but whether she was summoning a wind or ordering her troops to flee, Clary couldn't tell. The sparkling magic seemed to float by unaffected as if her power had little effect on what Vivian had done.

As the demoness had said, LaFaye hadn't seen her coming.

All at once, the sky went dark as dusk. She spun to see a dark mass covering the sun. Shading her eyes, she craned her neck to make out a dozen kite-like shapes. She instantly dropped to the stone in terror. Demons, probably something Tenebrius had cooked up. She'd seen the ragged scraps of darkness from a distance during the last battle, but here they were close enough to make out the wicked claws and inky feathers—or perhaps it was tiny paws and bristling fur. The creatures seemed to shift before her eyes, though the jet-black eyes remained fixed on her. They were coming to wreak punishment on someone for that spell, and Clary was visible. They swooped, a stink of dead flesh staggering her senses.

Clary ran for the stairs, but she hadn't gone a dozen steps when they got her. She screamed as five of the things snatched her up, clawing fingers grabbing handfuls of her clothes. She flew upward, hoisted from the rooftop like a bale of hay. Clary squirmed as a toenail stabbed into her back, but went still as the edge of the tower disappeared and the distance to solid ground grew suddenly far. Vertigo swam as wind scoured her face and roared in her ears. She fought the instinct to fight free, trying hard to go limp until the grass swung upward and the creatures let go. She fell to her hands and knees, teeth clacking with sudden impact. With a thundering flap, the creatures were gone, circling around with sudden urgency.

Clary scrambled to her feet. A handful of fae ran toward her, weapons in hand. Demon sparkles still drifted through the air, but with a sinking heart she realized they weren't having any effect. Merlin's spell wasn't working. Why not? Fear hit her like an icy wall.

As the cold-eyed fae crowded around her, a spear tip touched her throat. Then Morgan LaFaye shouldered her mare between the guards. The queen's gray gaze was as furious as her henchmen's were blank. "Oh, look," LaFaye said through gritted teeth. "Tenebrius brought me a present. Merlin's little witchling."

Chapter 29

"Bring her," said the queen. "Put her with the other hostage, but beware. She has a little magic."

A huge fae grabbed Clary's arm and pulled her forward while LaFaye returned her attention to the castle. "Call off your enchanter, Arthur," she cried. "Call him off or I will destroy your queen!"

Did she not realize that the spell was done, and that Merlin would have spent all his magic and possibly his life? Clary clenched her teeth, fighting back a scream of frustration and sorrow as the fae tossed her to the grass. Gwen was there already, her back to a tree, while the white mare she'd been riding cropped grass nearby.

"Are you all right?" Clary asked in a low voice. Her friend looked flushed, a faint sheen of sweat on her brow.

"Why are you here?" Gwen asked. "You should have stayed on the tower."

"The demons brought me."

"Where's Merlin?"

"In the dungeon, I think. It wasn't supposed to happen this way," Clary protested, that old, horrible feeling of incompetence washing over her. Anxiety sped her heart, making her light-headed. "The spell should have worked."

"What spell?" Gwen asked and then gripped her distended belly with a groan.

"Are you in labor?" Clary asked in horror. It was possible, she supposed. Gwen had been dragged through a portal and forced to ride. That couldn't be good this late in her pregnancy.

"Not yet," Gwen said firmly. "I refuse."

"Sure," Clary said doubtfully as Gwen moaned in pain again.

"Silence!" one of the fae guards commanded, prodding Gwen's shoulder with the butt of his spear. It was the same big fae that had dragged Clary to his spot, and the queen hissed in a breath and clutched her collarbone.

Clary's self-control snapped. She sprang to her feet, pushing the guard away. "Don't touch her!"

It had been a stupid move. He was armed, while she was not. The guard casually flipped his spear around and presented the blade-sharp tip. "The queen has value. You do not. Be careful how you try my patience."

Still shaking with anger, Clary didn't back down. Instead, she planted her feet and folded her arms, taking up a position in front of her friend. "Right back at ya, bud."

It wasn't the best line, but it made the point. The fae's brows bunched together. "Do you think to challenge me?" He sounded more bewildered than anything else. Evidently, disobedience didn't happen often in his world.

Their argument had attracted LaFaye's attention. "Deal with her," she said coldly.

The fae struck. Gwen screamed, but the sound was drowned by the noise of the spear splintering against the wall of Clary's magic. Toothpick-size bits of ash wood flew into the air. The fae ducked to guard his face, just avoiding the blunted spearhead that ricocheted past his shoulder. Clary's heart pounded, but she grinned. The spell was hers, but the reflexes and power were Vivian's.

Surely you didn't think I'd miss this fight? Vivian's voice was very faint, but it was there.

"Welcome back," Clary said softly, knowing she'd just

had a narrow escape. "I've never been so glad to have a demon for a friend."

That doesn't say much for your social life.

The faery queen was off her horse and coming their way. The light flashed off the sapphires decorating her dark gown, giving her the look of a serpent in motion. She flicked a hand and a massive force struck Clary from the side, sending her tumbling across the field and away from Gwen. It felt like a dragon's tail had thumped her, knocking the breath from her lungs. She dragged it back in with a whooping gasp as she scrambled to her knees. She lifted her head to see LaFaye regarding her with open contempt while the surrounding warriors laughed. The mocking sound held a dangerous edge that reminded Clary of hyenas.

"Is this how Merlin trains his apprentices?" the faery queen scoffed. "You're hardly fit to mend his robes."

Clary crawled to her feet, aching in every joint, but Vivian's power was rising, winding round and round in the strange, humming dynamo she'd felt on top of the tower. This time it seemed different, though. Harder. Darker. Sharper. She wasn't holding anything back because La-Faye had ordered her death and this was the moment of her vengeance.

When LaFaye flicked her hand again, Clary struck back, Vivian's power driving the blow. The queen doubled over with a scream of surprised agony. Clary danced back, energized by the small win. The demon's magic was filling her with a whirling sensation so vast it made her ears ring. She felt ten feet tall and crackling with potential. Fae warriors rushed to stop her, but she swept them aside like flies.

When she struck again, the queen deflected some of the power, but not all. Blood ran from LaFaye's nose in a thin, scarlet trickle. Clary was panting, exhausted and exhilarated at once. She feinted, struck, and feinted again, her blows lighter now but coming so much faster. She was moving as one with Vivian, relaxing into the flow of the battle.

But the demon had given too much of her strength already that day, and LaFaye wasn't so easily beaten. The faery queen made a two-handed gesture and a column of white fire sprang from the ground, trapping Clary in its midst. It squeezed inward to cut off her air, blinding her vision and numbing every other sense. She began to gag, her ribs unable to move.

Vivian's magic wobbled dangerously, and Clary grew unbearably hot as the fire began to consume her. Slowly, inexorably, her feet left the ground as LaFaye's geyser of flame forced her upward. Death seeped in like a stain.

Merlin staggered into the courtyard and squinted against the daylight. Between the backlash of magic and the blow to his skull, his head throbbed as if he'd been on a three-day bender. His memory of the last hour was a senseless montage of light, color and ear-splitting explosion. He had one clear thought and he clung to it stubbornly—where was Clary and why hadn't she told him that Vivian was anything but dormant? She'd lied, and it had been a dangerous lie. An irrational urge to strangle her pounded inside him.

He couldn't explain what had happened at the end of the spell, except that Vivian had saved his life. He fell against the courtyard wall, propping himself up because his legs would no longer hold him. Grief and confusion wrenched his core.

She'd sacrificed herself. A demon. Out of love.

Merlin's world had changed in that single moment, but it would take much longer to make sense of it. He'd used his bruised magic to call out to her, but received no answer. Had her sacrifice been worthwhile? He didn't know.

The spell would work and save the fae, or Arthur's forces were doomed.

Merlin had to know what had happened. He had to know if Clary was safe.

He looked around. Goblin soldiers milled about the courtyard, distributing weapons from the castle's armory. Sir Owen was tending to a horse's shoe while somewhere in the distance Lancelot argued with the king. Merlin recognized the French knight's voice and Arthur's terse reply. He followed the voices to the balcony, hoping for a clue to Clary's location.

"She has my wife!" Arthur bellowed, but it obviously hurt, because he gripped the side of his blood-stained tunic.

Dulac steadied the king with one hand, his brow furrowed with concern. "You are in no condition to ride or fight, and Gwen is in the middle of the enemy's forces. Let me go."

Merlin went suddenly cold. The blood, the look on Arthur's face, sent him forward. "You're hurt." He touched a hand to the king's side, murmuring a spell to stop the flow of blood. His demon ancestry meant that he'd never be a good healer, and the repair was crude, but it would do for the moment.

"Where were you?" Arthur demanded.

"Working," he replied, deliberately vague. It would take too much time to explain. "Have you seen Clary?"

"There." Dulac pointed to the battlefield. "LaFaye has her, along with Gwen."

Merlin froze, then raised his eyes to Arthur's and saw what he felt himself. Rage, terror and the overwhelming need to shield the woman he loved from a monster. The instinct to protect was an almost mindless drive.

He turned to see where Dulac pointed. At first he saw thousands of heavily armed fae attacking the castle's defenses. The goblins were holding them off, but that wouldn't last forever. Then he saw the gentle snow of his spell—which was doing exactly nothing. Merlin staggered, the enormity of a second failure ripping the strength from his spine. He sagged against the wall, only a last shred of pride keeping him upright. His mind balked, refusing to admit that he'd risked so much only to lose again. It didn't seem possible—and yet the evidence was plain.

And despite monumental failure, his work wasn't done. His gaze found the knot of guards surrounding LaFaye, who was facing off with Clary, Gwen huddled on the ground behind her.

"By the Abyss," Merlin muttered.

Broad shadows slithered over the field. He glanced skyward, receiving a fresh shock when he saw flying black demon-creatures above the castle's towers. An aerial attack was a whole other problem—but he saw something else, as well, first as specks on the horizon, and then like tiny, distant kites. Dragons! Some of the eagles had made it to the Crystal Mountains, and Rukon had brought his kin.

He'd never seen so many at once. There were red and green and blue dragons, some slender and some small, but most were huge males, their wingspans as wide as any house. They circled above the battlefield, coasting between lazy flaps as a ragged cheer went up from the castle's battlements. When one of the dragons shot a lick of blue-white flame and seared a handful of the black demon creatures from the sky, the demon's flapping attack receded like the tide.

"Rukon!" Merlin cried as the green dragon sailed past. "Rukon Shadow Wing!"

The whiskered head swung his way and he banked. "Enchanter?"

"LaFaye has my mate!" he shouted, gratified when

the dragon's head snapped around in surprise. "Take me there!"

Merlin jumped to the edge of the battlement and leaped as the dragon sailed past. He grabbed on to the long, sinuous neck and straddled the bony spine. It was a madman's move, but it took him straight toward Morgan LaFaye.

Rukon sailed low, daring spears and arrows to bring Merlin close to his destination. LaFaye shot a fireball, but it flew slowly through the sparkling snow, its magic confounded by the demonic energy. The dragon dodged it with lazy grace. When Merlin slid off Rukon's back, he landed in a knot of fae who rushed toward him with swords drawn. Merlin belatedly realized he was unarmed, but that was soon remedied. His magic wasn't hampered by the haze and soon he had a sword, and his closest attacker did not.

A fae sprang at him and he slashed, the sheer force of the blow sending his opponent reeling. It was then he saw the column of light trapping Clary, and he lost his mind.

Magic slammed through Merlin's body, lashing out from his palm to smash through Morgan's spell. It was pure instinct, firing along each nerve with complete clarity of purpose. He was there to protect.

The column flared a brilliant scarlet before flying to shards of light and energy. For an instant, he was blind. Then he bolted forward, for Clary was falling and needed his arms. He caught her, cradling her warm weight as he lowered her to the grass. With a relief that left him hollow, he saw the rise and fall of her chest.

Then he rounded on LaFaye, his anger turning to something distant and deadly. The fae around them must have sensed the threat, for there was a sudden silence in their corner of the battlefield. Morgan's broken spell had washed outward, absorbing into the sparkling haze and turning it scarlet. It looked as if the sky was snowing flakes of blood. The fae stared upward, seemingly befuddled by the sight.

The Queen of Faery stumbled, clearly weakened by the blows she'd taken and the unfamiliar magic clogging her powers. Fear paled her cheeks, but she was far from surrender. Merlin put himself between LaFaye and the women. He held the sword casually, every sense attuned to her slightest move.

"This is it, then," she said, making it a fact more than a question. "I will make you beg."

"Believe that if it gives you comfort," he replied.

She lashed out with her power, and this time she put all her force behind it, cutting through the haze. Merlin raised the sword, making a mirror of the bright steel and deflecting her power away. His counter tossed her to the ground. She rolled quickly to her feet and threw a spell that locked her power with his, grappling like a wrestler trying to pin her opponent.

This was it, as LaFaye had said. Merlin fell to one knee, shaken by her strength. The impact jolted him, focusing the truth in his mind. He was fighting for his life, and if he fell everyone he loved was vulnerable—Arthur, Gwen and all of Camelot. Most of all, Clary would be unprotected.

LaFaye's power dug deep, and he howled with pain as she sought pieces of his soul to rip free—hopes, dreams, memories. Some things he might have gladly surrendered, but others he could not part with. Clary's sleepy face over breakfast. Her laughter as they fell into the silken bed at the oasis.

LaFaye's gray gaze locked with his, and there was no mercy in it. Merlin struck with everything he had, and she fell, her mouth open in a silent scream.

He grabbed her throat, ready to throttle her, but she found her voice. "Help me, my warriors. I am your queen!"

But there was no answer. One by one, the fae were falling as Laren had fallen, shuddering and foaming at the mouth. It had taken Vivian's magic, and Merlin's power, and the catalyst of LaFaye's spell, but together they had turned the demon essence into a cure for the fae. After so many centuries, their nightmare was over.

LaFaye wailed in grief, but no one cared. Merlin continued to hold her down, his hands still around her slender neck because he dared not let go. Not yet.

There were many ways to bind power, most of them unpleasant. Merlin had no potions or syringes to use, as he had with Vivian, but he had the advantage of the demon essence still lingering like a mist of blood in the air. LaFaye had never bothered to learn its ways, and now it hobbled her like a crude anesthetic. Merlin reached inside the Queen of Faery's magic, twisting her own power tight around her so that the more she struggled, the more energy she fed to her own bonds. It was a painful kind of noose, but she had done nothing to earn his sympathy.

When he finally let go and backed away, she thrashed, howling with pain and rage. Merlin spared a quick glance at Clary, who was sitting up now, her arm around Guinevere. The two women looked back at him with faces blanched by shock, but they seemed unhurt. He yearned to go to Clary's side, but he could not risk it yet. Giving in to his need might jeopardize everything.

As if he'd foreseen it, LaFaye chose that moment to lunge. Even deprived of her powers, she was dangerous. He grabbed her wrists before she scratched out his eyes. Using his greater weight, he forced her down to her knees. She glared like a madwoman, hatred bright in her eyes.

"What do you want, wizard?" she snarled.

He thought of so many things: Uther, the fae, the war, and all the wars before this one. He recalled Lancelot holding Nimueh's exhausted body in the woods. If that was not enough, Morgan had endangered Gwen and Clary and ordered Vivian's death.

"I want justice," Merlin said, his voice cracking with anger.

LaFaye laughed, a harsh, contemptuous sound. "Oh, be careful of your prayers, wizard. You just might get your wish."

Chapter 30

"**W**ait!"

Merlin turned his head to see Angmar, Laren and those of the rebel fae who had survived the battle approaching the scene.

"She is our queen," said Laren. "We must have a voice in deciding a fit punishment."

Merlin nodded, but he did not take his hand from La-Faye's wrists. "She used your people. She kept the fae from healing and turned their hunger into a weapon. What would you have me do?"

"Return her to us."

Merlin stiffened. "What?"

"You were my lover," LaFaye whispered to Laren. "Surely you recall the pleasure we shared?"

Laren's face cleared of emotion, and it took a moment for Merlin to identify the expression as blackest shame. "I remember," he said, his voice as strained as the look in his eyes. "The fae do not forget."

"Then do not be foolish. Not all of our people are here," said the faery queen. "There are others who are still mine to command."

Laren came closer, but not so close that his feet touched LaFaye's skirts. The dark blue velvet pooled on the trampled ground, the hem richly embroidered, but he recoiled as if she were rotting with the plague. "We will help the others. Your power over us is broken and time will heal the afflicted."

LaFaye said nothing, but Merlin felt the tension cording her every muscle. His shoulders tightened in response, wondering what she might do.

Laren looked up into the sky, his lips forming a bittersweet smile. "What a difference there is when I look around me now. Without my soul, I saw the world, but I could not see the beauty in it. I knew I was blind, but I could not perceive what I missed. It was as if the universe had drained of all color."

LaFaye and Merlin both went utterly still. They shared the guilt for the fae's pain, and though neither said it, that guilt was the thing that bound their fates together.

"The nightmare we've lived will never leave altogether," Laren added, "but it is dawn at last."

As if on cue, the haunting note of Gawain's horn sounded over the trampled fields. The king was coming. Laren drew his sword, lowering the point to the Queen of Faery's throat. Angmar did the same, and then another fae joined in. Cautiously, Merlin released his grip and stood. LaFaye was trembling, the agony of her binding no doubt profound, but he doubted it cut her as deeply as her failure. All around, her army lay senseless in the mud, though here and there one of the fallen warriors was stirring. Above, the dragons circled with majestic grace, having cleared every last demon from the skies. Then the castle gates opened and the knights rode out, Arthur mounted on his charger and Dulac at his side. The king was upright, but even at a distance Merlin could see he was in pain.

But though Arthur would always be his king and his friend, Merlin's heart belonged to Clary. Now that LaFaye was no longer a threat, he turned to gather her in his arms. She was soft and warm, and he understood Laren's smile when he looked into the blue and lovely sky. In many ways Clary had restored his soul the way she'd healed Laren. She was everything.

"Are you well?" he asked.

"Yes," she whispered.

"I have many questions about what happened on the battlefield. Vivian—"

"Don't ask," she said, tears glittering in her lashes. "Please don't ask."

He wanted to, and in many ways had to, but he bowed to the plea in her eyes. Besides, she was free of the demon taint now, wasn't she? How could Vivian have survived such a spell? "Yes, it's over. Nothing else matters but that we are both safe."

Merlin pulled Clary close, content to breathe in the scent of her hair. Somewhere behind them, Gwen and Arthur were playing out a parallel scene, happy to be alive and embracing the one they loved. They had come through their personal version of the Abyss and were safe on the other side. What more could anyone ask?

Then LaFaye burst free, giving a mindless shriek of fury. She launched forward, heedless of the fae's swords even though they slashed her flesh without mercy. Like a dark arrow, she flew toward Guinevere, her hands outstretched like claws. LaFaye had one last way to hurt Arthur and Camelot, and she meant to take it.

"Stay here!" Merlin ordered Clary, and bolted after the faery queen. He had bound her power, but that didn't mean she was harmless. With a wordless shout of warning, he saw LaFaye launch herself through the air. Gwen tried to dodge, but she was weary and heavy with child and only managed to fall.

Excalibur flashed as Arthur drew it. There was a sudden silence as if the whole of the Forest Sauvage froze in shock—except for the graceful arc of the blade. It whistled through the air, somehow anticipating where LaFaye would be when she spun, black hair flying, to face the king. Her expression had hardened to lines of malice, only her eyes widening as she realized what was about to happen. The blade found its mark, beheading her as she lunged.

The impact was not merely physical, for Excalibur was an enchanted sword. The Queen of Faery's magic ignited as the blade sliced through it, sending a rush of flame into the air. Heedless of his injuries, Arthur swept his wife to safety. Merlin stopped his forward rush, the fire's hot draft against his face so intense it nearly burned him. The smell reminded him of acid and ash.

This was how Morgan LaFaye met her end. She had been the greatest threat Camelot had known—cruel, ambitious and half-mad with jealousy, and yet Merlin couldn't stop a twist of regret. She could have lived a life that was brighter than this fire. Instead, she had chosen a path that left no conclusion but this.

"She knew the fae would do far worse to her than a clean death," Laren said. He'd suddenly appeared at Merlin's elbow, his face painted by the hues of the dying fire. His eyes held more anger than pity for his queen, but there was still compassion in his words. "She chose her end on her own terms."

"By attacking a woman heavy with child," Merlin said drily.

"She was never kind or wise, only certain of what she wanted."

They both fell silent. As if LaFaye's death had broken the last chains that held the fae, more and more of the fallen warriors were coming to their senses. Some seemed transfixed by joy, others overwhelmed with sorrow. Many sobbed. Laren excused himself and joined the other rebel fae who walked among them, comforting where they could.

The scene, already chaotic, was unraveling as the armies realized the war was over. The goblins were calling for beer. Still reeling from the sudden change of fortunes,

Merlin turned from the smoldering patch of earth that had been one of the greatest enchantresses of all time. There could be peace now, rebuilding and time enough to plan a future. Merlin could afford to be happy now, couldn't he?

Then Clary gave a yelp of terror. Merlin snapped to attention to see Tenebrius stepping through a ragged portal to seize her by both arms. The demon towered over her by a full head and more. He pulled her back to his chest, bracing one thick arm under her chin.

"You!" Merlin roared, summoning his power. "How dare you show your face here?"

"I am here for justice!" Tenebrius bellowed, making Clary wince. "I demand retribution for what you did to us, Merlin Ambrosius—to the witches and fae and demons. None of what happened here today would have come to pass if it had not been for your deceptions."

Merlin's hands fisted at his sides. His eyes locked with Clary's, doing his best to exude confidence while he scrambled for a way to snatch her from the demon's arms. "You don't care for anyone but yourself, Tenebrius. You were counting on LaFaye's promises to free you from exile. Now that she can't keep them, you're playing your last card."

"And if that card is a long-overdue reckoning?" Tenebrius shrugged, making Clary clutch at the arm pressed against her windpipe. "You didn't think you could walk away a free man, did you, wizard?"

"Why should Camelot bow to your threats?"

"I have the hostage. Besides, Camelot claims justice should be for all. Why not for the demons, too? What about the wrongs done to our kind?"

Arthur approached, Dulac at his side. The king walked slowly and stiffly, his surcoat streaked with fresh blood as if the fight with LaFaye had reopened his wound.

"Tenebrius," said Arthur. "I wish I could say it was a

pleasure to see you once more. We last parted on much better terms than this." There had been a tourney in the Forest Sauvage, Arthur's knights on one side and LaFaye's on the other.

"It seems you've won against the Faery Queen once more," said the demon.

"Release Clary," said Arthur in frigid tones that signaled all pleasantries were over.

"No. While I have her I also have your attention," said the demon.

"You always have my attention, though not in the best way," Arthur replied. "The demons were banished because they tried to conquer and enslave everybody else. I have to protect my people from your kind."

Clary closed her eyes, her face strained with fear. Merlin strategized five different rescues, but each plan ended with her neck broken or all of them blown to bits. Force was not the answer.

"We need to conquer, that is true," the demon answered. "We have lost the path to our homeland and have no place of our own to rule. What would you have us do?" He looked directly at Merlin as he asked the question.

"That is not my decision to make," Merlin replied, nodding to Arthur. "It is the king's. However, I will trade my life for Clary's. Take me hostage, not her, and we will give you an answer."

Tenebrius gave a mocking smile. "Are you certain that is a trade you wish to make? I know how you regard demonkind."

Clary made a strangled noise and tried to twist from his grasp. Tenebrius gave a soft, bitter laugh. "The violent combination of magics in the field today fused what was left of Vivian into Clary's being. One soul, one body, one mind, one consciousness. Your snow-white witchling is tainted by the wild essence of my kin."

Clary shrieked. It was not shrill and filled with rage, but plaintive with fright and confusion. If she'd known something was different inside her, she hadn't understood.

Merlin surged forward, just as bewildered but knowing she needed him. Tenebrius held out a hand. "Wait, enchanter, do not approach. Let me consider your offer."

A beat passed, and a thousand thoughts crashed through his mind. Clary must have kept the truth about Vivian from him all the way along—or at least since the last time he'd knocked Vivian out. Clary had hated that, and no doubt sheltered the demoness from any more of his efforts to get rid of her. In return, he suspected Vivian had protected Clary.

And just as well. In the end, Vivian had saved them all because Clary had taught her what kindness meant. Vertigo swept through him as the truth became plain, and he took a long, steadying breath. There would be almost nothing left of Vivian now, but the effect on Clary would still be profound. She would be much more than a witch—she would be immortal, powerful, an enchantress in her own right.

But at the moment, she was staring at him with round, terror-stricken eyes. A complicated pain inside Merlin rose to all but strangle him as he held her gaze. He knew what it was like to be told he carried demon blood. But was it the same for her? Did she have Vivian's memories? Did she recoil as he had and believe herself corrupted?

But then, Clary had joined with a demon who had grown and changed and sacrificed herself for love. Perhaps Clary would make her own choices about who she would become, just like she always had.

Merlin took a deep breath and released it, making up his mind.

He loved her. Nothing else mattered. "What is there to consider, Tenebrius? My life for hers."

Clary's eyes went wide with shock. She hadn't expected

that. He tried not to look as the surprise faded to a confusion of grief and hope. This moment could still go wrong.

Tenebrius gave a fang-tipped grin. "You are a poor bargain, wizard. She is a tasty treat."

Merlin reached into the pocket of his jeans and withdrew the ruby amulet he had used to locate Clary. "Then I will add this to your compensation. It belonged to LaFaye."

He held it up, letting it spin on the long, gold chain. The ruby flashed in the sunlight, dazzling with the promise of power. The demon's goat eyes glowed with greed.

"I recognize the amulet and know its worth," said Tenebrius. "I will accept it as part of the bargain, but there is one thing more I want, and it is not gold nor is it an object of power."

"Name it," said Merlin.

"Truth." The word hung like doom over the battlefield, with its confusion of bodies and sobbing fae and the wounded king leaning on Excalibur.

"Tell your friends the truth about yourself." Tenebrius swept a hand across the scene. "Tell the truth of who you are and how you came by the spell that cast us into the Abyss. The fae deserve to know why they suffered, and your king should know the real nature of the man he calls his friend and protector."

Arthur's look was puzzled and angry. "What is this monster implying?"

"That I am equally a monster," Merlin said softly. He felt as if he was falling down, down a well and would not stop until he drowned. "Vivian cursed the spell I stole from her—that is why it caused such great damage."

"Who is this Vivian?" Arthur asked, looking from Merlin to Clary to the demon.

"A teacher of mine. And more."

So much more. Merlin closed his eyes, wishing one of the dragons circling far above would snatch him up and carry him far away. This was too private, too great a flaw to expose. Shame ate through him as if it would turn his bones to powder. From the day he'd discovered who his father was, he'd tried to scour away every hint of association with the hellspawn.

"Merlin?" Arthur asked in a voice that edged toward command.

He met Clary's eyes again, but quickly looked away. He'd told her she would not want to know him if she found out his true nature. After what she'd seen in the past few days, she would understand why. He hated demons because he was as much one of them as he was a part of the mortal world. As Tenebrius had pointed out, he had caused monumental devastation. Agoricus the Great would be proud.

The only thing good he could do was save Clary. No doubt it would be the last gift she would ever accept from him.

"I have my father's eyes," he said. Then he told them the rest.

Merlin talked, and he talked. After LaFaye's brutal end, Guinevere had been taken to the castle to rest, but Arthur and the knights remained, as did many of the fae. He was aware of them, but his gaze strayed most often to Clary, who listened with a fixed expression he could not read. He tried with all his might to guess what she was thinking, but she kept her thoughts completely guarded. The only movement she made was to swat the demon's claw away when he tried to stroke her cheek.

When Merlin had finished, he expected Excalibur's edge against his throat, or a fae blade or even the kiss of dragon breath. Instead, there was a soft murmur that died almost as soon as it began. The afternoon was fading, the shadows deepening to a dusky purple.

"I have no more to say," Merlin concluded. "I have upheld my side of the deal."

Tenebrius held out a clawed hand. "The amulet?"

Merlin tossed it to him and walked slowly forward. Tenebrius kept his word and pushed Clary away.

To Merlin's intense relief, she paused slightly as their paths crossed. Now her eyes were wide and thoughtful as if seeing him for the first time. For an instant he fell into their green depths. He expected to see elements of both Clary and Vivian there, but it was not so simple. She was neither and both, and yet someone new and stronger than before. He silently took Clary's hand and raised it to his lips, savoring the scent of her skin before letting her pass.

"Hello," he said.

The corners of her mouth turned up, the expression both fond and challenging. "Hello."

He desperately needed more, but urged her away to the safety of Camelot's knights. Then he turned to the demon. "I am your prisoner."

"And now," said Tenebrius, digging his claws into Merlin's shoulder, "you shall pay for your crimes, Merlin Ambrosius."

Chapter 31

"Not so fast," said King Arthur. "We have been patient and bargained generously, but you push too far, demon. At that tourney you judged, I won the prize. You promised me anything of my choosing that was in your power to grant."

Arthur had never claimed his prize. Merlin's breath caught and he turned to Arthur with a sudden, almost bewildered realization that his friend hadn't abandoned him after all, even if he was half a demon.

Tenebrius's face fell. "I don't remember," he said, although it was plain he did.

"I choose Merlin," said Arthur.

"Under one condition." Angmar stepped forward. "As the fae suffered in consequence of the stolen spell, we put a condition on Merlin's freedom."

"Oh?" Arthur said tightly. He had just ended a war with the fae and could not afford to offend them, especially not the rebels who had come to his aid. "What condition would that be?"

"That Vivian agrees," said Angmar. "She was deceived by her lover. It is up to her to decide if he has truly been redeemed."

Tenebrius burst into a belly laugh that made Merlin long to punch him. "You are asking a demoness to forgive?"

Merlin's heart plummeted. He could see Arthur drawing breath to argue, and held up a hand. "The decision is hers to make," he said softly. "I wronged her."

Tenebrius made a doubtful snort. "How would you

rather serve me, wizard? As a scullery boy or the slave who scrubs my dungeon's floors?"

Clary took a step forward, opened her mouth as if to speak and then hesitated. Licking her lips, she tried again. "A long time has passed. He deceived me, that is true."

She looked confused as if processing memories that were only half her own. Merlin tensed, wondering what memories Vivian had kept, and how much had slipped away before she'd fused with Clary. Some of those early times had been joyous.

Merlin took a step forward, and Tenebrius did not stop him. Merlin knelt at her feet, thinking how everything had come full circle. Vivian had taught him, and he had taught Clary and now Clary had taught them all about matters of the heart.

"My love," he said, feeling the words true but strange on his tongue. "Forgive me. Forgive what I did, and that I compounded that crime by distrusting you now. You saved me from a certain death, and you saved us all from defeat at the hands of LaFaye."

"Who are you speaking to?" she asked.

Merlin took her hands, feeling the slight bones of her fingers curl around his. Blood pounded in his ears at the thought of her walking away, dismissing him because he had betrayed her. "I thank both Clary and Vivian for our salvation, because you both saved us. It was not just Vivian's power and Clary's heart, but Clary's courage and Vivian's willingness to learn. If you are one, then you are the most wondrous creature to walk this enchanted forest."

"Even if I am a demon?"

Merlin bowed until his forehead touched her hands where he held them. "You are unique."

"So are you. We all are. That's the point."

He looked up, but she was scanning the crowd, her gaze going from the fae, to the king, and finally to Tenebrius.

"Merlin betrayed me, but he's also stitched my wounds and taught me the right way to build a portal and helped me clean up when I accidentally summoned all the chocolate custard in the Pacific Northwest. He's been a mentor when I chose to start my life over, and he's never held me back when I wanted to see what I can do." Clary paused, finally looking down to meet his eyes. Hers were warm, but with an edge of laughter. "I think I'll keep him. And in the end, he did cure the fae, so I suppose we all should forgive him. He has done much good in the world, although he cannot see it for himself."

Arthur cheered, and the men of Camelot cheered with him. After an initial hesitation, the fae applauded, too. They were too overjoyed to be cured to hold a grudge. As for the goblins, they had found the castle's cellars and were delighted with pretty much everything.

Merlin didn't need any more encouragement to rise and grab Clary so he could kiss her soundly. Nothing mattered but that she believed in him, and that he wanted her, and that there would be a future.

"And what of me?" Tenebrius asked Arthur. "Are the demons to remain locked away until we dwindle to nothing?"

The demon was fading around the edges, a sure sign that the pull of the Abyss was taking effect. He could not stay in the Forest Sauvage many more minutes, and it would be some time before he could visit again.

"What is Camelot," said Arthur, "unless there is justice for all?"

"Surely we owe the demons nothing?" complained Gawain.

Arthur put a hand on his friend's shoulder. "We don't. But justice is not solely the payment of a debt. It is meant to put things right, and sometimes that means growth and better choices. Last time I chose war against the hellspawn. This time I will ask the finest minds in all the realms to study the path the demons traveled to reach this place. If they have a homeland, there must be a road to send them back. With a little effort and common sense, maybe everybody can be happy."

After the battle came the sad business of mourning those who were lost. Then came feasts of celebration, and then came farewells. Arthur's allies returned to their homes. So did his former enemies, although the fae, with Angmar as their new king, left with promises of friendship. The war with the fae was over at last.

Eventually, the court of Camelot returned to their new homes in Carlyle, Washington. For Merlin and Clary, that meant his condominium. Except it didn't feel like his place anymore and he wasn't sure why. He wandered from room to room like a restless cat while Clary sat at the dining room table scowling at the scorch marks left by the possessed laptop.

"Are you going to come sit down?" she asked him. "We should order in. After all that roast beast and spiced wine, I'm dying for a good pad thai."

He came out of the bedroom and leaned against the wall. "Then order enough for two."

"Have you got some menus?"

Merlin went to the kitchen and began opening and closing drawers. "I thought I did, but I can't remember where I put them."

She laughed, and it was a wholesome, merry sound he'd come to count on. "Two of the most powerful beings on Earth, and we can't manage to order dinner."

Merlin closed the last drawer and turned to face her with a grin. His heart lurched at the sight of her at his table, wearing one of his old shirts because they hadn't moved her things in yet—but they would. They were together now in all the ways he'd never dreamed would happen.

At first, he'd worried it would be strange to be with a woman who was his first love and his current love in one. It wasn't. In the end it had felt like his heart coming home to him, healed and renewed. And those that knew Clary best, like Tamsin, had said that the biggest difference they could see was that she had much more magic and a whole lot more confidence, especially when it came to her wardrobe. They adored her just the same.

"I love you." He'd never actually said it like that before, all three words together.

"I love you back." Her smile was slow and a little wistful.

He finally spotted the stack of menus on top of the microwave, but he ignored them. The moment was too important.

"You don't think it's too weird, what happened to me?" Clary asked softly—and for the zillionth time. "It doesn't freak you out?"

"There are things that freak me out," he said, sliding onto the chair beside her. "Ghouls, animated slime, those purse dogs with bulgy eyes."

"Purse dogs?"

He kissed her forehead. "You don't freak me out, okay?"

On the contrary, she intrigued him. She had Vivian's passion and Clary's compassion, as well as Vivian's temper and Clary's stubborn streak. All of the Clary he loved was there, but with an added spice he truly appreciated— and if he had his way, they'd be together forever.

"I'm part demon," she said.

"So am I."

"You hate demons. You don't get over that in a couple of days."

They were simple words, but they held so many layers of feeling for both of them. He realized this was what was making him restless, this thing he needed to face. "I do not like what the demons did. I will never see the world the same way most of them do. But I've learned from what happened. I've had choices all along. Like you said, we're individuals and all of us get to pick who we become."

The statement made him think of Morgan LaFaye, the graceful girl she had been and the evil queen she'd grown into. An unutterable sadness twisted inside him.

"We do choose, and we do change," she said.

"I know that now," he said, holding her hand. "It's like I've been wearing dark glasses all my life and finally took them off. Everything is lighter."

And now, with a little help from his friends, the fae were cured. He'd only understood the complete weight of that guilt after it had lifted, and now he wanted to live.

"New beginnings," she said, sliding onto his lap and pressing her lips to his.

The kiss pushed the last thoughts of pad thai from his head. Things were just getting interesting when Clary's phone buzzed. To his profound annoyance, she answered it. "Hello?"

He watched her face light up. "Really? A second one?"

Merlin heard the babble of Tamsin's voice and guessed she was referring to yet another knight showing up at Arthur's door. Long ago Merlin had put one hundred and fifty knights into the stone sleep, but only a few had ever awakened. It had been another case where one of his spells had gone wrong, but now—perhaps with LaFaye's demise or Vivian's forgiveness—it had fixed itself. First Sir Bors had turned up at Arthur's door, then Sir Geraint, then Sir Kay, and on and on. Getting so many medieval warriors acclimated to the modern world was going to be a heroic task all on its own. Still, Merlin was glad to see each and every one. They were old friends, and with this many willing and brave hearts, there was a lot of good Camelot could do.

Clary thumbed the phone back to sleep. "Gwen's gone into labor."

Merlin's heart leaped. "How is she?"

"Just fine. She's had her boy. Now she's working on her daughter."

"Twins?" Merlin frowned. "No one said anything about twins."

Clary shrugged. "Arthur's delighted."

"Did he know?"

She grinned. "No. But Gwen and Tamsin did. Women have to have some secrets, after all."

"How did she get away with keeping two babies a secret? What about ultrasounds?"

"Arthur's old-fashioned." Then Clary cocked her head, peering into a future Merlin couldn't see. "But I'll bet he gets with the whole prenatal program next time around. I think this surprise package is Gwen's way of making him pay attention."

"I promise I'll pay attention when the time comes."

"I know you will," she said in a way that left no options.

They both laughed, although he wondered what Clary would try to get away with down the road. She'd already hid a demon from him, after all.

"I want to get married in Camelot. In your tower."

That was right—the tower was back. "Why not at the oasis?" he asked.

"That's just for you and me."

"Ah."

She chuckled. "Do you think we could tie tin cans to Rukon's tail and get him to fly us to our honeymoon?"

"I'm guessing no." Then it occurred to him he was missing a step. "Aren't I supposed to go down on bended knee?"

She looked up from under her lashes. "You've done that already in front of the king, a bunch of hysterical fae and an entire army of drunken goblins. Show me what else you've got."

He kissed her again, nibbling and nipping and making it count until, with a sigh, she tossed the phone onto the table. She straddled him, winding her arms around his neck and paying his affection back in kind. She was definitely the best kisser he'd met in his long, long life. This new amazing creature was going to take centuries to learn.

He couldn't wait.

Dinner was gleefully, gratefully forgotten for a good many hours.

* * * * *

LET'S TALK

For exclusive extracts, competitions
and special offers, find us online:

- facebook.com/millsandboon
- @millsandboonuk
- @millsandboon

Or get in touch on 0844 844 1351*

For all the latest titles coming soon, visit
millsandboon.co.uk/nextmonth